"The whole damn place is one huge powder keg."

"And I'm supposed to light the fuse," Bolan said, smiling ruefully.

"Not quite," Brognola said. "We're hoping a clean, strategic move against the syndicate may help defuse the situation. The Russians obviously have to clean their own house...but this particular unsightly mess is slopping over to the States, big time. The drugs are only part of it, as you're aware. The Russian mob will deal with anybody for a price, and that includes terrorists who will do anything for a pocket nuke. We know the Russian Mafia has no respect for anyone or anything beyond itself."

There was a cold gleam in Bolan's eyes. "Then it's time they learned a little healthy fear."

DON PENDLETON'S

MACK BOLAN®

STONY MAN™

Blood Star

A GOLD EAGLE BOOK FROM

WORLDWIDE®

TORONTO • NEW YORK • LONDON
AMSTERDAM • PARIS • SYDNEY • HAMBURG
STOCKHOLM • ATHENS • TOKYO • MILAN
MADRID • WARSAW • BUDAPEST • AUCKLAND

To the NATO pilots in Bosnia-Herzegovina,
who carried the cleansing fire. God keep.

First edition May 1997

ISBN 0-373-61912-X

Special thanks and acknowledgment to
Mike Newton for his contribution to this work.

BLOOD STAR

Printed in U.S.A.

Blood Star

PROLOGUE

Moscow

A drizzling rain had fallen on the city for the past three hours, leeching warmth from those pedestrians unfortunate enough to be abroad on such a night. Rain made the streets and sidewalks glisten, but no long-term resident of Russia's capital would be deceived by the illusion. It was still the same drab, heartless city underneath the temporary sheen.

Lieutenant Leonid Gromylko lit another cigarette—American, thank God; rank had its privileges—and stared out through the rain-streaked windshield of his black sedan. Beside him, wedged behind the steering wheel, his partner of eleven years was eating chestnuts from a paper bag and glaring at the night.

"He's late," Alexei Churbanov remarked.

There was no need to check the cheap watch on his hairy wrist. Their quarry had been due an hour earlier, and Sergeant Churbanov had been remarking on the subject's tardiness at fifteen-minute intervals, since nine o'clock.

"He'll be here," said Gromylko. "Everybody else is here. He wouldn't stand them up."

"Why not?" his partner asked. "The bastard thinks he's God. He thinks his shit smells like a rose garden. He wouldn't mind insulting Third World peasants."

"Too much money on the table," the lieutenant said. "His greed won't let him stay away."

"Where is he, then?"

"Just wait a bit."

The others had been waiting since 8:55 p.m. Gromylko and his partner had been waiting, watching, as the visitors arrived. The two Colombians were traveling with an interpreter and half a dozen bodyguards—four of their countrymen and two tough Chechens loaned out by the Moscow syndicate to make them feel secure. A welcoming committee from the local *mafiya* had been on hand to greet them at the safe house, off Scolkovskoie Sosse, but the man whom they had come so far to see was running overtime.

"Where *is* he, Leonid?"

"I wouldn't be surprised if he was still in bed," Gromylko said. "You've seen his little playmate."

"He can do that anytime," Churbanov said. "The man should keep his mind on business."

"What are you, his manager?"

"I'm sick of waiting for him, that's all."

"He'll be coming soon."

The truth was that Gromylko had grown sick and tired of waiting, too. He worried that they would be noticed, parked a half block from the safe house in the standard-issue Zil sedan of the *militsiya*. It stood out like a sore thumb in the Goljanovo district of northeastern Moscow, where the residents leaned more toward foreign cars, selected with an eye to luxury. The

Goljanovo precinct was entirely ignorant of the impending raid, kept in the dark because Gromylko feared the level of corruption that had spread like cancer through the ranks of the *militsiya* in recent years.

It had been one thing, when the Communists were in control, and some degree of bribery was accepted as a fact of life. But now, with the deregulation and the leap in crime statistics, violence in the streets and payoffs to police, Moscow was rapidly emerging as a clone of Chicago in the 1920s. It was never safe to trust a stranger these days just because he wore a matching uniform.

One of the men responsible for that corruption was the object of their stakeout on that rainy night in Moscow. Gregori Vasiliev was one of the top-ranking criminals in all of Russia, known as a *vor v zakonye*—a godfather—of the Vorovskoi Mir, the Thieves' Society. In fact, some said he was first among equals on the Bratskaya Semyorka—the fabled Brotherhood of Seven said to rule the Russian syndicate. Vasiliev maintained a range of interests in the world of crime, but his acknowledged specialty was *narco-bizness.* He supplied Muscovite addicts with a range of drugs, including *anasha,* or hashish, *khimka,* or Manchurian hemp, and *mak,* which was a weak opium derivative, typically ingested in liquid form. More recently, it was reported by informers on the street, Vasiliev was interested in large-scale shipments of cocaine imported from Colombia. To that end he had fixed a meeting with the spokesmen from Cali who waited for him now—and none too patiently, Gromylko thought—across the street and four doors down.

"What's this?" Churbanov pointed with his free hand, through the rain-slick windshield, toward a pair of headlights moving slowly down the street.

Gromylko was reminded of a cat's eyes shining in the dark, the mental image of a stalking panther large enough to swallow him without a second thought, and he felt the goose bumps rising on his arms.

"Let's wait and see," he said.

The car had slowed down to a crawl as it approached the safe house. Would the driver see them, sitting there and watching him? Gromylko fought the sudden urge to duck down, out of sight, aware that it would only make him more suspicious in appearance, if the new arrival noticed him at all. The best thing he could do was take his own advice, to wait and see what happened next.

"He's stopping!"

"I see that, Alexei." The lieutenant made a conscious effort to conceal his own excitement. If it was Vasiliev, they had their man. If not...

"Wipers," Gromylko said.

His partner twisted the ignition key and gave the windshield wipers one quick sweep, enough to clear the streaks of rain away without attracting undue notice from the new arrivals. Even as the rubber blades swept back and forth across the glass, Gromylko lifted the night glasses to his eyes and focused on the gray Mercedes-Benz downrange.

He saw a stocky man emerge on the passenger side, opening a black umbrella as he straightened up and closed the door behind him. Two strides brought him to the rear door of the Benz. He glanced each way along the street before he opened it, positioning the umbrella to shield the next man who stepped out of the car.

It was Vasiliev.

"We've got the bastard."

"Yes!" Churbanov reached out for the radio, but hesitated when Gromylko caught his wrist.

"Not yet, Alexei. Let him go inside, relax a little. Put his money on the table."

"Right. We've waited this long, I can last a few more minutes." Even so, Churbanov couldn't hide the tension in his voice.

Gromylko watched Vasiliev until the mobster and his escort disappeared from view. There was at least one man remaining in the Benz, and he would certainly be armed, as were the several bodyguards inside the house. They could anticipate resistance when they made their move, and they had come prepared for meeting force with force.

Two blocks away in each direction, north and south, another pair of black sedans stood, each with five policemen waiting in the dark. All ten were armed with pistols, shotguns, and AK-74 assault rifles, the folding-stock models chambered in 5.45 mm, produced as latter-day replacements for the venerable AK-47. Gromylko and Churbanov had handpicked the raiders, selecting officers they trusted, men above reproach, of unquestioned courage. There had been no leaks before the raid, and if they met resistance going in, his chosen troops were not afraid of fighting fire with fire.

It might be better that way, thought Gromylko, to avoid the Russian legal system with its quirks and loopholes, corrupt judges and terrorized witnesses. Dead men couldn't arrange a bargain with the court or buy their way out of a criminal indictment.

"Now?" Churbanov asked after several moments.

"Now."

His partner raised the microphone and mashed down the transmitter button with his thumb. "Move in!" he growled. "Repeat, move in!"

Gromylko drew his Makarov 9 mm pistol, flicked the safety off and reached across his body with his left hand, opening the door. His thinning hair was plastered down with rain before he straightened up beside the car, the cold water running down his collar making him grit his teeth. Churbanov slammed his own door, moving swiftly toward the gray Mercedes-Benz, Gromylko falling into step beside him, thumbing back the hammer on his Makarov.

Incredibly the driver didn't see them until they were right on top of him. When he noticed the two policemen looming over him, he mouthed a curse behind the glass and gave a long blast on the horn to warn his friends inside the house.

Churbanov swung his Makarov against the driver's window, shattering the glass and reaching through to strike the driver hard, across the face. The horn fell silent, but the damage had been done. Rushing toward the house with Churbanov behind him, Gromylko heard the hiss of tires on dampened pavement. The support troops would have to catch up as best they could.

They had no time to waste.

A hulking shadow moved behind the curtains of a

lighted window to his left. He spun in that direction, calling out to Churbanov and raising his pistol as the curtain was swept aside and a gun barrel jabbed through the glass. His finger tightened on the trigger as a burst of yellow flame erupted from the muzzle of the weapon in the window, and he flinched at the staccato sound of a Kalashnikov.

Gromylko fired two rounds. The Makarov jumped in his hand, its sharp reports barely audible over the rattle and crash of automatic fire. He heard Churbanov firing, glimpsed his partner's chunky outline from the corner of his eye as the man ran toward the house, his pistol spitting fire.

One of their shots hit the gunman silhouetted in the window, and he lurched backward, dragging flimsy curtains with him, the AK spitting more erratically as it withdrew.

Gromylko cleared the front steps in a rush and raised his leg to kick the heavy door with all his strength and weight behind it, slamming three times beside the latch before it gave.

The door swung open, and Gromylko saw a shadow just beyond the threshold, ducked in time to save himself and called his partner's name as he was diving to the floor. Another automatic weapon stuttered, this one lighter, sounding like a submachine gun, probably 9 mm. Bullets sizzled overhead as the lieutenant hugged the floor and squeezed off aimless rounds in answer to the hostile fusillade. Churbanov gave a startled cry behind him, and he heard the gunman grunt once.

He fired another round—two cartridges remaining

in his pistol, damn it!—and there could be no mistaking it this time, the sound a falling body makes on impact with the floor. He risked a glance ahead and found himself staring at the soles of the gunman's shoes, an inch or two of hairy calf protruding from each pant leg.

Scrambling to his feet, Gromylko kept the fallen gunman covered, checked to see if he was breathing, but couldn't be sure. The shooter's weapon was an Uzi SMG, and the lieutenant hastily retrieved it from the floor beside his adversary's outstretched hand.

Feeling more secure with a substantial weapon in his grasp, Gromylko turned to call his partner and spotted Churbanov reclining with his back against the doorjamb, knees drawn up against his chest, a dazed expression on his face.

"Come on, Alexei! There's no time for sitting on your backside—"

Churbanov's feet slid out in front of him, knees dropping, to reveal the crimson blotches on his shirt. As the lieutenant stood there watching, they expanded, dark blood soaking into the material, the separate stains combining into one. Churbanov tried to speak, lips moving, but he couldn't seem to catch his breath or form the necessary words. Before Gromylko came out of his trance and moved to help his partner, Churbanov put everything he had into a simple shrug and then slumped over on his side.

Gromylko checked his old friend for a pulse and thought he had it for a moment, faint and fading, but he lost it seconds later, and the precious beat of life didn't return. Churbanov's eyes were open, staring into space, until Gromylko closed them with his fingertips. His own eyes blurred and stung with sudden tears, but he couldn't allow himself to be immobilized by shock or grief. Not now, when everything—his life itself—depended on his personal reaction time.

Three of his men were charging up the sidewalk, toward the door. They stopped short at the sight of Churbanov stretched out across the threshold, and Gromylko snapped at them.

"Come on! You've all seen dead men!"

One or two of them would have the driver of the Benz in custody outside, while the remainder of the strike force would have rushed to close the other exits from the safe house, trying to make sure that no one slipped away. Gromylko wondered if they might already be too late, if his best friend of fifteen years had given up his life for nothing.

No! He would not let Vasiliev slip through his fingers. Not this time.

Gromylko lumbered to his feet and led the way inside the house, the captured Uzi warm against his skin. He ached to use it, feel the power rippling through his hands and through the weapon as he cut the bastards down and left them sprawled in blood. One provocation, anything at all, and he would—

Sudden gunfire from the rear part of the house alerted him to danger. He was on the move in a crouch, past open doorways and empty rooms. The house was large by Moscow standards, but it wasn't the palatial dwelling of a millionaire or former commissar. A passing glance into the parlor showed the chairs and table carefully arranged for a meeting, with some of the chairs tipped over in haste when the shooting had begun. There was no sign of anyone remaining in the house, other than the bodies he had left behind, and so Gromylko concentrated on the sound of gunfire, moving toward its source.

The fight had spilled into the darkened yard before he got there. Several gunmen from the house exchanged bursts of autofire with members of the raiding party still outside. Gromylko saw no one resembling Vasiliev before he started firing with the Uzi, heard his men cut loose behind him with their AK-74s. The storm of bullets ripped into gunmen who were taken by surprise, cut down before they could defend themselves.

Just like Alexei, *da.*

Outside, the shooting sputtered on for several seconds more, then silence fell across the scene. Gromylko closed his eyes for just a moment, breathing in the smell of gun smoke, blood and loosened bowels—the telltale odors of a battlefield. The first time he had smelled it, in Afghanistan, the stench had sickened him, but he was used to it these days.

Gromylko called a warning to his men outside, before he stepped across the bloody threshold. There was no point getting killed by friendly fire if he could help it. There were bodies scattered on the lawn, at least one of them a policeman who appeared to be alive.

"Somebody call an ambulance," Gromylko said. "And check the bodies for ID."

He turned back to the dead men sprawled around the back door of the safe house, watching as his raiders turned the bodies over so that each was facing toward the ceiling. Two of them were swarthy Latin types—Colombians, he recognized. The other two were Chechens, bullnecked thugs, undoubtedly the same two who had been assigned as escorts to the visitors from Cali. There would be no questioning them now, but that didn't concern Gromylko. These weren't the sort of men who blurted out confessions once they were in custody. A prison term for the attempted murder of policemen wouldn't have frightened them. Anyway, there would have been a fair chance they could beat the rap, as the Americans would say, once high-priced lawyers started twisting facts and spinning fairy tales in court.

No, it was better this way. The lieutenant only hoped that they would find Vasiliev among the dead outside. And yet, almost before the thought took shape, he knew it was too much to hope for. They were short on bodies; he could see that at a glance. And if anyone escaped, gut instinct told Gromylko that his longtime quarry was the man to pull it off.

The ambulance took thirteen minutes to arrive, a record in Gromylko's personal experience, no doubt accelerated by the combination of a call from the *militsiya* and the Goljanovo address. It may have disappointed the attendants to find out that they were hauling a policeman to the hospital instead of a celebrity, but they were wise enough to keep their mouths shut in the presence of so many angry officers with automatic weapons in their hands.

Colonel Yuri Renko reached the scene eight minutes later, stepping from his four-door Zil sedan as the forensic team from headquarters was setting up its floodlights and unpacking cameras. Gromylko met him on the porch without saluting, since both men were in civilian clothes. Displays of military courtesy were normally reserved for formal situations, when the parties were in uniform.

"I heard about Alexei on the radio," said Renko. "You have my condolences."

"*Spaseeba*, Colonel. Corporal Andropov was wounded, also."

"Ah. I'll check on his condition at the hospital when we are finished here. What happened, Leonid?"

Gromylko gave a brief recap of the events: the driver's warning to his comrades, the exchange of fire as they approached the house, the flight of Gregori Vasiliev and two Colombians before Gromylko's men were in position to prevent them from escaping out the back.

"So," Renko summarized the information, "you have one dead and one wounded on your side, against eight dead and one in custody, while all the big fish got away. Is that about the size of it?"

Gromylko frowned. "I wouldn't put it that way," he replied.

"I daresay," Renko answered, "but the facts seem plain enough. I shall look forward to your full report. This morning, if you please."

"Yes, sir."

"I'll leave you to it, then. *Spakoyni nochie.*"

"Good night, sir."

And to hell with you, Gromylko thought before he turned back toward the charnel house to finish with the dead.

CHAPTER ONE

Upstate New York

A two-lane road, flanked by trees on either side, ran north from Cannon Corners to the border. The blacktop had been patched repeatedly where winter sleet and ice had eaten potholes in its surface, creating a kind of sloppy checkerboard effect. Nobody special occupied the last four miles before New York turned into Canada, and highway maintenance had never been a top priority in that neck of the woods. In early-morning darkness, driving with his headlights off, Mack Bolan felt as if he could have been the last man on the planet, cruising toward a rendezvous with death.

The latter part, at least, was accurate.

He had the tip from "sources known for past reliability." The word had come to him from Hal Brognola, via Stony Man, and Bolan hadn't asked about its origins in any greater detail. Whether the alert was gleaned from wiretaps, physical surveillance or a mole within the syndicate, it made no difference to the Executioner. He knew enough to trust the information. That was all he needed, all he could expect.

It was supposed to be a relatively simple drug transaction, cut and dried. If anything distinguished the occasion, it would have to be the volume of narcotics riding on the line. A semitrailer filled with kilo bags of uncut China white was coming in from Canada, escorted by a troop of soldiers from the Russian *mafiya*, for delivery to agents of the Balderone crime family in New York. The rumored wholesale price for two tons of Asian heroin was forty million dollars, cash. That amounted to roughly ten percent of what the New York mob would realize from street sales once they finished stepping on the smack and pushing it in nickel bags.

It was the kind of bust any agent of the DEA would sell his sainted mother for, but Hal Brognola had his reasons for involving Bolan rather than delivering the stash and cash for interdiction by more common means.

The Russians were a major part of it, thought Bolan. It was coming up to ten years since the Soviet regime had crumbled into dust, and crime was still the largest single export of the Russian commonwealth. The *mafiya*, or Thieves' Society, had pointmen working overtime from Eastern Europe to the States and Canada, throughout the Third World, firming up alliances with mobsters in Japan and Southeast Asia, Sicily and Corsica, Colombia and Mexico, the Middle East—you name it. They were smuggling everything from weapons to undocumented immigrants and weapons-grade plutonium, but drugs were still the single largest moneymaker. That was true whether they were pushing them on Moscow's streets or acting as the middlemen for deals between American importers and the outlaw growers of the Golden Triangle. It was a multi*billion*-dollar industry, effectively immune to prosecution, thanks to payoffs in the millions in a dozen different countries.

There was only so much one man could expect to do against an operation of that size, but some of that depended on the man. Thus far the Russians and their allies in the States had given no thought to the Executioner.

They were about to learn from their mistake.

He checked the dashboard clock and saw that he had sixty-seven minutes left. It shouldn't be much farther to the access road where he would leave his car to make the last two hundred yards of the approach on foot. A deeper patch of darkness came at Bolan, on his left, and he confirmed it with a quick flash of his headlights, braking as he cranked the steering wheel and nosed his car into the unpaved country lane.

His gear was in the trunk. Five minutes saw him changed from street clothes into camouflage fatigues and dressed to kill. The rest of it was simply hiking north, the highway on his right to keep him oriented, and his targets would be waiting for him at the border.

Waiting for the semitrailer filled with poison to arrive.

He planned to join the welcoming committee, and to make it an occasion none of those on hand was likely to forget.

Assuming they survived.

VINNIE LUPO normally slept in till nine o'clock, but this was business, and he didn't plan to let his capo down. When Tony Sicca told his men to hit the road at 4:00 a.m., they hit the fucking road, no questions asked. And when the job involved delivery of a forty-million-dollar payoff—five suitcases stuffed with hundred-dollar bills—everyone involved made sure he had his eyes wide open, all the way. That kind of money made the trigger finger itchy, and a damn good thing. One slipup, with that kind of bankroll on the table, and the guy who blew it wouldn't just be killed. He would be fucking vaporized.

More to the point, the cash was only part of it. They had the forty million dollars going, and a semi full of pure skag coming back. It boggled Vinnie Lupo's mind to think how much two tons of dope was worth, but if the family was paying forty million to bring it in, you had to figure they were getting ten or maybe fifteen times that much back from the street.

Drop off the cash and bring the dope back home. Before they finished, Vinnie Lupo knew he would be ready for a good stiff drink, and then some. Heavy-duty tension always left him wired and anxious to un-wind. He thought of Marcie, waiting for him back in Queens, and reckoned that he might have something good and stiff for her when he got home.

Damn right.

For now, though, he would have to keep his mind on business. He had two crew wagons, twelve men altogether, one of them the driver who would take the semi over from the Russkies once they made the swap. Vinnie was set on riding shotgun in the truck, with one car leading by a quarter mile or so, the other right behind him all the way. His men were packing shot-guns, M-16s and Uzis, in addition to their side arms. Ten or fifteen federal violations on the guns alone, but that would be the least of Vinnie's problems if they ran into the heat.

Tony had spelled it out for him in no uncertain terms: *You lose the money or the smack, you're fucking dead.*

Okay. It was the kind of stipulation Vinnie Lupo understood. If anybody tried to stop him, *they* were fucking dead, and Vinnie didn't care if they were wearing federal badges or a bunch of clown suits from the circus. Lupo had his orders, and he never, ever, let the family down.

There was a mean chill in the air, but Vinnie had the Lincoln's engine running, with the heater on, to keep his soldiers warm. Some other time it might have made him drowsy, but the thought of forty million dollars in the trunk, two tons of China white approaching on the narrow highway up ahead, kept Lupo and the others on their toes. The Lincoln smelled like cig-arettes and gun oil, two familiar odors that were part of Vinnie's trade. Some people might have been re-pulsed, but it made Vinnie Lupo feel at home.

"Whazzis?" the driver asked nobody in particular.

Headlights appeared a mile or so in front of them, still on the wrong side of the border. Vinnie had a sudden feeling that he had to take a leak, and concen-trated on the job at hand to make it go away. He had an Ingram submachine gun in his lap, no silencer—it wouldn't matter if the shit came down—and now he closed the fingers of his right hand tight around the pistol grip.

"Be ready."

Vinnie waited till he knew for sure it was a semi, not some jerkoff farmer on his way to market at the crack of dawn. When he was positive, he had his driver flash the Lincoln's headlights in the signal they had arranged: two shorts, one long, another short. The semi slowed, its high beams flashing out the recognition signal.

Cool.

The breeze cut through his jacket as he stepped out of the car and closed the door behind him, standing with the Ingram pressed against his leg. He didn't want to make the semi driver or his escorts nervous, but you didn't dick around with forty million and a couple tons of skag. No way.

A car he hadn't seen before pulled up to pass the semi now, and slowed when it was thirty paces from the waiting crew wagons. Between the headlights in his eyes and tinted windows on the car, he gave up counting heads, but Vinnie calculated there could be no more than half a dozen soldiers in the escort vehicle. He gave the Russkies points for nerve and wondered if they took it as seriously as he did.

Vinnie Lupo stood and waited while the escorts climbed out of their car on either side, the hardware showing. He saw rifles, shotguns, pretty much the same as what his men were packing, spread out on the road behind him like a military firing squad. If someone popped a cap by accident, there would be hell to pay, with Vinnie in the middle of it. But he wasn't overly concerned. The Russkies were supposed to be professionals. What could go wrong?

He got his answer as the leader of the Russian escort team was moving forward, one hand raised in greeting, while the other held a pistol at his side. A comet came from nowhere, moving left to right across Lupo's field of vision, homing on the semi rig. On impact it exploded in a blinding ball of fire that flattened several of the Russian escorts where they stood, the shock wave rocking Vinnie Lupo on his heels.

There was barely time for him to think of what was happening before all hell broke loose.

THERE WAS NO RECOIL to speak of from the LAW rocket as its back-flash slipped over Bolan's shoulder, blooming from the rear end of the disposable launching tube. He dropped the fiberglass tube even as the hurtling rocket struck home, erupting in a ball of fire that tore the semitrailer open on the starboard side and left it twisted, like a toy made out of tinfoil. Reaching down beside him, while his enemies were scrambling for their lives, he found the Colt Commando and prepared to make his move.

The rifle is a smaller version of the classic M-16, with a shortened barrel and a telescoping stock, but all the deadly firepower of the original. In this case, it was loaded with a 100-round drum magazine, a live round in the chamber, with the safety off. The firelight helped him find a target, and he stroked the rifle's trigger lightly, sending off a 4-round burst that found one of the shadow men and spun him like a top before he fell.

The gunfire broke whatever spell the rocket's blast had cast over his enemies. The leaders started shouting orders—some in Russian, some in Brooklyn English—as they tried to rally the survivors and present a unified defense. The raw chaos in the aftermath of the explosion left both sides confused about exactly who was killing whom, which was fine with Bolan as he rose from hiding and advanced to meet the foe.

So far his targets had been members of the Russian team, and Bolan kept it going that way as he found the next mark, sprinting for the cover of a jet black BMW four-door, parked between the burning semitrailer and a pair of Continental crew wagons. From its position, the direction it was pointing, Bolan knew it had to be the escort for the two-ton heroin consignment, and he guessed it would have held six soldiers—seven, tops—but numbers weren't Bolan's primary concern.

The Executioner was firing for effect, and that meant a psychological, as well as physical, component. If anyone survived his strike, by luck or otherwise, Bolan was determined he should take a story home consistent with a violent break between two criminal fraternities. It was supposed to have the strong smell of a double cross, for all concerned.

He squeezed the Colt Commando's trigger, saw the runner stumble, tripped by some invisible obstruction, as he went down sprawling on his face. A couple of the New York boys were firing now, in the direction of the trees, but they had yet to find a solid target. Bolan's flash hider had done its work so far, and they were firing in the general direction of the rocket's glide path, yards to Bolan's left along the road. It made the five or six surviving Russians duck and cover, looking for a place to hide while they decided whether they were under fire or being rescued by the New York troops.

Bolan was first into the gap between uneasy allies, firing as he came. Another Russian staggered, clutching at his punctured chest and slumping back against the semi's grille. He slithered down the polished steel until he wound up seated on the blacktop, with his head cocked to one side, dead eyes locked open in the firelight. Seconds later hungry flames found diesel fuel, and an explosion flipped the semi cab so it was standing on its head, the lifeless Russian ground to paste beneath a ton of metal.

More shots came from the scattered soldiers, bullets hissing through the night. From his position at the tree line, Bolan saw a shadow breaking from the cover of the BMW, running back in the direction of the burning semi and the border, some three-quarters of a mile beyond. He just had time to drop the runner, had him in the Colt Commando's sights...and let him go.

One messenger was perfect. Let him spread the word of New York's treachery, while Bolan finished mopping up the rest. His face was grim as he went back to work.

SERGEI SHIKULOV wasn't a religious man. His parents had been Communists—a calculated ploy to keep their jobs secure and get a break on state-owned housing—and their only son was educated to believe that God was fabricated by oppressors to delude the proletariat, keep workers focused on the beauties of the afterlife while they were treated like a pack of slaves on earth. He still believed that, more or less, although his bent toward crime and personal reward had drawn him far afield from other party teachings ever since he'd been old enough to smash a window, grab a can of meat or loaf of bread and run away. But there were times when Shikulov wished that he knew how to pray.

Like now.

He was the leader of the Russian escort, charged with dropping off the semitrailer filled with heroin and picking up the payoff. Forty million U.S. dollars, he was told. The captain of his troop wasn't concerned that Shikulov and the others would go into business for themselves, take off and split the cash. That would have been five million dollars each, unless they snuffed the semi driver, but it made no difference. Each and every one of them had seen firsthand the vengeance meted out to traitors by the family.

Five million dollars simply wasn't worth the risk.

But now…

Shikulov ducked behind the BMW, grimacing as bullets ricocheted above his head. He clutched a Czech-made Skorpion machine pistol, still unfired, since he hadn't found a target yet and he worried about wasting precious ammunition when his life might yet depend on every round.

It had to be the gunmen from New York, he reasoned. The American police came in with lights and sirens, bullhorns amplifying voices till they sounded like a race of angry robots. Shikulov had observed that much on CNN and in the movies. Everybody knew that the *Amerikanski* pigs were bound by law to read your rights before they started shooting—and they wouldn't use a rocket launcher even then.

That part of it confused Sergei. Why would the gunmen from New York incinerate two tons of heroin if they were bent on stealing it? An accident, perhaps. If the appointed marksman was a novice with a rocket launcher, or if he got frightened at the crucial moment, it was possible that he was aiming for the BMW, got it wrong somehow and blew the truck instead.

Another burst of automatic fire distracted Sergei Shikulov from private thoughts. Behind him Pavel Bagdasarian squeezed off a burst from his Kalashnikov in the direction of the long, black Lincoln Continentals.

"Bastards!" Bagdasarian muttered as he ducked back under cover of the car. "They set us up."

"We've lost the merchandise," Shikulov said. "We have to try and get the money now."

"There are too many!" his partner answered.

"Even so. Would you go back without it, empty-handed?"

Bagdasarian thought about that question for a moment, making his decision. *"Nyet."*

"All right, then. What are we to do?"

"It's not for me to say, Sergei."

"How many of us still remain?" asked Shikulov.

Bagdasarian glanced at the men behind him, sheltered by the car. Two more that he could see, and one of them the lorry driver, crouching with a pistol in his hand.

"It looks like four."

Against a dozen, maybe more, thought Shikulov. He also thought about the grim alternative, returning to his captain and attempting to explain that he had lost two tons of heroin *and* forty million dollars, without doing anything to mitigate the double tragedy. Shikulov thought he would be lucky if the family's torpedoes only tortured him for six or seven days before they let him die.

"You know what we must do," he said to Pavel Bagdasarian.

"I know," the gunner said, "but I don't like it."

"We don't have to like it, Pavel."

"Da." The soldier's voice was grim, befitting the occasion. "We should get it over with, in that case."

"Right."

Sergei Shikulov snapped an order to the other men, waited to hear if either one of them had an objection to the suicidal plan and nodded when they chose to keep their mouths shut.

"After me," he said, and rose from cover, making out a line of shadow men with weapons blazing in their hands before he cut loose with the Skorpion. Behind him Bagdasarian and the other two were up and firing, two more automatic weapons and the handgun barking out staccato messages of death.

He saw one of the ten or twelve Italians fall, immediately followed by another, jerking as the bullets ripped into their bodies, spinning them around. Some of the others were turning even as he fired, the muzzles of their guns still spitting flame. In *his* direction now, instead of toward the trees.

Why were they firing at the trees? Sergei Shikulov wondered.

It would be his last coherent thought on earth, before he died.

FOR SEVERAL SECONDS Bolan watched the New York gunners trading fire with the depleted force of Russians. Two of Balderone's men went down in the initial exchange, a third staggering and dropping to his knees a heartbeat later, but the Russians were still outnumbered two to one, despite the casualties they had inflicted on their would-be allies, now their mortal enemies. A spray of automatic fire ripped through their ranks, stray bullets gouging divots in the BMW's paint job, shattering the windows, flattening both starboard tires. The Russians went down kicking, jerking, squeezing off their final rounds at nothing as they fell.

A sudden hush fell on the scene, but Bolan wouldn't let it last. He palmed a frag grenade and yanked the safety pin, wound up and threw it overhand. It landed between the Lincoln crew wagons, a yard or so behind the New York firing squad. Nobody seemed to notice it until the lethal egg exploded, shrapnel peppering the mafiosi where they stood, the shock wave dropping all but two of them.

One of the men who kept his balance had blood streaming from a ragged scalp wound, while the other seemed unscathed but shaken, looking for a target in the smoky no-man's-land. He held a stubby SMG, and as Bolan watched, he fired a long burst toward the tree line, obviously still convinced the premier danger came from that direction.

He was right.

A burst of 5.56 mm parabellum tumblers ripped into his chest and slammed him backward, draping him across the fender of the nearest Lincoln Continental.

Bolan stepped out of the shadows, moving toward the middle of the battlefield. Three of the gunners dropped by his grenade were dead before they hit the ground, another on his way, with shrapnel in his belly, chest and face. That left two others dazed and groggy, bleeding from assorted lesser wounds, but still in shape to fight.

As Bolan reached them, one of the gunners was on all fours and reaching for the submachine gun he had dropped when he went down. He never made it, as a single round from Bolan's Colt Commando drilled a hole behind his ear and punched him facedown on the pavement.

That left one, a stocky soldier, on his knees and fumbling in a pocket filled with shotgun shells. He brought a handful out, dropped most of them, but kept his grip on two, inserting one into the loading port of what appeared to be a 12-gauge riot gun with a folding stock. He was about to load the second round when Bolan shot him from a range of fifteen feet and punched him backward in a boneless sprawl.

All done with killing for the moment, Bolan checked the cars. There would be cash in one of them. When he found no luggage in the passenger compartments of the Lincolns, he walked back to check the trunks. Instead of searching corpses for the keys, he used the universal lockpick, firing one round from his rifle into each keyhole. When the trunks were open,

Bolan found three suitcases in one, two in the other. They were matching Samsonites, jet black, and none of them was locked.

He stood and stared at forty million dollars for a moment, doing the division, finally extracting one suitcase from each crew wagon, while he left the others open, in their places. Stepping back, he placed the two bags in the middle of the road, then turned and fired a short burst from his rifle into each car's trunk. In seconds flat he heard the trickling, dripping sound of gasoline as it began to drain from punctured tanks. He lit a book of matches, dropped it on the pavement, stepping backward as the winking flames met fumes and both cars were engulfed by fire.

Money to burn, Bolan thought, and now he had money to spend. Something in the neighborhood of sixteen million dollars, if they split the stash up evenly among five bags. No matter if it fell a little short; he had his war chest for the rest of the campaign, and then some.

Time to go.

He slung the Colt Commando, took a heavy bag in each hand and began the long, dark walk back to his car.

CHAPTER TWO

Manhattan

The predawn raid had been a fitting prelude for the Executioner's campaign in New York City. It wasn't the end of anything, but rather the beginning of a new defensive effort, heading off a double threat to the United States.

The home-grown Mafia had put down roots in New York City sometime in the nineteenth century, and it had prospered ever since, to varying degrees. Of late a rash of state and federal prosecutions had created vacuums at the top of the traditional Five Families, reorganizing the established power structure with a vengeance. It had been inevitable, Bolan realized, that someone from the ranks would try to grab the reins and pull himself into the saddle.

That someone was Louis Balderone.

It was a testament to federal law enforcement and the Executioner's long battle of attrition that a man like Balderone could even hope to boss the New York underworld. A lowly capo before John Gotti went away and other bosses found themselves in court or on a slab, Louis the Louse—as he was known behind his back to many "brothers" in La Cosa Nostra—had been elevated in the Brooklyn family almost by default. Of course, he had ambition and a ruthless style that helped him rise, but those were standard attributes of every mafiosi worth his salt. Intelligence and courage were the qualities that *kept* a godfather on top, and no one in New York was betting heavily on Balderone to reach a ripe old age once he attained the pinnacle of power in the mob.

Which meant that there would be no losers, other than Balderone himself, when he bought the farm.

Too bad.

It would have pleased the Executioner to cost his enemies more money, but it was more than he had any right to hope for. The Manhattan gig was only part of it, another step along the hellfire trail, and Bolan had no plans to tarry in the Apple any longer than was absolutely necessary.

At 10:15 a.m. he had a fair idea of where Don Balderone should be and what he would be doing. *Where* was the penthouse office suite on West Sixty-sixth Street, a block north of the Metropolitan Opera House. *What* was dissecting the morning's action near Cannon Corners, trying to find out how he had lost his forty million dollars *and* two tons of uncut China white. To get those answers, Balderone would be asking questions, none too gently. Regardless of the answers he received, there would be hell to pay.

That much the Executioner could guarantee.

The parking in Manhattan is a bitch, as anyone who's ever driven something larger than a bicycle around the city will attest. It helps to have a service vehicle and multiple permits, the kind of cover items Bolan had secured within an hour, after speaking on the telephone to Washington. The logo on his three-year-old Dodge van announced that he was part of Acme Heating/Air-Conditioning Repair, a nonexistent firm whose phone number, if dialed, would offer the weather forecast for the afternoon.

He wondered briefly if the "Acme" tag was taken from an old Three Stooges movie or the series of cartoons where a coyote ordered tools and bombs by mail in his attempts to snare a beeping roadrunner. Bolan wouldn't have put it past the brains at Stony Man, a little joke to make him smile as he was knocking on Death's door, but it made zero difference either way.

There had been two options to approach Don Balderone and make the tag: up close or from a distance. Bolan could have called on him at home, but he had opted for the office, judging that a high-rise suite downtown would mean a smaller number of civilian bystanders than going after Balderone in a residential neighborhood. As for the manner of approach, he chose long-distance over close and personal, another safety measure for bystanders *and* himself.

Reach out and touch someone, damn right.

The New York tour guides will tell you that there are no alleys in Manhattan. Every outdoor passageway, no matter how unkempt or claustrophobic, is officially regarded as a street. It was semantic bullshit, but Bolan didn't care if New York's alleyways were paved in gold and named for passages of scripture.

All he wanted was a place to park the van.

He found it three doors down and across the street

from Balderone's high rise. He nosed into the alley and killed the engine, zipped his denim jumpsuit almost to the throat and reached back for the heavy metal box of tools behind the driver's seat. He locked the driver's door behind him, paused to open up the double doors in back and lifted out a pair of bright orange rubber cones, which he deposited behind the van, in plain view from the street beyond. It made the setting look more official, and would hopefully prevent some jerk from cutting in and rear-ending the van while he was gone.

He grabbed the toolbox, hefting it as if the heavy iron inside weighed nothing, and began his walk back toward the sniper's nest.

Louis the Louse was pissed. He got that way sometimes—in fact, his rage was legendary—but there were degrees of anger, some more serious for the souls unfortunate enough to be within his orbit when he lost his cool.

Today his rage was off the scale.

"What do you fuckin' *mean*, nobody knows what happened?"

Louis Balderone's three underbosses were assembled in a semicircle, facing him across the antique desk that was a shade too small to let a Piper Cub touch down and taxi on its polished surface.

Philip Sacco, Anthony Sarducci, Tommy Vega—all were glancing nervously at one another, none of them exactly eager to respond.

Louis the Louse slammed down an open palm

against the desktop, doing his impression of a pistol shot. "I asked a fuckin' question, people!"

"Well, uh…" Sacco hesitated, swallowed hard and tried again. "Nobody knows what happened, boss, because our people didn't make it back."

"I know that, shithead! Do you think I'm fuckin' stupid?"

"No, sir."

"Then don't treat me like I'm fuckin' stupid, 'kay? I want to know what happened to our people, that they don't come back."

"They all got wasted," Tommy Vega answered, smiling like a little kid who gets the answer right in class for the first time in his life.

The open hand came down three times in swift succession. Balderone watched his underbosses jump as if their chairs were hot-wired to a generator.

"*They all got wasted,*" Balderone whined as he mimicked Vega's answer. "You must really think I'm fuckin' stupid if you're gonna tell me shit like that."

"No, boss. No fuckin' way."

"Well, lemme see. I *know* they all got wasted, right? Somebody woke me up at fuckin' 3:00 a.m. to tell me they got wasted, and I lost my forty million dollars, *plus* the China white. I know all that, but you keep tellin' me the same thing, Tommy, so I'd say you gotta think I'm fuckin' stupid."

"Maybe I disunderstood the question," Tommy Vega muttered.

Balderone swore through gritted teeth. "I wanna know *who* killed my people, 'kay? I wanna know *who* stole my forty mil. *Who* torched a semitrailer full of uncut skag from Bangkok. Are we on the same page, now?''

"My money's on the fuckin' Russkies," Anthony Sarducci said.

"How's that? They lost their people, too."

"They lost *some* people, sure, but we don't know how many they sent out. It could be Vinnie and his boys got lucky with a few, before the others took 'em out."

"And why would they be doin' this, the Russians?" Balderone asked.

"Same reason I would, in their place," Sarducci said. "They grab the forty mil for nothin', right?"

"So, what about the merchandise they lost?"

"They lost a *truck* is all I know for sure. Could be it was an empty truck. Or maybe they put just enough skag in there so it shows up when the pigs go through the ashes with their scientific shit, you know? I mean, why not?"

"A fuckin' setup, huh?"

"It's what I'd do."

"That's twice you said that, Anthony. You make me wonder."

"Huh? Hey, boss—"

"Relax, I'm playin' with ya. You may have the right idea on this thing, after all."

"We oughta check it out," Phil Sacco said.

"No shit, Sherlock."

"How would we do that, do ya think?"

The question came from Tommy Vega, making Balderone smile against his will. A guy like Vega got promoted for his muscle and his loyalty, not his brains.

In fact, Louis the Louse was wise enough to know that underbosses shouldn't be too smart, or they would start to scheme against their chief and try to grab the whole thing for themselves. He liked them loyal and stupid, with a hint of panic when he blew his stack, but stupid was a drawback when it came to plotting strategy.

"First thing you do—"

The thought was right there, balanced on his tongue, but Balderone never got it out. Before he had a chance to finish, something struck the picture window to his right, and Tommy Vega's head exploded like a melon with a cherry bomb inside. One second he was leaning forward, hanging on his capo's every word, and then his tattered neck was spewing blood and shit like a volcano, while his body started flopping, jerking from his chair, down to the floor.

Louis the Louse had time to curse once more before his whole world went to hell.

THE WALTHER WA2000 is the sniper's weapon of the Space Age, built for accuracy and convenience. It's a jungle fighter's weapon, more a match piece with a lethal edge, but Bolan had become accustomed to it, using one whenever it was handy and his mission called for killing from a distance. A semiautomatic rifle of the short, bullpup design, the Walther sported a 25-inch barrel fluted for cooling and reduction of vibrations, clamped fore and aft for stability. It fed .300 Winchester Magnum rounds from a 6-shot detachable box magazine, with a Schmidt & Binder 2.5 × 10-power scope providing the optical edge.

Peering through the telescopic sight, Bolan almost felt as if he were inside the office with Don Balderone and his three lieutenants. He was no lip-reader, but it didn't take an expert to know that Louis the Louse was ripping his underbosses up one side and down the other, looking for solutions to the massacre at Cannon Corners. Bolan waited for the tirade to wind down a little, chose one of the don's lieutenants on a whim and fixed the crosshairs on his anxious-looking face.

Show time.

The Walther's trigger had a three-pound pull, and Bolan waited for the kick against his shoulder, watching through the scope as his first steel-jacketed round drilled through double-pane glass and found its target on the other side. The guy was dead before he knew what hit him, more or less decapitated by the Magnum round that cored a hole below his nose and sheared off most of what was located above the impact point.

One down and three to go.

He swiveled back toward Balderone, in time to see the capo gaping, at a sudden loss for words. His target pushed back from the desk, prepared to dive for cover, but Louis the Louse had run out of time. The second round was dead on target from a hundred yards, punching through Balderone's chest and slamming him back against the nearest wall, high-backed swivel chair and all. The capo's mouth fell open in astonishment, as if his last thought was a rage of disbelief that anyone could reach him in his inner sanctum. Too damn late to tighten his security by that time, as his body seemed to lose its substance, giving in to gravity and sliding toward the floor.

The two survivors had gained a fair idea of what was happening, and both were on their feet as Bolan pivoted to find them with his telescopic sight. At times like this, the Walther's semiautomatic action was a blessing, sparing him the time it would have taken to finesse a standard bolt action between his shots. Line up and squeeze, no sweat, the taller of the targets vaulting forward as a bullet slammed between his shoulder blades. He struck the office door facefirst and left a crimson smear from flattened nostrils as he slithered to the deck.

His buddy reached the doorknob, gave a tug and found the door obstructed by the latest corpse. He reached down for the dead man, mouthing silent curses as the crosshairs found his profile, locking in. The shot that killed him bored a tidy hole about an inch below his temple, on the left, before the right side of his head erupted in a crimson spray that blotched the door and wall with gore.

Four up, four down.

It took a moment, breaking down the Walther and replacing it in the toolbox, a metal tray of wrenches, screwdrivers and pliers fitting over it to hide the killing instrument. Bolan rode the service elevator down and had it to himself, walked back to find the Dodge van unmolested, with no parking ticket on the windshield.

Perfect.

He was on a roll, but Bolan wasn't finished yet. He had another team to deal with before he wrapped the action in New York, and anything could happen in the second half.

In fact, the Executioner was counting on it.

MIKHAIL VASILIEV was troubled, pacing restlessly around his hotel suite and shooting glances at the silent telephone. He was expecting news at any moment, a report that it was safe for him to leave the Belvedere—in fact, to leave the city, putting it behind him while he still had time. He felt himself in danger, and while he wasn't afraid, he didn't relish staying in Manhattan any longer than he absolutely had to, now that any chance of an agreement with the New York syndicate had been destroyed.

One member of the team he had dispatched to guard the China white and bring his money back had managed to survive the carnage in upstate New York. The man described an ambush, with a rocket launcher used to detonate the semitrailer with its tons of heroin inside, while automatic weapons cut loose on the Russian escorts. It was madness, but he understood the ruthless mind behind such actions, and was willing to agree that the initial rocket may have been misplaced by a distracted marksman. If that were the case, he would assume that Louis Balderone had already killed the man responsible. It was exactly what Mikhail Vasiliev would have done in his place.

The upshot was that he, Vasiliev, was out two tons of heroin and forty million dollars in cash. His brother, back in Moscow, would be furious when he found out, and while Mikhail wasn't actually afraid of Gregori, he was relieved that he could break the news by transatlantic telephone. Let someone else endure the screaming tantrum that was sure to follow. By the time Mikhail was safely back in Canada, his older brother would have calmed himself enough to set about devising suitable revenge.

This much Mikhail could say with certainty: Gregori's vengeance would be ruthless and extreme. His brother was predictable in that respect, had been from childhood, when the slightest insult prompted him to sudden, brutal violence. Mikhail had wondered more than once if Gregori might be possessed of something in the nature of a fractured personality, enabling him to charm a woman or negotiate a multimillion-ruble business deal one moment, while exploding into homicidal savagery the next. In any case, his personality had served them well as they were rising up the ladder of Vorovskoi Mir to reach their current prominence. Mikhail tried hard to emulate his brother and was fairly good at it by now, but he could never truly rival Gregori's apparent fearlessness where violence was involved.

Today, for instance. He was jumpy, anxious to be gone, put New York City far behind him and leave Louis Balderone to gloat over his triumph for a while, until Gregori's plans were finalized and the ax fell on Balderone's neck. The city was a death trap for him in the meantime. The Italians would think nothing of eliminating one Vasiliev when they had gone this far to place the brothers on the brink of war.

He veered off track, still pacing, moving toward the telephone that mocked him with its silence. Viktor should have had the limousine downstairs by now. Arkady should have called to tell him everything was ready for departure. Brooding in his suite, Mikhail Vasiliev imagined that some new disaster had befallen his remaining soldiers. What if Balderone had found out where the limousine was kept and sent his gunmen out to lie in wait? What if Mikhail was alone in New York City, stranded, miles from the safe haven he had found in Canada, with no way to get back?

He pulled his thoughts up short, his anger focused inward now. It was one thing to hide from enemies of flesh and blood when you were visibly outnumbered and outgunned, but fabricating adversaries out of thin air was a sign of cowardice. Mikhail Vasiliev wasn't a coward, and he wouldn't let himself fall prey to idle fears.

As if on cue, the telephone demanded his attention, shrill and strident. Mikhail answered on the second ring, made no attempt to mask the tension in his voice.

"Anno!"

"The car is here," Arkady told him, speaking from the hotel lobby. "I've already checked the street."

"Well, check again," Mikhail instructed his chief bodyguard. "I'm coming down."

Three soldiers waited for him in the main room of his suite, expensive jackets looking bulky and misshapen with the military hardware underneath. They were prepared for anything, he thought, and there were three more guns downstairs. He was as safe as he could ever hope to be, until they crossed the border once more, passing into Canada.

A few short hours now. Perhaps one stop for gas on the way, and he could let himself relax again until the orders came from Gregori and it was time to punish those responsible for his embarrassment. Mikhail was looking forward to that opportunity.

"Let's go," he told the gunmen, waiting while they lumbered to their feet and moved before him out into the hallway and toward the elevator. In another moment they were all descending toward the street and freedom, anxious to be out of there and gone.

HE COULD HAVE SNIPED the Russians, but the idea of shooting toward the sidewalk and a crush of innocent civilians left Bolan cold. Instead, he opted for the more direct approach, with all of its inherent risks, and planned his move accordingly.

The stakeout was no problem. No one really noticed one man standing on the sidewalk of West Twenty-eighth Street. He was caught up in window-shopping at a lingerie shop, maybe checking out a present for his mistress, killing time before he went back to the office to complete the daily grind. If anyone gave him a second glance, it may have been a woman passing by, intrigued by Bolan's looks and by the seeming focus of his interest, maybe wishing she could be on the receiving end of such a gift from such a man. None dared approach him, though—not in a city where you could be murdered on the street, with several dozen people watching it, none caring enough to get involved.

Bolan saw the limousine pull up and stop in a no-parking zone. A stocky gunner moved from the hotel lobby to the curb and leaned in to check the car, the driver, for himself. After the massacre upstate, it seemed the Russians weren't taking any chances.

Bolan slipped open the single button on his jacket, reached inside to touch the grip of the Beretta 93-R automatic pistol nestled in its custom shoulder rig. The holster was designed to take a pistol with a compact silencer attached, and while his plan left little chance that passersby would fail to notice him, the natural confusion of the moment, coupled with the silence of his weapon, would at least confuse descriptions from the handful who would remain to speak with the police when he was done.

He drifted slowly toward the hotel entrance, stalling, knowing it would be a grave mistake to get there prematurely. On the other hand, he couldn't give his targets too much room; he would then have to sprint along behind them, drawing more attention to himself. It was a matter of finesse, split-second timing. A mistake in one direction or the other would be fatal to him.

Bolan was thirty feet east of the hotel entrance when the stock gunner reappeared, trailing others in his wake. Four bodyguards were behind him, in a rough diamond formation, with a fifth man in the middle, covering all sides. That made six shooters, if they had the driver packing, plus the one man he couldn't afford to miss. The Beretta's magazine held twenty parabellum rounds, with one more in the chamber.

It would have to be enough.

He drew the pistol, tried to keep the movement unobtrusive, walking toward the Russian party with his weapon down against his thigh. The target's escorts looked in all directions, but they had no reason to suspect a well-dressed businessman, his side arm blocked from view by an obese man running interference.

Perfect.

At the final instant, Bolan sidestepped, raising the Beretta in a firm two-handed grip. The piece was capable of 3-round bursts, but he couldn't afford to waste his rounds on automatic fire. He went for head shots, quick and clean, within three paces of his targets when he opened up.

The first two bodyguards died before the others had a clue that anything was wrong. Blood spattered anxious faces as the shocked survivors tried to close ranks, reaching for their hardware, knowing it was too damn late to save their boss, no matter what they did from that point on.

His next two rounds were allocated for Mikhail Vasiliev, one shot between the eyes, another to the heart, before the Russian's brain could register the fact of death. A couple of the bodyguards had guns in hand by that time, lining up their shots, but Bolan stood his ground, aware that any movement to avoid the confrontation would place unarmed bystanders at even greater risk. Instead of running for his life, he put his faith in Kevlar and a steady hand.

His fifth shot plugged one of Vasiliev's torpedoes right between the eyes, a submachine gun tumbling from the dead man's grasp before he had a chance to fire. Half turning toward the last two, on his left, Bolan saw a muzzle-flash and staggered as the close-range bullet slammed into his Kevlar vest with all the impact of a hammer blow. It took iron will to keep him on his feet and firing back, but Bolan pulled it off, the shooter sprawling backward as a parabellum round drilled through his chest.

That left the stocky leader of the team, still grappling with a pistol that had stuck inside his waistband, and the driver, even now emerging from the limousine. A head shot put the grappler down and out, but Bolan waited for the wheelman to expose himself, unwilling to waste bullets on the bodywork and windows of an armored car.

The driver was a young man, with more balls than brains. He rushed around the vehicle to meet his adversary, squeezing off a wild round from his nickel-plated pistol as he came. The sidewalk crowd was scattering by then, recoiling from the scene of carnage, footsteps smearing blood that spread across the pavement, screams and curses rising from the lips of panicked men and women.

It took three shots to stop the driver, not because he was a large man, but because momentum kept him moving forward, even with two bullets in his chest. The third round drilled his heart and punched him through an awkward pirouette, legs tangled as he fell.

All done.

The Executioner returned his pistol to its holster, pressed against his aching ribs, and swiftly lost himself in the disorder of the crowd.

CHAPTER THREE

Stony Man Farm

The little Cessna was a switch from military and commercial aircraft. There was no more leg room, but the crowding didn't make Bolan feel as if he had been crammed into a sardine can. Despite their many safety features, Bolan always thought of flying in a small prop plane as more of an adventure, tempting fate—as if he didn't get enough of that in daily life. He understood the Cessna's physics and mechanics well enough, but still experienced the unexpected thrill of turbulence the way a child looks forward to his next ride on a roller coaster.

"Getting there," the pilot said unnecessarily. He didn't know his silent passenger from Adam, and the odds were excellent they would never meet again. He had no way of knowing that the Executioner had made this trip, by land and air, on numerous occasions in the past.

They followed Skyline Drive along the rugged backbone of the Blue Ridge Mountains, in Virginia, less than fifty miles southwest of Washington, D.C. A casual observer would never make the capital connection, staring out the Cessna's window at the two-lane highway down below and the forest that pressed close on either side. It was impossible to look upon that wilderness and postulate a concrete world of scheming politicians, limousines and bodyguards, high-rise hotels and reeking slums.

The Farm looked somewhat out of place when studied from a bird's-eye view. It seemed incongruous that someone would clear acreage here when he could drive a few miles east or west and find much larger tracts of open land, but that was Southern farmers for you. Once the first surprise wore off, the farm that Hal Brognola christened Stony Man, after a nearby mountain, seemed predictably routine in all respects. There was a farmhouse, cultivated fields and orchards, outbuildings, even a mobile home, some distance from the other buildings, where the hired help would bed down.

Special clearance was needed for anyone to be briefed on what went on inside those buildings. Similarly, what appeared to be a long, bare stretch of fallow ground was actually an airstrip, camouflaged with paint and a thin layer of topsoil, carefully maintained. The "mobile home" that sat astride the north-south runway was, in fact, a spotter's post and gun emplacement, mounting radar and a quad of 20 mm Gatling guns, concealed behind hinged walls, that could lay down a concentrated fire exceeding 20,000 rounds per minute in emergencies. Any uninvited pilot trying for a touchdown on the Stony Man airstrip would discover that the trailer blocked his best approach. If he persisted anyway, he could expect to have a catastrophic accident.

The Cessna was expected, though, and as they circled once above the Farm, a tractor was already coupled to the double-wide command post, moving it aside to let the small plane land. A narrow road ran from the airstrip to the central complex, and a Chevy Blazer was approaching as the pilot leveled into his approach and throttled back, the little aircraft touching down without a hitch.

"Smooth ride," said Bolan as they taxied through a U-turn and he reached back for his duffel bag.

"We aim to please," the pilot answered with a cocky smile.

Flyboys.

Deplaning, Bolan recognized the Blazer's wheelman, and smiled with real pleasure at the stocky, grayhaired man. "You're looking good," he said.

"This is retirement?" Yakov Katzenelenbogen grumbled, putting on his gruff act one more time. "A chauffeur now, I am. I should have let them shoot me while I had the chance."

"The job's all right, I take it?"

"It beats working," Katz replied. "I can't complain."

They shook left-handed, since the tough Israeli's right hand had been a casualty of war, long years ago. His grip was firm, and he was smiling now, despite himself.

"We'd better go," Katz said. "The natives have been getting restless since you called."

THE WAR ROOM was downstairs, with access via elevator from the ground floor of the farmhouse. The remainder of the basement level was reserved for office space, auxiliary communications and a well-stocked arsenal, a generator and the storage of supplies. A conference table occupied the center of the room, six chairs on either side, while Hal Brognola took his place at the table's head. Three of the dozen chairs were occupied, by Bolan, Katz, and Barbara Price, the Farm's honey blond mission controller. Aaron "the Bear" Kurtzman sat off to one side in his wheelchair, manning a high-tech console that controlled the room's lights and audiovisual displays.

"That was a good job in New York," Brognola said when everyone was settled, steaming mugs of coffee close at hand. "I wish that was the end of it."

Bolan waited, knowing there was bad news on the way. It was the only kind delivered in this room.

"But," Hal continued, "we've got problems with the Russian mob that won't be settled by eliminating Louis Balderone and company."

"I'm listening."

Brognola nodded to the Bear, and Kurtzman stroked a button on his console, bringing down the lights. Another tap, and Bolan watched a slab of paneling slide back to reveal a six-foot TV screen. The first face that came into focus was familiar, round and scarred from teenage acne, sandy hair buzzed in a crew cut that was better suited for low maintenance than any sense of style. The last time he had seen that face, thought Bolan, it was streaming crimson from a fresh hole in the forehead.

"You met this one in New York," Brognola said. "Mikhail Vasiliev. He was the front man for the so-called Chechen Mafia in North America. In case you're not up on your Russian sociology, the Chechens—out of Chechnya, no less—are the Sicilians of the Eastern Bloc. They raise their kids to honor family above all else and treat outsiders like they have the plague. That led to problems with the KGB and the militia in the bad old days, and Chechens were among the first real Russian gangsters, well before the country fell apart in '89. By then, in fact, they were the richest criminals in Moscow, and considered some of the most ruthless. These days they're involved in everything from drugs and vice to bootleg nukes. They're in the forefront of the move to spread the Russian mob around the world, making alliances with hoods from Sicily and Tokyo to Medellín and Queens."

"Vasiliev?" said Bolan, prodding.

"Right. The guy you dusted in Manhattan was the younger brother of a hard-nosed pair. Gregori calls the shots in Moscow—not without some competition, granted, but he's generally regarded as a *vor v zakonye,* literally a 'thief within the code,' or what our friends from Sicily would call a godfather."

"He won't be pleased about his brother," Katzenelenbogen said.

"Bet on it," Brognola replied. "Of course, the chances are he'll blame the Balderone connection. Not much he can do to Louis now."

"He won't stop pushing for a foothold in the States, though," Bolan advised.

"Hell, he's already got a foothold," said Brognola.

"You know all about the FBI's exchange program, I guess?"

"The basics," Bolan answered.

"Okay. Long story short, they've got a team in Moscow as we speak. Been there for better than a year, rotating agents in and out to help the Russians get their act together on the org-crime angle. Nothing in the Soviet experience prepared them for the crime explosion they've seen since Yeltsin blew the party off. It's like Chicago in the 1920s, ten times over. They've got neighborhoods in Moscow and St. Petersburg where you can pick up rocket launchers and machine guns off the street. The dealers line up in their cars and try to undersell the competition like some kind of Arab street bazaar."

"Which helps explain the body count," said Barbara Price.

"In spades," Brognola agreed. "The other thing is runaway inflation. Everybody wants 'hard currency,' which basically means dollars, though they won't turn up their noses at a deutsche mark, either. Anybody keeping up on the inflation rate in Russia these days?"

"I just know it's high," said Bolan.

"That's the understatement of the century, my friend. In November 1990, one ruble was equal to a dollar seventy-five in U.S. currency. By September 1992, a dollar bought two hundred rubles. Today it's closer to thirty-five hundred. Imagine living in a country where the value of your income dropped from twenty grand to the equivalent of six or seven bucks a year. You have to be a millionaire to pay the rent."

"It sounds like Germany after the Treaty of Versailles," said Kurtzman.

"Close enough," Hal said. "Which helps explain a strong trend toward religion as the hope runs out, plus all the far-right groups that have sprung up in Russia in the past few years. Some of the neo-fascist crowd are so extreme they dig black magic on the side and talk the same old anti-Jewish crap that got Hitler rolling back in 1933. Toss in the old guard, who can't wait to take another shot at communism, and I'm telling you, the whole damn place is one huge powder keg."

"And I'm supposed to light the fuse," said Bolan, smiling ruefully.

"Not quite," Brognola said. "We're hoping that a clean, strategic move against the syndicate may help *de*fuse the situation—or a part of it, at least. The Russians obviously have to clean their own house, with some foreign aid to help them buy the mops and brooms, but this particular unsightly mess is slopping over to the States, big time. The drugs are only part of it, as you're aware. The Russian mob will deal with *anybody* for a price, and that includes your half-assed terrorist who won't mind robbing six or seven banks to get the money for a pocket nuke. We know the Russian Mafia has no respect for anyone or anything beyond itself. It's time they learned a little healthy fear."

"So, what's the plan?" asked Bolan.

"One of Gregori Vasiliev's most valued contacts is a Turkish poppy grower, Kenan Bey. His fields alone provide approximately one-third of the heroin consumed in Moscow at the present time. If you decide to take this job, your first priority is shutting down the Turkish pipeline. You'll have Phoenix Force on loan, along with someone from the Russian team. They tell me he's a little on the rough side, by militia standards. Spetsnaz training as a background, lost his partner not too long ago. A drug raid went to hell, with the Vasilievs behind it. These days he's the man they use for no-win situations."

"That's encouraging," said Bolan. "And what happens after Turkey?"

"You let nature take its course," Brognola replied. "Officially the Russians won't know anything about the operation. They'll be going through the motions to preserve the peace, but it's primarily a new excuse to clean house on the syndicate."

"I see." The Executioner considered it for all of thirty seconds, then he said, "Okay. I'm in."

"YOU COULD HAVE TURNED the mission down, you know."

"And miss a free trip to the Russian Commonwealth?"

"I'm serious," said Barbara Price. "This whole thing smells."

"That's just the borscht," said Bolan.

"God, you're hopeless."

"So I'm told."

They were alone in Price's quarters, on the second floor, directly over the computer room. A subtle, sexy fragrance permeated every corner of the room.

"You *will* be careful, right?"

"My middle name."

"Bullshit."

"Such language, from a lady."

Price smiled and tugged the zipper on her jumpsuit downward to her waist. "You ain't heard nothing yet," she said.

"Is that a promise?"

"Yes, indeed."

She stepped into his arms and kissed him deeply, meeting Bolan's tongue with hers, her fingers busy with the buttons of his shirt. He drew the jumpsuit's zipper down a few more inches, slipped his hands inside and felt her shudder as he cupped her breasts, the nipples stiffening as he began to tease them with his thumbs. She whimpered into Bolan's open mouth and struggled with the jumpsuit, desperate to be free of it. He helped her with the sleeves, then knelt before her, sliding fabric down across her hips and thighs, her panties going with it, leaning in to taste her. Her fingers tangled in his hair, and Price arched her back to meet his lips, unable to suppress a moan.

Bolan cupped her buttocks, holding her upright as her legs began to tremble, shudders rippling through her body. When she was on the verge of falling, nearly helpless to control herself, he drew his lips away and rose, led her to the nearby bed. She sat down on the mattress, tried to help him with his clothing, but her hands were trembling so that Bolan took a short step back and finished undressing himself.

"Oh, my," she said. "Is that for me?"

"Assuming that you want it," Bolan said.

"Yes, please."

She scooted backward on the mattress, stretched out on her back and raised her knees as Bolan joined her. Reaching down between their bodies, she found him, showing him the way.

"Oh, God!"

He moved against her, cautiously at first, and then with greater urgency as she opened for him, locked her ankles tight behind his buttocks, pressing downward with her heels. She made good on her promise in a breathless whisper, telling Bolan everything she wanted him to do, explicit details spilling from her lips as she began to pant, her body writhing, squirming, matching Bolan's lusty rhythm thrust for thrust.

He tried to make it last, but there is only so much pleasure mortal flesh can tolerate. He felt Price's convulsions starting, heard her gasp his name and then his climax overtook him in a rush. They clung together, straining toward the ultimate release, until the tide of passion crested, ebbed and left them stranded in the afterglow.

"Not bad," she told him moments later, when she had her voice back. "For the first time, anyway."

"Excuse me?"

"I mean, we're just getting started, right?"

"Well, I—"

"That's what I thought." She grinned and reached for him, trapped him with her fingers, working at his tender flesh.

"I wouldn't hope for much right now," he said.

"There's always hope."

"I wouldn't be so sure."

"Where there's a will…"

He felt an unexpected stirring, glanced down at her hand. "You may be right," he said.

"I told you so."

"Be gentle with me," Bolan said.

Her smile turned wicked as she rolled him over on his back.

"I'm sure."

CHAPTER FOUR

Istanbul

Once upon a time, this city of over six million was called Constantinople, after Constantine the Great, an emperor of Rome. It is the last outpost of Eastern Europe, perched upon the Bosporus and facing eastward into Asia Minor. Even so, the atmosphere is predominantly Eastern here, with the vast majority of all inhabitants professing their allegiance to the Muslim faith. The sights and sounds and smells are those of Asia, and the same could easily be said of the prevailing attitude toward human life.

The cultivation, processing and sale of opium is banned in Turkey, where a first arrest for transportation of narcotics means a prison sentence in conditions said to rival Devil's Island. Even so, raw opium and processed heroin remain two of the largest Turkish exports, right up there with coffee and tobacco. Drugs mean money, in the East as in the West, and Turkish cops are no more incorruptible than any of their colleagues in the States.

The sun was setting over Istanbul as Bolan moved along a narrow street in the Samatya district, near the waterfront. A soft breeze blew in from the Sea of Marmara, carrying the salt-and-fish smell to his nostrils, mingling with the fragrances of cooking food that wafted out of kitchens close at hand. He had a sense of being watched, and hoped that it was only T. J. Hawkins, waiting in the car.

Hawkins had filled the empty slot in Phoenix Force when Yakov Katzenelenbogen shifted to the staff at Stony Man. A thirty-something veteran of the Rangers who had seen his share of action in Grenada, Panama and Desert Storm—the latter conflict earning him a Silver Star—he had been separated from the service after executing a Somalian warlord to protect a group of unarmed villagers. A threat of murder charges had evaporated in the face of bad publicity, and Hawkins had been honorably discharged from the Army, signing on with Phoenix Force once Hal Brognola and a friend from Delta Force convinced him the appointment meant he would see action on the firing line, and not behind a desk in Washington.

It had been Bolan's choice to break the six-man party into teams of two, thus covering more ground and saving time on their campaign in Istanbul. The others would be busy, even now, as he approached his target on the waterfront, the stubby MP-5K submachine gun snug beneath his jacket on its swivel rig.

The target was a Turkish "travel agency" that booked no tours and sold no tickets, even though it did a multimillion-dollar business every year. Its customers were Europeans and Americans who represented various narcotics syndicates, arranging shipments in the guise of tour bookings, with the prices registered in fractions of the actual amount. Thus, a booking for six at two thousand dollars a head denoted sixty kilos of pure Turkish heroin, delivered at a price of twenty thousand dollars per kilo. It was a thriving business for the godfather of Istanbul, one Kenan Bey, but Bolan meant to change all that.

It was five minutes short of closing time when Bolan stepped into the office, his arrival heralded by a brass bell suspended from the door frame. One look at the young receptionist, and he decided she should live, if only as a witness to the fate awaiting Kenan Bey's associates. Her smile went sour as he flashed the submachine gun, standing back and nodding toward the door.

"Gitmek hemen!" said Bolan, using one of several Turkish phrases he had memorized for such emergencies.

The lady blinked at him and followed orders, heading swiftly for the street and safety.

Bolan watched her go, then moved beyond her desk, in the direction of the private offices in back. He followed voices, muffled laughter, to a door that stood ajar, emblazoned with a placard and a name he couldn't read.

As he toed the door wide open, Bolan recognized the men he had come looking for. He didn't know their faces, but the type had grown familiar from the first days of his one-man war against the syndicate back home. Rough faces, even with the perfect haircuts, sunlamp tans and waxed mustaches. There were three of them, and Bolan thought that they would all look more at home on Wanted posters than in three-piece suits, pretending to be honest businessmen.

They started scrambling at first sight of Bolan's weapon, one man grabbing for a pistol in his top desk drawer, the others breaking right and left, both wishing they were armed. He shot them anyway, short bursts that spun them off in opposite directions, one man bouncing off a filing cabinet, while the other kissed a wall and slumped down to his knees, a praying supplicant with nothing left to ask the Man upstairs.

That left the owner of the office, caught with one hand in the open drawer, his other braced against the desk. He looked Death in the face and tried to snarl defiance, but it came out sounding like a whimper, covered by the racket of a burst that slammed him back against the wall and left him lolling boneless in his swivel chair.

It was another thirty seconds' work to empty out the filing cabinets, yanking drawers and dumping great handfuls of paper on the floor, with no attempt to read or sort it out. The plan was slash and burn, with Bolan hoping that the loss of active files might cause some inconvenience down the road for Kenan Bey and company. He palmed a slim incendiary stick and dropped it on the heap of papers in the middle of the floor, retreating as it popped and sizzled into life.

Smoke followed him outside, and Bolan walked back to the car, ignoring the pedestrians who passed him on his way. It made no difference if some of them recalled his face, as long as he and Hawkins were away from there when the police arrived.

"No problems?" Hawkins asked as he slid into the shotgun seat.

"We're one for one," the Executioner replied.

"All right."

"I'M IN," David McCarter, the Phoenix Force leader, told the little hand-held radio. "Two minutes, starting...now."

He switched the two-way off to keep stray bursts of static from betraying him to any nearby ears, and slipped it back into the inside pocket of his coat. The micro-Uzi that replaced it in his hand was fitted with a silencer that made it muzzle heavy, prompting him to favor a two-handed grip.

The brothel, a longtime fixture in the Hasköy district, was owned by Kenan Bey and managed for him by a second cousin on his mother's side to keep it in the family. McCarter had gained entry through the basement, pausing briefly at the foot of wooden stairs that led up to a door. If his nose was not mistaken, the door opened on a kitchen presently in use. The live-in hookers occupied three floors above the swank ground level, where they advertised their wares and were selected by the paying customers before a trip upstairs to show what they could do.

So much for romance, right.

McCarter had been elevated to the leadership of Phoenix Force when Katz retired from active field-work—though the gruff Israeli's job at Stony Man could hardly be called retirement—but the change in rank hadn't removed McCarter from the firing line. Each member of the team was fully operational on every mission, barring injuries, and McCarter's experience in combat with the SAS had taught him early on that it was easier to lead men than to shove them from behind.

Besides, he thought, without the action, what in bloody hell would be the point?

He trusted Rafael Encizo to be glancing at his watch outside, waiting for the proper moment to come knocking on the brothel's door. The Cuban passed for Turkish at a glance, as long as no one drew him into conversation, and between the two of them, McCarter thought they stood a decent chance of bringing down the house.

Of course, there was a chance that something unforeseen could still go wrong, but that was what made life more interesting.

He took the stairs two at a time and tried the doorknob with his left hand, balancing the silenced Uzi in his right. The knob turned easily, without resistance, and McCarter edged the door back inch by inch. He was awash in spicy cooking smells that brought saliva to his mouth, but he dismissed the sudden craving, concentrating on the three chefs who were busy at the stove, their backs turned toward the doorway where he stood. It would have been no trick to kill them, but McCarter drew the line at shooting innocent civilians in cold blood. They had one chance to live, and if they blew it, he would send them off to meet Allah without a second thought.

He whistled softly, catching their attention, waiting for all three to turn and face him. He didn't speak Turkish, but they got the message loud and clear, discarding floppy hats and aprons as they made a beeline for the nearest exit, following McCarter's nod and gesture with the gun.

He left a giant pot of something simmering behind him, stepped into an empty dining room and kept on going toward the lounge. Cigar smoke, clinking glasses and recorded music waited for him on the far side of the door. He hesitated, checked his watch and started counting off the thirty seconds left before Encizo made his play at the front door.

The bell rang right on time, and startled voices told him Encizo had flashed the hardware. Pushing through the tall door from the dining room, McCarter joined his partner, ready to complete the cross fire if their momentary hostages had any kind of violent disobedience in mind. He counted off six women wearing next to nothing, plus the older madam, a bartender and four male customers with fading bulges in their slacks.

No more party time.

McCarter faced the madam. "Something tells me you speak English, yes?"

"I do." Her voice was gritty with the sound of too much alcohol, too many cigarettes.

"How many more upstairs?" McCarter asked.

"Four girls, three customers," she said.

"I hate to spoil a party, but it's time to bring them down."

"Is this a robbery?" the madam asked. "If so, you're making a mistake."

"I'll risk the consequences," McCarter declared, "but we didn't come for money."

"No? What, then?"

"We've got a message for your boss," McCarter said. "That would be Kenan Bey?" When she made no reply, McCarter said, "He's going out of business, love. It starts right here, right now."

"You're fools," she snapped.

"That may turn out to be the case. Just now, though, we're the fools in charge. Now, would you like to bring the others down, or shall I burn the place with them upstairs?"

The madam passed in front of him to reach a button mounted on the wall, beside the mantel of a decorative fireplace. When she pressed it, muffled chimes began to sound upstairs, and they heard footsteps scrambling overhead. In moments flat the other girls were in the parlor, three of them stark naked, while the fourth was decked out in a low-cut mockery of a nurse's uniform. The three johns took a little longer, grappling with their clothes, but they made decent time responding to the sound of an alarm that probably had been installed for the event of raids by the police.

"This is your lucky day," McCarter told them, wondering how many members of his audience could understand a word he said. "You can go home right now, instead of getting shot or fried. Of course, if anybody wants to stay and argue, we'll be glad to kill you where you stand."

As the madam translated, McCarter watched frightened faces lose what little color they had left after they saw the automatic weapons. Still, nobody moved, as if they thought his offer was some kind of deadly trick. At last he fired a muffled burst into the ceiling, shouting, *"Go!"* and watched them stampede toward the street.

The madam was a trifle slower, pausing in the foyer to glance back and frown at him. "You'll die for this," she said.

McCarter shrugged. "We all die, ma'am," he responded. "If we know why, I reckon that's a lucky break."

The madam shook her head and turned away, proceeding to the door and out into the night. When she was gone, McCarter reached inside his jacket and unclipped the thermite canister that weighted down his belt.

"What was that cowboy song again?" he asked.

Encizo smiled. "You mean 'There'll Be a Hot Time in the Old Town Tonight'?"

"Just so," McCarter said, and pulled the pin. "I wouldn't miss it for the world."

RAGE SWEPT OVER KENAN BEY in waves, another surge of livid anger cresting in his brain just when he thought he had managed to control himself, think clearly once again. The *raki* didn't help, but he drank anyway from force of habit, welcoming the fire it lit inside his stomach to compete with that already burning in his skull.

How could this happen? Who would dare insult him in this way, right there in Istanbul, where it was known the word of Kenan Bey—indeed, his very whim—possessed the force of law?

Of course, the Turkish mobster had his enemies, and some of them were reckless men, but none of them was suicidal…were they? There were thugs whom he expected to lay plots behind his back, to steal from him in minor ways and hope they wouldn't be caught. He knew them all, and tolerated them when he was in the mood, because corruption made the world go around.

But this…

It had been years, more than a decade, since he had been called upon to face this kind of challenge. He could only think that someone had misjudged him out of ignorance, or else the men involved were simply not afraid to die.

Such men were dangerous.

He knew that it was more than one man, since the raids had been coordinated, carried out in different parts of Istanbul on a schedule that wouldn't have allowed the same man to rush from one scene to another in the necessary time. Also his Hasköy whores had seen two men inside the brothel, which told Bey that his enemies were working in teams.

How many were there? Why were they attacking him? And why now?

The obvious answers revolved around the wealth and power Bey had managed to accumulate in Istanbul—in all of Turkey, for that matter. He was known to be a wealthy man, something of a celebrity, in fact. By definition he was envied by the lower classes—which included ninety-five percent of all his fellow Turks—and it was only logical that some of them, somewhere, would seek to steal what Kenan Bey had worked long years to earn. It happened every day, in little ways, a *lira* here, five *lira* there. Sometimes, if the amount was small enough, the thief particularly clever—or, at least, respectful in defeat—he let it go.

But this…

There was no petty theft of cash or merchandise involved this time, no room for generosity, much less forgiveness. This was nothing less than an all-out frontal assault on Bey himself, his reputation and his empire, challenging the man whom all of Turkey feared to prove himself once more.

The business had been relatively quiet lately. Six or seven months had passed since he'd been forced to order anybody's death, and it was nearly three years since Bey had killed a man himself. You never lost the skill, of course, but he had hoped that part of it was well behind him. Bey would have been perfectly content to spend the remainder of his years counting money and women, letting the business details take care of themselves, but that was clearly not his fate. Instead, to stay on top, he must display once more the powers that had put him there to start with.

And he had one trick up his sleeve that hadn't been there in the old days. He could call on the authorities to help him, rather than avoiding them as if they were the plague. He was paying them enough each month to let him operate in peace, and nothing that had happened in the past two hours could be logically described as peaceful. There were wild men in the streets of Istanbul, committing brutal murders, starting fires, endangering the lives and livelihoods of men and women whose prosperity was constantly reflected in the secret envelopes of cash distributed by ranking officers among their men.

Now it was time for them to earn their money by decisive action, not just by looking in the wrong direction as a truck rolled past. He might offer a tidy bonus, in addition to the glory that would reward whichever man or men destroyed these menaces to Istanbul society.

The thought calmed Bey enough for him to pour another glass of *raki,* but his hands were trembling slightly as he drank. That brought the anger back full force, and made him clench the glass until it shattered in his hand, sharp slivers gouging at his palm. Blood mingled with the *raki* dripping on his carpet, but the godfather of Istanbul was too pissed off to care.

He wanted blood, all right, but it would have to come from someone else. And soon.

He had a reputation to protect at any cost, and the embarrassment inflicted on him by a pack of snarling jackals had already gone on long enough.

"MY TURN?" asked T. J. Hawkins.

Bolan thought about it, shrugged and told him, "Be my guest."

Hawkins stepped out of the car and felt it rock as Bolan slid into the driver's seat. The MP-5 SD-3 submachine gun slung beneath his long coat weighed almost nine pounds, but it felt featherlight as Hawkins moved along the sidewalk, savoring the rush that came from knowing he was just about to cross that line into a situation where the stakes were life-and-death. He wondered sometimes if his father had experienced that same rush when he went to Vietnam, or on those last hours of the Tet Offensive, when he lost it all.

But living in the past was one sure way to become part of it. One slipup on the firing line, and you were history. He had enough experience with killing—and of almost *being* killed—to know when it was time for him to put the memories away, lock in on here and now.

The target was a warehouse on the Yenikapi waterfront. They had it figured for a one-man job, with instant wheels on tap, and Hawkins had no problem letting Bolan sit it out. His greatest difficulty so far, as the new kid on a five-man team, had been in nailing down his fair share of the action. Not that Hawkins relished killing for its own sake, but he loved the way plans came together, heading off the bad guys at the pass, presumably inflicting damage on a predator who could be snacking down on *him* tomorrow if the good guys let him roam at will.

Another forty yards to reach the warehouse, and he glanced back at the car. He could see Bolan sitting ramrod straight behind the wheel. It was supposed to be a one-man show, and Hawk didn't anticipate a problem. There were no lookouts in evidence, no gunmen hiding in the shadows of the loading dock as he approached. A light was showing from inside, but well back from the tiny window in the first door he approached. The door was locked, but Hawkins checked it out and beat the lock in thirty seconds, once he knew there was no opposition waiting on the other side.

Across the threshold, he pursued the sound of tinny Arab music emanating from a cheap boom box. It led him to an office cubicle constructed out of cheap plywood partitions, with no wall on the side that faced the warehouse proper. Lounging at the desk, a fat slob of a watchman showed more interest in his sandwich, made of stringy meat and pita bread, than in security. He gaped at Hawkins as the younger man appeared, his submachine gun leveled at the watchman's face.

"Do you speak English?" Hawkins asked.

The fat man shrugged and said, "A leetle, yez."

"Okay. You want to die?"

"*Neyir!* No, sir!"

"Then take the gun out of your holster, nice and easy. Leave it on the desk, and take a hike."

"A hike?"

"Get out!"

A jerky nod was followed by the thunk of an antique revolver on the desktop. Hawkins blocked the fat man's path and pressed his silencer against the flabby chest.

"Next time you see your boss," he said, "I've got a message for him."

"Message?"

"Tell him that he's going out of business. Can you do that?"

"Yez, sir."

"Fair enough."

He stood aside and let the fat man go, suspecting he would place a call to his superiors as soon as he was safely out of killing range—by which time it would be too late.

The Yenikapi warehouse, owned by Kenan Bey, was well-known as a depot for assorted contraband both entering and leaving Istanbul. Hawk had no way of knowing whether there were drugs around the place this night, nor did he care. It was enough to strike another costly blow at Kenan Bey's machine—and at the man himself—as they proceeded with the Turkish phase of the campaign.

Beneath his jacket two round thermite canisters were clipped onto his belt. He let his submachine gun dangle from its shoulder strap and took one in each hand, released the safety pins and lobbed them in opposite directions from where he stood, outside the office cubicle. When they went off, in six or seven seconds, the erupting white-hot coals would get a fair spread through the warehouse, eating through concrete and steel, along with any other substance in their path, igniting fires that water wouldn't drown.

Hawk took himself away from there before they blew, was halfway to the car before the first pale tentacles of smoke began to wriggle from the open doorway on the loading dock. It didn't matter if the warehouse had a sprinkler system, or if someone passing by should call the fire brigade right now. The place would be a total loss, one more slap at the godfather of Istanbul.

"Who was the uniform?" asked Bolan as he twisted the ignition key.

"Some rent-a-cop. He'd rather switch than fight. I left the word."

"Sounds fair," the Executioner replied, and switched the headlights on, already rolling toward another mark.

"YOU KNOW, I don't exactly fit the local color scheme," said Calvin James.

The comment brought a smile to Gary Manning's face. "No problem, Cal," he said. "If anybody asks, I'll tell them you're my personal valet."

The black man made a sour face. "I've got your personal valet right here," he said.

"Now, now. Can't we all get along?"

"You're watching that Bill Maher again," said James. "I knew it."

"Not at all. I simply think—"

"Heads up," James interrupted him. "We've got a visual."

Across the street two young men were emerging from the entrance of a nightclub, pausing on the narrow sidewalk as they both lit cigarettes. Bright neon from the club behind them highlighted their faces, but it didn't reach the alleyway where James and Manning waited in their small Fiat sedan.

"That's Maras on the left," James said.

"Looks like. The other one must be a shooter."

Achmed Maras was described by sources in the know as one of three top-ranking officers in the crime syndicate controlled by Kenan Bey. His nightly habits were predictable—a fatal error for a man who made his living with a knife and gun—which meant that on a Tuesday evening he would be found killing time at Club Barsaklarim.

"You ready?" James asked, one hand on the ignition key.

Beside him Manning switched the safety off the Uzi submachine gun in his lap and said, "I feel like Sly Stallone."

"You *look* like Sly Stallone," James said.

"There's no excuse for rudeness, Calvin."

"Sorry."

"There they go."

"I see 'em."

Maras and his friend had turned right, moving north along the street, in the direction of a smallish parking lot. They would have wheels there, waiting for them, and the last thing Manning wanted was a running battle through those narrow streets.

"Let's do it."

"Right."

The Fiat's engine came to life, and James nosed out of the alley, turning left to put the marks on Manning's side. Manning had cranked his window down while they were waiting in the alley, thankful for a breeze that dried the perspiration on his forehead. He was ready now, the Uzi's muzzle braced across his windowsill.

"We're sure about this guy, correct?"

"You memorized the snaps," James said, "the same as me."

"Okay."

James kept the headlights off until the final moment, pulling up beside the targets. Manning spoke to Maras from his open window, calling him by name, and saw the dark face swivel toward his own. It was enough. He depressed the Uzi's trigger, hosing both men with a stream of parabellum manglers where they stood, their bodies twitching, dancing from the impact of the slugs.

James stood on the accelerator, taking them away from there before the echoes died away. Behind them

two discarded rag dolls huddled on the sidewalk under
winking lights, dark pools of blood beneath them
changing color in the garish neon.

"Scratch one underboss," James said, and aimed
the Fiat through the darkness, rolling toward the next
live target on their list.

CHAPTER FIVE

The yacht was moored at Samataya. Bolan navigated by the light of a three-quarter moon and cut his head-lights. There was no point in warning anyone ahead of time, and it stood to reason that the yacht would have at least some marginal security on board, to guard against theft and vandalism.

"I could come along," T. J. Hawkins offered as he watched Bolan's profile in the darkness of the car.

"Thanks anyway," Bolan replied, "but I'd rather know for sure I have a ride."

"Okay. Your call."

"It's made." He took a canvas satchel, from the back seat as he left the car.

The yacht was named *Karbizim,* and it measured out to forty meters of conspicuous consumption. Kenan Bey had let his fantasies run wild and piled on every luxury that he could think of, from a radar dish to hot tubs in the cabins, an elaborate galley that could turn out gourmet fare, a full gym and a helipad located near the stern. The good ship *Karbizim* had set him back at least two million dollars, and Kenan Bey could live at sea for weeks if he was so inclined.

In fact, word had it that he rarely used the yacht

these days. A weekend outing now and then, but rarely more than half a dozen trips per year. His business with the Russians lately had been taking up more of his time…and fattening his bank account at such a rate that he couldn't afford to let his wits go drifting with the tide.

Still, if the yacht was an abandoned toy, it still remained a damn expensive one, and Bolan knew that Bey would feel its loss, especially if it was taken from him in a manner that cast doubt upon his knack for taking care of business.

Striding boldly down the dock toward the *Karbizim,* Bolan saw the gangplank lowered, as if ready to receive arriving passengers. He slipped a hand into the outer pocket of his lightweight overcoat and found the MP-5K hanging on its swivel mount. His fingers wrapped around the pistol grip, and Bolan thumbed the safety off. He climbed the gangplank, scanning left and right along the rail in search of lookouts, but he reached the deck before a swarthy shooter popped out of a doorway to his left and challenged him.

He didn't understand the gunman's words, but there was nothing in the tone or scowl that called for an interpreter. The young man had a pistol in his hand, some kind of European semiauto piece, and Bolan didn't wait for him to raise it from his side. The MP-5K nosed its way into the night and spit a 3-round burst from twenty feet away. The gunman lurched backward and collapsed on the deck.

That tore it. Bolan moved with grim determination toward the doorway where his adversary had emerged a moment earlier. The sounds of running feet and startled, anxious voices reached his ears from somewhere down below—the reinforcements, coming to investigate the sound of gunfire.

Bolan waited for them at the head of the companionway, his compact submachine gun braced in a two-handed grip. There was a risk in facing several guns at once in a restricted space, but it wouldn't help Bolan if he let them scatter and surround him; they would then move through the passageways and cabins of a ship they knew by heart, while he would be fighting for his life on unfamiliar ground.

There was a light below, not brilliant but enough to cast the shadows of his enemies in front of them as they came racing toward the stairs. He had them lined up as they showed themselves, stood waiting as the three of them rushed up the steps, discovering their danger just a beat too late to make a difference. Bolan held the MP-5K's trigger down and swung the stubby muzzle in a zigzag pattern, making sure each one of the defenders got his share.

They fell together at the bottom of the stairway in a tangled mass of arms and legs, dead faces turned up toward the ceiling. Bolan ditched the empty magazine, reloading as he started down the stairs to check them out. No signs of life were visible as he stood over them, and he resisted the temptation to supply a point-blank coup de grace.

Instead, he moved along the corridor immediately to their right, in the direction of the engine room. *Karbizim*'s power plant was silent at the moment, its surroundings spotless, spit and polish the apparent order of the day. He reached inside the canvas satchel hanging from his shoulder, lifted out a half-pound Semtex charge with timer and detonator already in place and placed it where he thought it would do the most harm to the big yacht's heart. He gave himself fifteen minutes on the clock, retraced his steps to forward, past the dead men, moving toward the master's cabin with determined strides.

He left a larger Semtex charge in Kenan Bey's plush home away from home, pressed tight against the hull where it would detonate a foot or so above the water-line. A glance at Bolan's watch told him two minutes had elapsed. He set the timer's simple clock accordingly and left the cabin, moving aft, back toward the stairway that would lead him to the deck and freedom. On the way he planted two more plastic charges in guest cabins, one on either side of the *Karbizim,* and synchronized the timers for a simultaneous explosion that would lift the yacht clear of the water just before it settled to the bottom of the bay.

Topside he took the time to look for any watchdogs who might have been hanging back, relying on an ambush to succeed where their impetuous associates had failed. He had the deck all to himself, no sign of any passersby attracted by the sounds of gunfire, and he hurried down the gangplank, turning back in the direction of the car, where Hawk was waiting.

"Did you want to wait?" Hawk asked.

"No need," the Executioner replied. "We've still got work to do."

MAHOMET HISARÖNU YAWNED and checked his wristwatch, scowling as he saw that he had four more hours left on watch before he would be relieved to go back home to sleep. It was an easy job but boring, standing watch outside a pawnshop in the Kuruçesme neighborhood in case an enemy of Kenan Bey should come around and try to raid the place.

It was the guns that worried his boss, of course. The pawnshop was a blind for one of Master Kenan's private arsenals in Istanbul, a stockpile that included everything from small arms and their ammunition to explosives. There was probably enough hardware inside the place to fight a minor war. There wasn't that much call for paramilitary weapons anymore—anyway, there hadn't been before tonight—but Master Bey believed in preparation as a hedge against his enemies.

And they were out in force tonight, from all appearances. Hisarönu didn't have the details, but he knew there had been several violent strikes against the property of Master Bey, in Istanbul. He wondered, as he sat there killing time, what kind of men were brave enough—or fool enough—to challenge Master Bey on his home ground.

It takes all kinds, he thought, and shifted in the shotgun seat of the Peugeot. The pawnshop was across the street, all dark and shuttered. In the driver's seat beside him, Turhan Bitlis lit another cigarette and filled the little car with smoke. Hisarönu rolled his window down another inch or two but offered no complaint.

"This is a waste of time," Bitlis complained.

"Maybe so."

"We should be out there looking for the bastards," Bitlis insisted.

"We were told to wait," his partner reminded him.

"I *know* what we were told. I'm saying it's a waste of time."

"The guns—"

"Nobody knows about the guns," Bitlis interrupted him. "They're safe, and we're stuck here while others get the glory."

There was probably some truth to that, Hisarönu thought, but then who outside the family had known about the other targets hit so far? He had been trained to follow orders without question, knowing that his life was forfeit if he disobeyed. It didn't matter if his disobedience caused problems for the family or not. He could be executed for an act of insubordination that resulted in a benefit to Bey as easily as for an act that harmed his master. There was nothing more important than obedience and loyalty.

"I should call Malik and tell him nothing's happening," the driver grumbled, dragging on his cigarette, not caring when the ash fell in his lap.

"Call if you want," Hisarönu said. "Just leave me out of it."

"I'm telling you—"

Whatever Turhan Bitlis had in mind, he lost his train of thought as the pawnshop exploded, yellow flame erupting from the plate-glass windows, the front door projected from its mountings to the middle of the street. The shock wave rocked their car, and Bitlis dropped his cigarette somewhere between his legs, unmindful of it as he focused on the larger fire across the street.

"Allah preserve us!"

Bitlis bolted from the car, taking his submachine

gun with him, moving toward the middle of the street. Hisarönu followed him, his pistol drawn, but heat kept them well back from the demolished pawnshop. In another moment they could hear the sharp, staccato popping sound of ammunition detonating in the fire. A few more seconds and the darkened side street would become a combat zone, with phantom warriors dueling in the heart of the inferno.

"Let's get out of here," Hisarönu urged.

No sooner had he spoken than a silhouette detached itself from shadows cast by one of the surviving shops across the street. It ran in the direction of the nearest cross street, gaining speed. Bitlis was startled, but recovered quickly, following the runner with his submachine gun, squeezing off a burst before he had a chance to aim.

"Don't stand there like a fool!" the driver snapped. "We have to stop him!"

That made sense. Hisarönu raised his pistol, sighting down the slide, but something struck him in the legs before he fired. The impact toppled him, dark pavement rushing up to meet his face. He heard the shots a heartbeat later, raised his head in time to catch a glimpse of Turhan Bitlis reeling, clutching at his chest and going down.

Incredibly the shooter was on their side of the street. Hisarönu saw him step out of the shadows there, his automatic weapon leveled from the waist. He seemed to be an African, but it was difficult to say with any certainty, between the firelight and the shadows, the shock and pain. He knew he was bleeding badly, felt the blood soaking through the fabric of his slacks, but there was nothing he could do about it at the moment. First he had to stop this man from killing him, assuming he had not already done the job.

Hisarönu raised his pistol, braced his elbow on the pavement, but his hand was trembling with the effort, and he couldn't find his mark. His eyes swam in and out of focus, while the firelight tried to trick him, casting giant leaping shadows on the walls around his enemy.

He managed two wild shots and knew that they were wasted even as they left the muzzle of his gun. The black man—if he *was* a black man—didn't even bother trying to avoid the bullets. Standing fast, he fired another short burst from his submachine gun, muzzle-flashes winking, speeding death toward where Hisarönu lay.

Incredibly the rounds that struck him in the chest produced no pain. There was a stunning impact, pitching him onto his back, but nothing more. Instead of pain, an icy numbness settled over him, and while he couldn't move his arms or legs, it didn't seem to matter anymore.

A killer from the age of sixteen years, Mahomet Hisarönu had been moved to wonder, more than once, exactly how it felt to die.

And suddenly he knew.

"*HIJO DE CHINGADA,*" Rafael Encizo muttered underneath his breath. "Come on and move your sorry ass."

The object of his anger was a young man standing in the shadows, several yards in front of him, just lighting up another cigarette. He was the kind whose visage came to mind when you said "punk" in any language: greasy hair and sallow, sunken cheeks; a pair of shifty eyes; lips curled in what appeared to be a constant sneer. In Cuban jails you would expect a kid like that to be the one who grabbed his ankles for the bully boys and tried to stick a shiv in anyone who laughed about it afterward. As long as he could stab them in the back.

Right now the kid was an obstruction. He was standing watch outside the back door of a Topkapi nightclub owned by Kenan Bey, and Encizo had two minutes left before he had to be inside. McCarter would be starting the festivities without him if he didn't hurry, and Encizo didn't plan to let his partner down.

"Tough luck, kid," Encizo spoke softly as he crossed the two-lane blacktop. *"Lo siento mucho."*

As he walked, he drew the long, bone-handled switchblade he had purchased at a market stall that afternoon and snapped it open, holding it against his leg and out of sight. The young punk saw him coming, squared his shoulders, putting on his personal impression of a soldier to be reckoned with. The flat bulge of a pistol underneath his shirttail was the only thing that kept his act from being laughable.

Encizo started speaking Spanish to him as he hit the sidewalk, saw incomprehension in the young man's eyes. It changed to shock a moment later as Encizo rushed him, slammed him back against the brick wall with a forearm locked across his throat, his free hand pumping with the switchblade down below. It took two thrusts to do the job, a third to satisfy Encizo that the kid wasn't about to drag himself away somewhere and summon help before he died.

He propped the punk against a nearby Dumpster, hidden by its shadow, wiped the switchblade on the dead man's shirt and stowed it in his pocket. Reaching underneath his windbreaker, Encizo drew the mini-Uzi from concealment, still attached to its all-purpose shoulder rig. There was a live round in the chamber, spare mags in the inside pockets of his windbreaker. He thumbed the safety off and let himself in through the back door of the club to join the party that was coming down in less than ninety seconds.

The club was open to the public, and although they didn't plan a general slaughter, there would be guns inside, as well. The message they were sending back to Bey required disruption of the Turkish mobster's day-to-day routine, a forceful interdiction of his cash flow, with whatever that entailed. If some high rollers suffered nervous trauma in the process, that was too damn bad.

The Cuban passed the kitchen, where a group of sweaty teenagers was working underneath the watchful eye of a middle-aged chef. Encizo left them to it, seeing no threat there, convinced that they would scatter when the lead began to fly. He trailed the sound of music to a doorway masked by hanging strings of beads, and peered out into the main room of the club. The joint was obviously SRO, with several dozen booths and tables occupied, a four-piece band onstage, two dark-haired women grinding through a version of the dance of seven veils.

Encizo watched them for a moment, then went back

to looking for McCarter. His companion was supposed to come in through the front, posing as a customer, and wait until eleven-thirty to begin the party. It was coming up on time, and Encizo was feeling more than slightly nervous when he spied McCarter, seated at a table by himself off to the left.

Encizo had his earplugs already in place, the kind favored by shooters, which protect the eardrums from explosive sounds while still allowing normal conversation to proceed. McCarter wore a pair, as well, unnoticed by his fellow customers and waiters in the dim light of the club. A harder trick was hiding the concussion bombs—without a bulge to show for it—beneath the jacket of his suit, so he had taped them to his calves. Encizo smiled as he saw the Briton cross his legs and grimace, wincing as the tape uprooted hair.

Encizo stepped back from the doorway, standing with the mini-Uzi ready in his hand, and closed his eyes. The flash produced by stun grenades was every bit as dangerous as the concussion—not that there was any lasting damage, but the brilliant light caused temporary blindness, lasting several moments, and a soldier on the firing line couldn't afford to lose his sight.

Encizo waited, pictured McCarter priming one of the grenades and rolling it away from him, across the floor, before he ducked his head as if to fetch a fallen napkin from the floor. The blast felt like a swift punch to the solar plexus, even with the plaster wall protecting him, and Encizo could only hope McCarter was in good shape to continue with his work. The second bomb could use a windup pitch, and the Cuban was moving in as his partner lobbed it toward the bar.

Encizo ducked behind a table as it blew and came up in time to see a pair of groggy-looking shooters moving toward McCarter from the general direction of the cloakroom, shiny pistols in their hands.

It was a tricky shot, with dazed and blinded people staggering across his field of fire, but Encizo couldn't afford to hesitate. He hit the forward gunner with a 3-round burst that ruined his tuxedo for all time and pitched him over backward in a lifeless sprawl.

The second shooter had enough wits left to know that he was under fire, but tracking down the source was something else again. Encizo waited while a woman and her escort lurched in front of him, and found the gunman standing in the same place, not quite crouching, dark eyes searching desperately for somebody to kill. The burst that took him down was neat and clean, no wasted rounds, no through-and-through to jeopardize civilians on the other side.

McCarter had his own gun out by now, unleashing several rounds in the direction of the roof. He started shouting at the crowd in English, anything that came to mind, the added element of chaos prompting a stampede in the direction of the nearest exit. Encizo stayed where he was, alert to any sign of other gunmen on the premises, and watched the cream of Istanbul society brawl shamelessly for access to the street.

McCarter saw him, had begun to move in his direction when another shooter popped up from behind the bar. His first round missed its mark by six or seven feet, and McCarter pivoted to bring him under fire before Encizo could respond. A burst from the Phoenix Force leader's automatic weapon took the soldier down and dropped him out of sight back behind the bar.

"Ready?" asked McCarter with a grin as he drew closer.

"I believe the party's over," Encizo replied.

"Life's one big party, if you just know where to go," McCarter said.

"Shall we?"

Another grin. "I thought you'd never ask."

LEONID GROMYLKO TOOK a sip of coffee, grimaced as it burned his tongue and set the cup back down. Instead of anger he felt weariness, but he couldn't blame jet lag for the feeling. There was only one hour's difference between Istanbul and Moscow, not enough to make him feel as if he had been going strong for days without a wink of sleep.

It was a deep soul-weariness, Gromylko realized, which had afflicted him in varying degrees since the night Alexei Churbanov was killed, the night Vasiliev and his Colombian associates had given them the slip. It wouldn't pass, he realized, until he found a way to make things right, avenge himself against the Chechen godfather once and for all.

That knowledge had encouraged him to make the flight to Istanbul. It hadn't been an order—not exactly—but the news that the Americans were interested in taking on Vasiliev had galvanized him. There was no way he could pass on the assignment once it was offered to him. He couldn't expect another officer

to share his personal commitment to dismantling Vasiliev's corrupt empire and seeing justice done at any
cost. Some officers of the *militsiya* were certainly corrupt, while others had a vested interest in preserving
their careers, in going by the book. All that had
changed for Leonid Gromylko on the night his partner
died.

He had no wife or children to protect, no living
relatives the syndicate could threaten, use as pawns in
an attempt to slow him down. It would require a bomb
or blade or bullet, and he knew Vasiliev wouldn't stop
short of murdering one more policeman.

But the bastard had to find him first.

It was true that working in Istanbul had certain ad-
vantages. Gromylko was away from Moscow for the
moment, but still in position to damage Vasiliev and
the rest of the Thieves' Society at the same time. It
remained to be seen how the Americans would shape
up, but they were clearly not running the standard FBI
operation, with reams of paperwork to file and slim
results to show for it. Unless Gromylko missed his
guess, the recent spate of violence rocking Istanbul
had much to do with the American campaign, a no-
holds-barred approach to shutting down the Turkish
drug pipeline that meshed well with Gromylko's personal aversion to going by the book. He would be
pleased to help them if he could, as long as they
agreed upon the common goal of crushing Gregori
Vasiliev.

Gromylko wondered how the rough approach would
fare when they were back in Russia, how his various
superiors in the *militsiya* would take to having armed

Amerikanski running wild in their backyard and targeting the very criminals who made such huge investments in the system, via massive bribes. He pictured Colonel Yuri Renko looking down his crooked nose and scowling at the notion, taking steps to intervene wherever possible and put the Yankees in their place—perhaps a prison cell, perhaps a shallow grave. And if Gromylko should be cut down in the cross fire, he suspected Renko would spend little time in mourning.

Still, the new approach was worth a try. He had considered trying something of the sort alone, but knew it would be suicide. This way there would be others on his side, to watch his back, and they would have at least the theoretical support of certain ranking officers in the *militsiya*. With any luck it might just be enough to keep the likes of Renko and his men at bay, but Gromylko wouldn't bet his life on that.

Not yet.

Before he started trusting the *Amerikanski*, he would have to wait and see.

CHAPTER SIX

There was still an hour left before the break of day as Bolan made his way along the sidewalk, moving toward the massive monument to Ataturk. He was five minutes early, but he felt like scouting out the territory on his own after surveillance from a distance through a sniper scope. He knew that Hawkins would be tracking him with field glasses, perhaps the Walther WA2000's telescopic sight, with frequent sweeps to check for any evidence that he was entering a trap.

Too late, in any case, thought Bolan as he neared the point selected for the predawn rendezvous. If there were shooters waiting for him, they were hidden well enough that he had failed to spot them, and presumably they would elude Hawk's scrutiny, as well—at least, until they opened fire. By that time there wouldn't be much his one-man backup could achieve in terms of saving Bolan's ass, but he could still repay the enemy in kind.

And sometimes payback was the best that you could hope for.

Sometimes, in the real world, vengeance was enough.

Almost.

He tried to sketch a mental picture of the Russian and came up with a laughable caricature: double chin, bushy eyebrows, pale complexion underneath a round fur hat, with a militia uniform in gray or olive drab. That much, at least, he knew couldn't be accurate. The officer detailed to meet him was a long way from his lawful jurisdiction now, and he wouldn't be advertising his connection to the Russian state police.

It was a sign of Moscow's desperation that the proud militia would not only welcome help from the United States—a precedent established earlier, when doors were opened to the FBI—but that it would cooperate with Bolan's style of war against the homegrown *mafiya.* He knew that crime was running wild in Russia, and that syndicate activities abroad were threatening the foreign aid that Moscow's present rulers needed to survive, but it was still a quantum leap from borrowing a team of Washington advisers to the kind of blitz that Bolan had in mind.

He wondered if the men behind the scenes in Russia had really known what they were getting into when they cut their deal with Hal and Stony Man. If not, they would find out before the smoke had cleared in Turkey, and there would be time enough for them to weasel out if they were so inclined.

In which case, Bolan thought, he might be forced to go ahead without official sanction. It would multiply the risks a thousandfold, but that was SOP in Bolan's kind of war. He weighed the risks at the beginning, figured out if the potential gain was worth it and then he went ahead, with no more personal regard than any other soldier, cop or fireman when the chips were down.

It was the only way to fly, and it had served him well so far.

He checked the plaza, peering into shadows that defied the nearest streetlights, wondering if death were waiting for him there. It made no sense to think the Russians would prepare an ambush for him here, in Istanbul. He had opposed their interests in the past, under the Soviet regime, but that was ancient history, and those in power now had no idea who Bolan was, much less that Hal would send him on this mission to assist their government.

He found a bench a few yards from the looming monument and sat down at one end, placing a portion of the plaza at his back. There was little he could do about that, short of staying on his feet and moving constantly, like some demented street person jumping at shadows. He would trust Hawkins to watch his back, and let it go at that. As for the Russian, if he brought a tail…well, they would have to deal with that event if and when it occurred.

In the meantime there was nothing for the Executioner to do but sit and wait to see what happened next.

GROMYLKO PARKED his rented car three blocks from the appointed rendezvous, sacrificing convenience in the interest of security and personal survival. Walking three blocks to the monument, he would have ample time to see if he was being followed or observed, and no one could pursue him in a vehicle without creeping along at the curb, making himself painfully obvious in the process.

Before he left the car, he double-checked his Makarov and slipped it down inside the waistband of his trousers, at the back, where he could reach it easily with either hand. The gun had passed unnoticed in his check-through luggage, hidden in a hardback copy of *War and Peace* that he had hollowed out specifically for moving contraband. The crude system wouldn't defeat a metal detector or X-ray device, but few airports other than Israel still X-rayed luggage that was destined for the cargo hold. If he was caught, he would plead ignorance of local laws and flash the diplomatic passport that had been provided for his trip to Istanbul.

The special paperwork said much about how the *militsiya* brass regarded his present assignment. It was important enough for them to pull strings with the Office of Passport Control and the Ministry of Foreign Affairs, but Gromylko still wondered exactly how much support he could expect if things went sour in Turkey. The diplomatic passport would prevent him from being jailed, but Gromylko still had to consider the consequences of any embarrassment once he got home.

If he got home.

The course of action he had chosen could well result in his death. Gromylko had no illusions on that score, nor did the prospect of impending mayhem intimidate him. Whatever squeamishness remained after seventeen years in the service, he had lost it in the aftermath of Churbanov's murder.

Lately he was focused more precisely on revenge.

He didn't know if the *Amerikanski* operatives could even help him when it counted. They had done all right so far, assuming they were actually responsible for the recent series of attacks in Istanbul, but they were fighting Turks, an altogether different breed from Chechen mobsters. Gromylko was happy to give them a chance, the benefit of the doubt...but in the death game they were playing, there would be no second chance, and doubts could get you killed.

He wondered whom the bold *Amerikanski* represented, which one of the alphabet agencies spawned by Washington they were assigned to serve. The Yanks had several elite military units—the Rangers, Special Forces, Navy SEALs, the black berets of Delta Force—but none of them was normally assigned to stalking ordinary criminals. Their specialty was counterterrorism, plucking hostages from danger, crushing Third World revolutions. They were more like the Spetsnaz in his homeland, which would gladly kill the people of Afghanistan or even Georgia, but wouldn't feel at home in Moscow, trailing homegrown villains through the streets and alleyways.

Who, then?

There was a time when Leonid Gromylko would have guessed at CIA involvement, but he knew enough of politics in the United States since Nixon to believe that Langley's old swashbuckling days were gone forever, lost beyond recall. The Company no doubt had gunmen on its payroll, more than likely contract agents from some criminal fraternity to rent for certain dirty jobs, but oversight from Congress had derailed the CIA's ability to mount extensive covert operations, much less active paramilitary teams like those rocking Istanbul since early afternoon.

Still, the Yankees already had Gromylko's admiration. He had lost count of all the times he wished that he could simply walk up to a criminal, pull out his Makarov and shoot the bastard dead, without the paperwork and second-guessing from his own superiors. In Russia the *militsiya* had much more freedom than American police—to search without a warrant, for example, or to hold a suspect for extended questioning—but the demise of communism was inevitably bringing on reforms. Some of the changes were long overdue, in Gromylko's opinion, while others simply hampered the police in their attempts to deal with violent crime. The end result, he feared, would be a stronger syndicate, greater corruption in the ranks of government and law enforcement, greater violence in the streets.

Unless the man he was supposed to meet had a solution for the problem tucked under his hat.

It was unlikely, Gromylko told himself. Americans had simple notions about life in Russia, some of them encouraged by the very rulers of the USSR under communism. In the Western eye, most Russians were lethargic, vodka-swilling trolls who waited endlessly in line to get a piece of moldy cheese, whose women either mainlined steroids to become athletic prodigies, or else gained ninety pounds the morning after they were married and began an endless round of cooking, cleaning house and giving birth.

Gromylko, for his part, had never owned or worn a fur hat in his life, and he had never joined the Communist Party, even though his reluctance meant he would never rise above the rank of first lieutenant in his chosen field. He *did* drink vodka, but there was some truth in every caricature, every stereotype. It was how the distorted generalizations got started in the first place.

The monument to Ataturk was half a block ahead. Gromylko slowed his pace and glanced behind him one more time to satisfy himself that he hadn't been followed. There was no good reason to believe that anyone employed by Gregori Vasiliev knew where he was, much less why he had come to Istanbul, but there was no such thing as too much caution.

He began to sweep the plaza with his eyes, picked out a solitary figure seated on a bench perhaps a hundred yards to the south. He had no physical description of his contact, but the big man matched Gromylko's general impression of Americans. His mind dredged up the coded ID phrase he had been given back in Moscow, and he started toward the bench. His windbreaker hung open, granting speedy access to the Makarov.

Gromylko hoped the gun wouldn't turn out to be his only friend in Istanbul.

HIS ROOFTOP PERCH let T. J. Hawkins cover all four corners of the plaza down below, and he had checked the square repeatedly with night glasses before and after Bolan took up his position on the bench. The Walther WA2000 sat beside his elbow, muzzle elevated by the bipod that was factory standard on the Space Age rifles. If a target showed itself below him, he could switch from night glasses to the Walther's telescopic sight in a heartbeat, covering Bolan's retreat all the way.

If Bolan was in any shape to get away.

The very notion of the rendezvous didn't sit well with Hawkins. He didn't mind the place, but he objected to the hour—too damn early for civilians to be running interference, too damn dark to let him absolutely guarantee a safe approach—and he had argued that they ought to push it back an hour, maybe two or three, at least until the sun came up. Bolan was adamant about the timing, even though they had a backup rendezvous arranged. They would proceed on schedule, do their best to minimize the risk and let the chips fall where they may.

But Hawkins didn't have to like it. Not even a little bit.

He didn't trust the Russians; that was one thing. Thirteen years in active military service, most of that under the Reagan-Bush administrations, and he *knew* the Russians wanted power, just like everybody else. He had been up against a number of their Cuban flunkies in Grenada, dodging bullets from Russian AK-47s and machine guns. Even granting that the Communist regime in Moscow was no more, the diehard Marxists had controlled Russia for almost three-quarters of a century. Thousands, maybe tens of thousands, had mourned the old order's demise, watching their party perks and privileges evaporate before their eyes. The KGB was forced to change its name, if not its mission. It would be fatally naive, in Hawk's humble opinion, to believe that every Russian had experienced a sudden change of heart, transforming Moscow and the Kremlin into a new cradle of world liberty.

In Hawk's experience the lust for power transcended political parties and traditional ideology. Repression of dissent, for instance, was common to both right- and left-wing regimes around the world. You only had to glance around the Balkan states, of late, to get a clue that Russia hadn't wholly changed her ways.

Still, Hawkins didn't mind assisting Moscow with specific problems, like the arresting of the spread of syndicated crime—especially where that problem was exported to the States. He couldn't make himself believe that one campaign would slam the door on Russian mafiosi spreading into Europe and America, but it was well past time to make a start on cleaning up the mess.

There were a few pedestrians at large despite the hour, heading off to early-morning jobs, and Hawkins studied each of them who crossed the plaza down below. If anything went wrong for Bolan, it wouldn't be due to negligence on his part. Hawkins had discretionary power to remove approaching targets if he satisfied himself that they posed a threat to Bolan. Technically he wasn't bound to let the suspect draw a weapon and take aim before he intervened, but he wasn't about to turn the square into a shooting gallery without good reason, either.

Bolan was a pro at this, Hawk realized. The guy had lived through shit that would have made another soldier's hair turn white, and he was still around, still going strong. Somewhere along the line, of course, the odds caught up with every man. It was inevitable, nature's way, but T. J. Hawkins was determined that it wouldn't happen on *his* watch.

Not this time.

Not today.

He saw a lone man coming from the north, approaching Bolan's bench. He looked like anybody else from that distance, nothing obvious to set him apart, like a hammer-and-sickle armband or a nice pair of horns atop his head. Still, there was something about him....

Hawkins laid his night glasses aside and scooted over to the Walther, wrapped his hand around the sculpted pistol grip and found his target with the scope.

Say cheese, he thought, and waited, trying to decide if this man he had never seen before should live or die.

"TURKEY IS WARM this time of year," the stranger said.

Bolan returned his level gaze and said, "But weather changes by the day."

"That's why I always carry an umbrella," replied the stranger, who had no umbrella in his hands.

Their ID ritual complete, the Russian sat down next to Bolan, leaving some two feet of empty space between them on the bench. He studied Bolan's face for several moments, frowning to himself, then said, "I've never cared much for this cloak-and-dagger business."

"No," said Bolan, "but at least it does the job."

"I am Lieutenant Leonid Gromylko," the Russian stated.

"Mike Belasko," Bolan replied. "No rank, per se."

Gromylko's grip was firm and dry, possessed of strength without the need to demonstrate by grinding knuckles. "Have you been in Turkey long?" he asked.

"About twelve hours," Bolan said.

"You have been busy, I believe."

"We had some time to kill before the meeting," Bolan said. "I didn't want to waste it, so we introduced ourselves to Kenan Bey."

"And quite effectively, from what I've made out of the local news. When you say 'we,' how many men are you referring to?"

Bolan considered lying to Gromylko, but he couldn't see the point. The trust had to begin somewhere. "Six guns, including mine."

"Regretfully I've come alone," Gromylko said.

"No sweat. I'm counting on you more for information and direction than a frontline presence," Bolan said.

The Russian frowned at that, his disappointment obvious. "I plan to do my share."

"I only thought—"

"Three months ago my partner was assassinated during an attempt to pick up Gregori Vasiliev in Moscow. Since then, my superiors in the *militsiya* have done their best to keep me at a desk, coordinating paperwork and chasing information on the telephone. I'm only here because they can spare no one else... and no one else knows the *bandity* as I do. My information is at your disposal, but I have a price."

"Which is?"

"I want—how you say it?—a piece of the action. You don't handle me with kid gloves or expect me to watch idly from the sidelines."

"Fair enough. You know the risks involved."

"My partner knew them, too."

"I've been there," Bolan told him, "but I don't advise you let your heart start thinking for your head."

"I've thought enough," Gromylko said. "It's time to act."

"You know the Turkish action?"

"Well enough. You've done all right so far, from what I know."

"We're moving on to Ankara this morning," Bolan said. "My information is that Kenan Bey is headed for his home away from home. He thinks the capital may be a little cooler for him, with the heat in Istanbul."

"So, now you plan on turning up the heat in Ankara?"

"That's it. When we get done with this end of the pipeline, we'll be ready to change theaters of operation. After that it's your show all the way. You call the shots."

"I'd rather *make* the shots."

"Well," Bolan said, "there's no time like the present to get started, if you want to take a look at Ankara."

Gromylko smiled. "I understand it's warm this time of year."

"And getting warmer all the time," the Executioner replied.

"One question," Gromylko said.

"What?"

"We're covered, I assume?"

"That's right. You mind?"

Gromylko shook his head. "It's reassuring," he told Bolan. "I prefer to risk my life with men who know their business."

"Then you've come to the right place."

"I hope so."

"One way to find out," Bolan said.

"Shall we take my car?"

"Where is it?"

"Three blocks that way." Gromylko pointed to the north.

"Another cautious man."

"I'm still alive."

"Let's try to keep it that way."

"For a time, at least," Gromylko said. "I still have work to do."

"I'll wait here while you get the car, then we can have mine brought around."

Gromylko rose. "Ten minutes, then."

"Ten minutes."

Bolan watched him turn away, retrace his steps. Hawk would be watching, too, but they were clear for now. He didn't trust the Russian absolutely, but he was prepared to give the guy a chance.

Ankara would provide the testing ground.

And anyone who failed wouldn't be coming out alive.

CHAPTER SEVEN

Ankara

"This is it?" Hawkins asked.

"Right."

It was another warehouse, this one on the outskirts of the Turkish capital. The deed and other legal paperwork might not reveal the name of Kenan Bey, but Stony Man had verified the link through Interpol, and Bolan was prepared to take it at face value. One more stop on the circuitous route for all manner of contraband, including drugs and weapons, stolen property and bootleg articles, even the occasional fugitive from justice. As in Istanbul, he had no way of knowing what the warehouse held right now, nor did it matter. It was enough to know that Bey would suffer from the loss of anything inside.

"You're armed?" he asked Gromylko.

"Da." The Russian flipped his jacket aside to show a semiauto pistol tucked inside his waistband at the back.

"That's it?"

Gromylko shrugged. "I must admit, I didn't come prepared for total war."

"We did," Hawkins said, reaching back into a gym bag on the floor behind the driver's seat. He came out with a loaded mini-Uzi and reached back again to find its matching silencer, together with a pair of extra magazines.

"You've handled one of these before?" Bolan asked.

"I can manage," Gromylko replied as he screwed the silencer onto the Uzi's threaded muzzle.

"Then I guess we're set."

Gromylko pocketed the two spare magazines and tucked the Uzi underneath his jacket as he left the vehicle. Hawkins stayed behind the wheel and kept the engine running as his partners crossed the street and closed in on the warehouse, painfully aware that daylight made them easy targets. There had been no sign of lookouts on their drive-by, but you never really knew about a place until you made your move.

And by the time all hell broke lose, it was too late to change your mind.

Two canvas-covered trucks were parked against the loading dock, with a Mercedes-Benz sedan around the west side of the aging warehouse. Leaving trucks would be routine, but Bolan seriously doubted that anyone would leave a Benz unguarded overnight. That told him there were men inside, but he would have to find out for himself if they were armed and dangerous.

No turning back.

They left the loading dock alone and found a door around in back. The lock was no great challenge, and the door hadn't been wired with an alarm as far as Bolan could determine. As it closed behind them, Gromylko drew the borrowed submachine gun from beneath his jacket, flicking off the safety with his thumb.

The warehouse was three-quarters filled with wooden crates and cardboard boxes, stacked up halfway to the ceiling, leaving aisles between them wide enough to let a forklift pass. Bolan couldn't read the labels, but it hardly mattered if the tags were fraudulent. They stood and listened for a moment, picked up on the sound of an electric motor several aisles away, and Bolan moved in that direction, carrying his MP-5K with the custom silencer attached.

They met the forklift operator in the third aisle over from the door where they had slipped into the warehouse. He wore denim coveralls and a black shoulder holster, with a heavy autoloader slung beneath his left arm for a cross-hand draw. The Turk's eyes widened at the sight of strangers on his turf, and he released the throttle of his clumsy vehicle, his right hand groping for the pistol in a reflex action.

Bolan shot him in the chest, a 3-round burst that slapped him off the driver's seat, one foot hung up so that he dangled like a fallen scarecrow from the rear deck of the forklift. Passing by the vehicle, Gromylko switched the motor off. It hadn't been that loud, and yet the sudden silence seemed oppressive as they moved along the aisle together, toward the north end of the warehouse.

It wasn't completely silent, though. The sound of muted voices drew them onward to the far end of the aisle. Bolan took a brief glance around a wooden crate the size of an industrial refrigerator and saw four men sitting at a card table. Three of them were smoking, all four wearing pistols and playing some card game Bolan didn't recognize.

He turned back toward Gromylko and raised four fingers. The Russian nodded in reply, then they stepped out of the aisle together, spreading out enough that they wouldn't present a single target to the four cardplayers. Even then, it took another moment for the Turks to notice them.

The fat man facing Bolan and Gromylko glanced upward from his cards and lost his cigar stub as his mouth dropped open. Porky blurted out a warning to his friends.

The others turned and reached for their side arms, but the effort was too little and too late.

Bolan and his companion cut loose with their SMGs, the muffled sound reminiscent of playing cards fanned by the spokes of a bicycle wheel rather than gunfire. A storm of 9 mm parabellum rounds ripped into flesh and fabric, spinning the cardplayers around, one bringing the flimsy table down beneath his weight, the others sprawling out beside it, spilling crimson on the concrete floor.

Gromylko moved to stand above them, checking visually for signs of life. When he was satisfied that they were dead, with no more shooters waiting in the wings, he turned back to the Executioner and nodded. Bolan took a thermite canister from underneath his coat and tossed it to the Russian.

"Be my guest."

"A fire sale, I believe you call it?"

"More or less."

Gromylko yanked the pin and lobbed the canister

downrange, toward the far end of the warehouse. By the time it blew, they were outside and jogging toward the car.

"So, this is how you fight your war," the Russian said.

"It's how we start," Bolan replied as he took the shotgun seat and closed the door behind him.

T. J. Hawkins met Gromylko's flat gaze in the rear-view mirror. "You ain't seen nothing, yet," Hawkins said.

THE HOUSE would have been advertised as ranch-style in America. David McCarter didn't have a clue what they would call the architectural design in Turkey, and he frankly didn't give a damn. The dwelling was a bloody target, nothing more.

Located in a northern suburb of Ankara, it stood on three or four acres of land, screened from its neighbors by strategically located trees, surrounded by a wall of sun-bleached brick, with broken glass on top, lodged in concrete. There were no other visible security devices, but McCarter wasn't taking any chances. He had opted for a long-range strike, across the wall, which had the added benefit of helping with a speedy getaway.

The target was a high-priced thug named Süleyman Izmir, described by Stony Man and Interpol as number two in Kenan Bey's crime family. It would have taken more than luck to tag him in his own backyard in broad daylight, but it was easier to hurt him where it mattered—his pride and pocketbook.

McCarter's weapon of choice was a Russian

RPG-7, part of the mobile arsenal they had acquired from savvy "businessmen" in Istanbul, surrendered on a strictly cash-and-carry basis. Bolan had paid the tab from what he called his private war chest, and McCarter hadn't argued. Now, as he prepared to launch his strike on Izmir, McCarter was relieved that they had come prepared.

The RPG launcher is one meter in length, a 40 mm weapon constructed on the classic bazooka design. Its rockets weigh five pounds apiece, and are so bulky in construction that the warhead protrudes from the RPG's muzzle like a football loaded with high explosives. The effective range for stationary targets is rated at five hundred meters, with a muzzle velocity of 120 meters per second. There is no recoil, since all the back-flash is expelled behind the shooter—to the everlasting detriment of anyone who stands too close.

McCarter balanced atop the cab of a truck they had "borrowed" for the occasion, sighting the RPG while Rafael Encizo sat behind the wheel below and kept the engine running for a swift departure. Extra rockets, three in all, were nestled in a canvas satchel slung across McCarter's left shoulder, while the launcher was braced on his right.

He didn't know the floor plan of the house, so he broke it down logically, aiming his first HE round at the tall double doors. He squeezed the trigger, smelled a whiff of dragon's breath and was reloading by the time the rocket found its mark, erupting into smoke and flame downrange.

McCarter shifted targets for his second shot, lined up the RPG's sights on the northwest corner of the house, aiming at the broad windows that offered easy access to the room beyond. Concern for innocent civilians was tempered by information that Izmir was a bachelor with no children, no live-in family of any kind. As for the staff, those workers who weren't employed to carry guns and keep the master safe drew their paychecks from the number-two gangster in Turkey. McCarter reckoned they could take their chances with the boss.

Two away, and he watched the fiery comet find its mark, punching through fragile glass to detonate inside the house, spewing smoke and shrapnel from the shattered window. Drawing the third rocket from his satchel, McCarter reloaded, watching and waiting for the inevitable reaction.

It came as he was lining up the penultimate shot. A half-dozen men charged around from the back of the house, all armed with shotguns or rifles. They gaped at the house, then turned in McCarter's direction, seeking the source of so much destruction, squinting in brilliant sunlight.

McCarter helped them with another rocket, ignoring the soldiers as he put a third HE round into the house, this one midway between the first two impact sites. Three rockets would probably not destroy Izmir's house, even if they started more-extensive fires, but there would be one hell of a mess to clean up. And more importantly, Bey's number-two would carry the message back to his master that no one was safe, not even at home behind walls and hired guns.

Beyond the initial shock now, the soldiers were reacting, big time. Two started sprinting for the wall, their starting point perhaps a hundred yards from where McCarter stood atop the truck, while their four companions piled into a gray sedan, revving its engine and rolling toward the gate.

The RPG's effective range for moving targets is roughly half the distance recommended for stationary marks, but McCarter was well within the limit. Even so, it took a hunter's eye to lead the gray sedan, time the release of rocket number four so that it flew to meet the racing vehicle instead of missing clean and hurtling on through empty air.

McCarter took his time about it, ignoring the gunners on foot, who were already firing from the hip, well beyond their own effective range. He had all the time he needed to do it right, and his hand was steady as he squeezed the trigger one last time, dispatching sudden death to meet his enemies.

The gray sedan was halfway to the main gate of the property when it exploded, swerving violently off course from the impact of the rocket, trailing flames and oily smoke as it limped to a halt. McCarter saw one man bail out and run for it before the gas tank blew, then he was scrambling down from his high perch, sliding into the shotgun seat as Encizo put the truck in gear.

"All done?" the Cuban asked.

"I doubt they'll invite us back," McCarter said.

THE NEWS HIT Kenan Bey like a swift punch in the solar plexus, stealing his breath away for a moment as he listened to Izmir ranting on the telephone. The younger man was livid, frantic, calling from a public telephone because his own had been knocked out by rockets of all things. The house that Izmir doted on was in a shambles, with damage running into the millions of *lira*, while his pride and personal sense of security lay in smoking ruins.

"Enough!" Bey interrupted him, cutting off the angry, frightened flow of words. "Find a safe place for yourself and your men. Call me when you're settled. I will deal with the police."

Police were not the problem, Bey decided. Everybody knew that there were violent dissidents in Turkey—Kurds among them, if not foremost in the cast of characters—and that they often vented mindless rage against the affluent, including lawyers, politicians and respected businessmen. The risk of terrorist attack explained why Izmir had armed guards on his property. Police who had been paid for years to overlook the foreign trade in heroin and other contraband weren't about to suddenly regain their eyesight now.

The move to Ankara had been designed to take the heat off Bey while the police and his own men tracked down the individuals responsible for his embarrassment in Istanbul. Now, it appeared, the problem had pursued him to the capital, three more attacks within the past two hours, telling him in no uncertain terms that there was nowhere he could hide.

He had not been fond of running in the first place. Instinct told him he should stand and fight, but that required at least some notion of the enemy's identity. There was no man, no weapon, that could kill a shadow. If he could not find his enemies, he could not fight.

A nagging dread told Kenan Bey that finding his assailants wouldn't be a problem in the long run. *They* would come to *him* in time. He must be ready for them, see to his defenses and prepare himself to snatch victory from the jaws of apparent defeat.

And that meant knowing who they were, if not precisely where.

Kerim Kürek was one possibility, a tough drug runner from Kars, near the Armenian border. They had clashed on more than one occasion over customers and territory, Kürek always managing to smell the traps arranged by Kenan Bey and save himself before his head was in the noose. Kürek had shown himself capable of violent reprisals in the past, but the recent attacks had been too well organized, too military to be Kürek's handiwork. The drive-by shooting that had taken Achmed Maras might have been arranged by Kürek, but as for the rest of it...

If not Kürek, then who?

It was a point of pride with Bey that few of his true enemies were still alive, and fewer still posed any significant threat to his illicit empire. Death came swift and soon to those who jeopardized his profit margin, much less his personal safety. The downside of Bey's scorched-earth policy, however, was the fact that it left a severely depleted field of suspects when anything went wrong.

Like now.

He thought of the Sicilians next. There had been disagreements lately over price, but Bey was still their major source of heroin, despite increasing trade between the Mafia and Chinese Triads moving China white. His price per kilogram wasn't unreasonable, and he never failed to strike a bargain with his favored customers. Polite disputes aside, it seemed unlikely that the mafiosi would attempt to kill him—even less likely that they would mount such a determined, wide-ranging campaign on Turkish soil.

The Russians? Kenan Bey was almost moved to smile at the idea. They were his new, best customers, and Gregori Vasiliev seemed eminently satisfied with both the price and quality of merchandise. He wouldn't put it past the wily Chechen to attempt a coup, eliminate the middleman if it was feasible, but such an effort would require Vasiliev to run the Turkish operation on his own, and that was so improbable that it produced a barking laugh from Bey.

The change of mood was short-lived, instantly extinguished as the Turkish mobster realized that he had come full circle, back to total ignorance of who his adversaries were and why they would attempt to ruin everything that he had worked and fought for.

It was damn frustrating, this lack of crucial knowledge, when his life was riding on the line. How could he hope to save himself and hold his world intact if he had no idea of who was trying to subvert him? Raw determination might not be enough, even with luck to help him out. He needed information and a gesture that would build new confidence within the ranks of his employees, his defenders.

Most of all, he needed time.

It galled the Turkish godfather to think of running, hiding like a frightened child, but the attack on Izmir had shown him that a house, a wall and bodyguards might not protect a man from those committed to destroying him. Some distance would be helpful. If a change of cities didn't do the trick, then Bey would choose his own ground for the showdown.

As it so happened, Kenan Bey had such a place in mind.

He would allow his enemies to find him, if they had the wits and courage to confront him on the killing ground he chose.

And it would be their last mistake.

THE OPERATION of a hashish parlor is illegal in Ankara, as throughout the country, but such parlors still exist. Their thriving trade is an open secret in Turkish society, as well-known to police as to any civilian on the street. From time to time a new wave of reform demands that they be raided, closed and padlocked, but the rules of play are understood by all concerned. The hashish parlors easily relocate, at a moderate expense to management, while the police forfeit their standard bribes during a "cleanup," ranking officers content to reap the harvest of publicity that makes them look efficient in the public eye. Within a week or less, business returns to normal, and the status quo is left inviolate.

The hashish parlor located in downtown Ankara was one of Turkey's largest, certainly the largest in the city, with a list of clients including businessmen and politicians who preferred to have their fun in circumstances that were easily, effectively controlled, instead of taking trouble home at night. Because of its exalted clientele, this parlor had gone seven years without a raid.

Until today.

The gas mask was uncomfortable, but it would be helpful once he got inside the place, thought Calvin James. He made a last adjustment to the tight elastic straps, then checked his wristwatch, verifying that he still had twenty seconds left.

He had already picked the cheap lock on the basement access door, and had his MP-5 SD-3 ready, with a live round in the firing chamber and the safety off. Another eighteen seconds now, and Gary Manning should be coming through the skylight, making it a pincer movement, catching their intended targets in a deadly squeeze. The parlor's management and guards should be discernible from customers by armament and attitude, if not attire. Whatever happened in the next few moments, the ex-SEAL told himself that anyone who fell had brought it on himself.

Drugs were a major sore point for the soldier from Chicago, ever since his only sister died from an overdose. James didn't blame the world at large for her mistake, but he had seen too much of suffering around the Windy City, later on a broader scale, to regard the organized drug trade as "victimless" crime.

Now it was time to move. James crossed the threshold with his submachine gun ready, closing the door behind him, and followed a faint light to the nearby stairs. Taking the steps three at a time, he poked his head into a kind of pantry. Seeing that he had it to himself, he closed the second door and kept on moving through an empty kitchen, following a muffled sound of voices to the party room.

The hashish parlor offered privacy for bashful customers, but several had collected in a kind of sunken living room, just off the corridor to James's left. Their fancy water pipes were percolating merrily, and a pungent smoke cloud was hanging overhead. James couldn't smell it with his mask on, but he had inhaled enough secondhand weed in his time to know what he was missing.

He stood and watched the patrons for a moment, wondering which ones were so-called civil servants, which were taking time away from industry and commerce to relax with some imported hemp. The women, dressed in next to nothing, were employees of the house, dubbed "hostesses," who dealt with any cravings the hashish failed to satisfy. They left the smoking to their "guests" and concentrated on a lot of sweet talk, making sure the pipes stayed full and busy, running up the tab.

One of the women noticed James in the doorway, with his mask and SMG. She gave a little cry that failed to rouse the groggy patrons, but it captured the attention of two bruisers to the left, the first watchdogs he had seen since entering the house. Both men reached for pistols underneath their stylish jackets as they caught a glimpse of James and knew they had bad trouble on their hands.

It was too easy, pivoting to meet them with the submachine gun, squeezing off a silent burst that toppled both men, flinging them away like broken mannequins. The pair went down without a protest, guns still holstered, crimson streamers painted on the wall near where they had stood a heartbeat earlier.

A couple of the women started screaming, loud enough to let their guests know something was amiss. A fat man, middle-aged and balding, staggered to his feet and tipped his hookah over in the process, blurting out an angry challenge that he never would have made if he was sober. James was in his face with two long strides, the muzzle of his weapon lashing out to wipe the sneer from Tubby's face and slam him back down to the sofa.

Shouts and more screaming from upstairs told James that Manning had announced himself. A heartbeat later pistol shots rang out, and he was ready as a shooter burst into view on the second-floor landing, pausing at the head of the stairs to line up another shot.

James stitched him with a burst that sent him tumbling headlong down the stairs. The shooter landed in a heap, limbs crumpled underneath him like the bent legs of a dying spider. Another short burst pinned him there and guaranteed that he wouldn't get up again.

A rush of half-dressed men and naked women followed. James watched as they pounded down the stairs and leaped across the fallen shooter. Bringing up the rear was Gary Manning. The tall Canadian resembled an escapee from a sci-fi movie in his mask, and those he drove before him were plainly worried that their last day on the planet had arrived.

James gambled on the odds that some of them spoke English. He waved toward the nearest exit with his SMG and shouted through the gas mask, telling them to get the hell out in the street. They got the point, but James had to stop a couple of the women in their rush and send them back to help the fat man he had subdued moments earlier. They were the last three out the door, two slender figures struggling under Tubby's weight.

"That's it?" James asked as Manning reached the sunken living room.

"One more upstairs. I think he was the manager."

Past tense, which meant the man was past coming down.

"Okay," James said. "Let's light her up."

A thermite canister was in his hand before he finished speaking, and Manning withdrew another from beneath his jacket. The Canadian pitched his up toward the second floor, while James was satisfied to drop his on the sofa, in the center of the party room.

Five seconds doesn't feel like much, especially when you're running to escape a blast of searing heat. They made it to the alley out in back and slowed down for the walk back to their car, removing gas masks and tucking weapons out of sight. Behind them, still unseen, the white-hot flames had started to consume another property of Kenan Bey.

CHAPTER EIGHT

The information wasn't that hard to come by when they got down to it. Bolan had been watching Kenan Bey's estate with Hawkins and Gromylko for about three hours, with no sign of Mr. Big, when they decided it was time to try another angle of attack. The Chechen syndicate was known to have a unit based in Turkey, for coordination of deliveries. Gromylko had no trouble spotting one of them—a piece of muscle named Piotr Kubichek—when they drove by a favored Russian hangout. Pulling off the lift with three on one was child's play, and Hawk and Bolan left their new comrade with the hostage for three-quarters of an hour once he was secured.

It worked.

After he had spent a little time in private with Gromylko, the Chechen leg-breaker suddenly remembered that his boss, one Vladimir Mikhasevich, had gone to visit Bey at a major processing plant a few miles north of Ankara. Mikhasevich had joked about the call from Bey, explaining that he had to hold the Turkish mobster's hand and help him through a rough time he was having with some competition from the hinterlands. Directions to the hardsite were included, free of charge, with Kubichek surmising that he had a chance to save himself by spilling everything he knew.

It was his last mistake.

The drive took fifteen minutes, with another ten to scout the place, before they left the car and suited up for battle. Gromylko took his introduction to the rest of Phoenix Force in stride, concealing any apprehension that he may have felt at being outnumbered by Western agents. The troop had no fatigues to fit him, but his denims passed inspection well enough, and he borrowed an AK-47 and a bandolier of extra magazines from Bolan's mobile arsenal.

A quarter of an hour later they were in position, covering the rural compound from all sides. The hardsite stood on twenty acres, mostly wooded, which afforded decent cover for the team's approach. For reasons best known to the man in charge, there were no spotters in the woods, though sentries prowled the open ground around a clutch of buildings that comprised the processing facility. They carried automatic weapons, and the Executioner stopped counting when he got to twenty-five.

It made no difference. Bolan and his colleagues had come prepared, and they were going in regardless of the odds.

The layout could have been mistaken for a ranch on cursory inspection. Bolan eyed the house, a kind of barn and several other outbuildings, including a detached four-car garage. He calculated that the opium processing would be carried out inside the "barn," though it could just as easily be for storage or quarters for live-in troops. In any case both the house and the barn were marked for long-range hits before they made their rush against the plant.

Their arsenal included three RPG-7 launchers, one of which was braced on Bolan's shoulder while he sighted on the broad doors of the barn downrange. McCarter and James had placed the other launchers for triangulated fire, while Hawkins, Manning, Encizo and Gromylko were stationed around the perimeter with automatic weapons, prepared to move in when the shit hit the fan.

Any second now, right.

It had been raining earlier, so the ground was damp, and Bolan saw no danger that the back-flash from his RPG would set the woods on fire. With that threat banished from his mind, he took a breath and held it, stroked the weapon's trigger and was reaching for a second rocket as the first one sailed toward impact, riding on a tongue of fire.

He saw a couple of the sentries glance in his direction, trying to decipher what was happening before the missile found its mark and detonated in a smoky thunderclap. By that time two more rockets from different points on the perimeter were already hurtling toward selected targets, and holy hell was breaking loose down there.

Reloading in a single, practiced motion, Bolan found his second mark and let the rocket go.

He wished his adversaries luck.

All bad.

GROMYLKO HAD BEEN WAITING for the rockets, but the first one startled him, regardless. Streaking out of nowhere, it ripped through the wide doors of the barn and spewed shards of broken, smoking lumber much like shrapnel from a fragmentation bomb. The next two RPG rounds came almost immediately, striking at the house from different angles, one explosive warhead peeling back a corner of the roof, the other plowing through a window and exploding well inside.

The guards were going crazy, several of them firing toward the tree line, even though they had no targets. Lying prone in shadow, the *militsiya* lieutenant picked one of the gunmen out at random, fixed the AK-47's sights upon his chest and triggered off a 4-round burst that knocked his human target sprawling on the grass.

It was amazing to Gromylko, how the killing came so easily, despite his years of service to the law. He had killed men before, but always in the line of duty as defined by the *militsiya* manuals and prevailing Russian law. This time, despite the tacit blessing of his own superiors and the Americans who were his allies of the moment, it felt different. Liberating. Almost therapeutic.

It was frightening, how much he liked the feeling of the weapon in his hands, the targets scurrying before him, knowing that he didn't have to build a case in court and watch some perjured witness ruin everything with unadulterated bullshit. Gromylko thought the feeling could become addictive, and a part of him already wondered whether anything about his life would ever be the same again.

Instead of dwelling on his doubts just then, Gromylko concentrated on his marksmanship. From counting sentries, estimating how many might be inside the house and barn, he reckoned that they were outnumbered by a minimum of five or six to one. Beyond a certain point the numbers hardly mattered. Gromylko simply knew that he must shave the odds as much as possible, by any means at his disposal, while they still had time.

Before they rushed the enemy.

He watched more soldiers spilling from the damaged, smoking house, all armed with automatic rifles, submachine guns, shotguns. Gromylko raised his estimate of opposition to the range of eight or nine to one, and then immediately did his best to forget about the odds as he sighted down the Kalashnikov's barrel, his index finger taking up the trigger slack.

The range was seventy-five or eighty yards, with the open ground falling slightly away from Gromylko's position at the tree line, and he adjusted his aim. The rifle bucked against his shoulder, but he held it steady, sweeping the field before him with a burst that tracked from left to right. Another sentry stumbled, spinning as he fell, collapsing in a rag-doll attitude upon the grass. Beyond him others ducked and scattered, dodging rifle fire or shrapnel from the latest round of RPG projectiles.

A handful of the gunmen seemed to have him spotted now. Three dropped prone and hosed automatic fire toward his position, while two others started moving toward the tree line, closing in.

Gromylko squinted as a stream of bullets raked the tree trunk overhead and showered him with shards of bark. He had done well to hide himself in shadow, and his enemies were firing with the bright sun in their eyes, thus spoiling their aim. Still, they were doing fairly well, and he couldn't afford to take them lightly, not if he wanted to survive.

The pointmen first.

Gromylko framed the nearer of them in his sights and fired a burst that opened up the gunman's chest and propelled him backward in a spray of crimson mist. The man was dead before he hit the ground, but he kept firing as he fell, and stopped only when his lifeless fingers lost their purchase on the weapon.

The other brave man hesitated, dropping to a crouch, but there was no way he could hide himself. Gromylko grimaced as a burst of submachine-gun fire came closer than the rest so far, but he held steady with the AK-47, sighting carefully and squeezing off, remembering that it would spoil his aim to jerk the trigger.

Five rounds stitched the crouching gunman's torso in a ragged line, slamming him down on his backside and through a clumsy backward somersault. The dead man wound up lying on his stomach, with his weapon pinned beneath him, and Gromylko shifted his attention to the three men giving cover.

Two of them were up and running by the time their second comrade hit the ground, apparently deciding to save themselves. Gromylko chased them with a burst that dropped one sprawling in his tracks and missed the other by at least a yard, then the lieutenant swung his piece around to face the one man who had held his post, still firing from a prone position on the lawn.

It felt like shooting at a mirror image of himself, but while Gromylko had the trees and shade to cover him, his adversary lay in sunlight, totally exposed. The Turk appeared to recognize his danger, but he had no recourse now that he was under fire. The last rounds from Gromylko's magazine ripped through the shooter's face and shoulders, scattering his brains across the lawn.

Gromylko's hands were trembling slightly as he fed another magazine to the Kalashnikov and chambered up a live round, ready to resume his duel with death. Downrange the Turkish sentries were retreating, seeking cover, as converging streams of fire and three more rockets tore into their ranks.

Perhaps, Gromylko thought, the odds wouldn't be such a problem after all.

Then it was time to go, and he was on the move, legs pumping, heading toward the clustered buildings of the compound on the strength of nerve alone.

CALVIN JAMES WAS on his feet as the last of nine rockets exploded in the middle of the compound, taking out approximately half the front porch of the house. It vaporized two gunners in the process, and James watched them die, already moving out at a dead run, cutting a diagonal across the broad expanse of lawn.

Before he had covered much ground, four guns were closing in to intercept him. James saw them coming, felt the vulnerability of his position out there in the open. But retreat would only give them a clear shot at his back, while leaving Bolan and the rest with greater obstacles to overcome.

So James kept going, firing from the hip with his

Kalashnikov and taking down the closest of the four men, on his left, with a rising burst from knee-level to throat.

And that left three, for starters.

James kept firing short precision bursts as he continued on his long run toward the southwest corner of the damaged house. He heard bullets humming in the air around him, felt one pluck his sleeve, but slowing down would only give his enemies a stationary target. If he was meant to die this afternoon, James intended to go down fighting, taking as many of the opposition with him as he could.

He took a second adversary with a burst to the chest, saw the 7.62 mm bullets ripping through the gunman's flimsy shirt, blood spurting from the wounds as the gunner vaulted over backward, going down. A last burst from the shooter's submachine gun was directed toward the cloudless sky.

The third man was too busy shouting and shooting to be conscious of the fate that had befallen his companions. Charging on a collision course with James, he emptied his magazine in one long burst, then seemed incredulous when the bolt of his weapon locked open on an empty chamber.

Stopping to reload meant instant death. The shooter knew it, and he chose the only viable option, reversing the SMG in his grip and charging with a throaty battle cry, brandishing his useless firearm like a club. James shot him in the face without breaking stride, caught his fall from the corner of one eye as he ran past, continuing on his way toward the house.

Each member of Phoenix Force had studied recent

photographs of Kenan Bey. There would be no mistaking him if one of them should meet him on the battlefield. Assuming he was in the house, James thought the Turkish godfather would be intent on getting out by now. The place was on fire after several RPG hits, and while much of the structure was brick, the roof would burn, collapse and bury those inside unless they made a prompt escape.

James didn't know or care if he would be the one who met and finished Bey. He wasn't on a trophy hunt, but rather fighting for a cause—and for his life. Defeat meant more than simple failure; it meant death.

The house was fifty yards ahead of him. Smoke poured from beneath the eaves on one side, to the north, while James was upwind. His visibility wasn't impaired so far, but that meant that the field of fire was open for his enemies, as well.

At once, as if in answer to his silent thoughts, two weapons opened up on James, one from a window to his left, off toward the nearest corner of the house, while the second was situated on the roof itself. He had a clear view of the rooftop sniper, who was down on one knee with a rifle braced against his shoulder, silhouetted by the open sky behind him.

The Phoenix pro fired by reflex, let the years of training and experience direct him as he swung the AK-47 up and squeezed off six or seven rounds. The rooftop gunman seemed to shiver, as if stricken with a sudden chill, then lost his balance and pitched off the sloping roof. James saw him hit the ground and turned his full attention to the live gunner who was sniping at him from the window on his left.

Another moment and his angle of approach would take him well beyond the shooter's line of sight, but that would leave an adversary who could track him down and point him out to others, still alive and dangerous. He hosed the window with a long burst from his AK-47, saw the bullets flinging brick dust high and low. Then the gunman caught his share and lurched back from the open window, arms outflung, his weapon toppling to the flower bed outside.

James reached the wall and pressed his back against it, breathing heavily. He used the moment to inspect his rifle's magazine, replacing it when he discovered only three rounds left. For what came next, he would need every break he could get.

Beginning now.

"I SHOULDN'T EVEN BE HERE, damn it!" Vladimir Mikhasevich was seething as he glared at Kenan Bey. "This is *your* fight, not mine."

"It's our fight now," the Turk informed him, sniffing at the air and almost smiling as he spoke. "They want to cook us both, you see?"

So, now the goddamn house was burning, thought Mikhasevich. He cursed the impulse that had brought him there to hold the damn Turk's hand and comfort him while he was running from his enemies. It had been foolish to expose himself that way, and it seemed he was about to pay the price—unless he left the losing game.

"I'm getting out of here," the Russian said.

"You think they'll let you?" Bey asked. He snorted laughter, finishing his glass of *raki* in a single gulp and flinging it aside to smash against the nearest wall. "We're all in this together, *comrade*."

"Then you'd better move your ass," Mikhasevich shot back, "because I don't intend to wait for you."

The good news was that he had his own car parked outside. It was a classic Porsche convertible, ideally suited to the sunny Turkish climate, though he could have wished for something more appropriate—perhaps an armored limousine—just now. In any case it was a fast car and had never failed him yet.

If he could only reach it.

If the bastards hadn't blown it into pieces with their rockets.

Mikhasevich was halfway to the door and moving swiftly when his host retrieved two automatic rifles from a cabinet on the wall and fell in step behind him.

"If we're going," Bey remarked, "we ought to be prepared."

Mikhasevich accepted one of the Kalashnikovs and cocked it, scowling at the Turk. "If you had been prepared," he said, "we wouldn't be in this position now."

"For all I know, it's someone after *you*," Bey replied.

"That's why they hunt your men all over Istanbul and Ankara, of course." Mikhasevich made no attempt to hide the scorn he felt for Bey.

The Turk had been a prime connection in the early days, when the Vasilievs were building up their empire in the Russian homeland, reaching out for merchandise from any source available. These days, however, they could buy a better grade of heroin at cheaper rates from Triad dealers in the East. Progress was whittling down the Turkish portion of their business, and today might be as good a time as any to sever the connection.

Mikhasevich was tempted. All he had to do was turn around and shoot the bastard point-blank in the chest, and that would finish it. Unfortunately he would still be trapped inside the burning house, with unknown enemies outside. There was a possibility that Bey could help with his escape, but only if he lived.

When they were well away, though, that would be a different matter. There would be nothing to restrain his homicidal impulse then, and he could always tell his master that the Turk was killed by those who hunted him from Istanbul to Ankara. Vasiliev might not be pleased at first, but in the long run it would make things easier, switching to dealing strictly with the Chinese for their product from the Golden Triangle.

Drugs were better than oil these days on the international market. As a constantly renewable product, they would never run out, and the retail price was vastly higher. Drugs caused no air pollution, nor damage to the environment—in fact, they were a clear-cut part of nature's plan, derived from poppies, coca leaves, whatever. Better yet, drugs reached a wider market, including countless addicts who were still too young to drive a vehicle.

As Mikhasevich opened the door, an acrid stench of smoke recalled his mind to the here and now. His immediate problem was survival, not economics. If his thoughts began to wander, he would end up dead, and *he* would be the cause of air pollution as his body rotted underneath the Turkish sun.

But not today, he told himself, and took a firmer grip on the Kalashnikov. Even if his car had been damaged, there were other vehicles about—a veritable fleet, in fact. Should all else fail, he could escape on foot. All he'd have to do was make it to the trees and find a place to hide, while Bey's unknown assailants finished mopping up around the place.

Mikhasevich felt certain that the Turks would lose this battle. They had suffered too much damage in the first few moments, and while he had no idea how many gunners had been killed or wounded, his instinct told him they were losing. They might not be wiped out, but if enough men broke and ran, it would achieve the same effect.

I'm running, thought Mikhasevich, and felt no shame. A man was obligated to defend his honor, but there was no Russian honor riding on the line in Ankara. The only loss of face he stood to suffer in the present situation was if he allowed himself to be dragged down with Kenan Bey.

And that wasn't about to happen.

Not as long as Vladimir Mikhasevich could point a gun.

McCARTER DROPPED the RPG and grabbed his AK-47, rising from the cover of a fern bed that was withered from the heat of rockets fired two feet above ground level. He had slammed two HE rounds into the house and one into the barn, and now it was time to move in close and finish off the job.

It would have been a better gig at nighttime, but the darkness would have given him away as he was firing with the RPG. In fact there was no perfect time to rush a compound occupied by armed and angry men. To some extent the battlefield was what each soldier made of it, with private courage, individual experience and expertise. In this case the advantage of surprise had let them whittle down the odds a bit, and while the opposition still had greater numbers, they were scattered, dazed, disorganized.

McCarter reckoned there would never be a better time to strike.

He broke for the detached garage, which had been spared from RPG projectiles on the theory that it might attract important targets if they managed to escape the house. A pair of groggy-looking shooters stood between McCarter and his destination, both blinking at him as he burst out of the tree line, running on a collision course with them.

They managed to recover fairly rapidly, their weapons swinging up and into target acquisition as McCarter closed the gap between them. He fired from the hip at a range of thirty yards, nailing the shooter on his right with a short burst that staggered him, slamming the SMG from his hands as he fell over backward and sprawled on the ground.

The other Turk dropped to a crouch and swiveled sideways, trying to reduce the target area he offered to his enemy. It was a good idea, but poorly executed, as he lost his target fix and sent the next burst from his weapon flying off some distance to McCarter's left. In other circumstances the mistake might have been something he could live with, but McCarter wasn't playing war games, and he had an unforgiving nature when his life was on the line.

A second burst from the Kalashnikov he carried struck the Turk around chest level, rising until two or three rounds hit him in the face. He wriggled on the grass, but in a few more seconds he lay still.

The long four-car garage was fifty yards in front of him. McCarter ran with his head down, watching out for adversaries even as he poured on speed, his knees and elbows pumping as he ran. It seemed that he had found a window on the killing ground, poorly defended, while the great majority of sentries fell back on the house and guarded the direct approaches to its three main entrances. Since none of those was visible from where McCarter stood, he had discovered something of a fluke, a veritable no-man's-land.

Now all he had to do was get to the garage alive.

And wait to see who came along.

GARY MANNING DROPPED the empty magazine from his MP-5 submachine gun and reloaded on the run. No more than thirty paces from the smoking barn now, he had left four Turks dead in his wake. His left biceps was burning from a bullet graze, and blood was soaking through his sleeve, but the wound was nothing serious.

It could have been a good deal worse, he realized, if his assailant had been thinking clearly, taking time to aim before he jerked the trigger on his SMG. Of half a dozen rounds or so, at least five had been wasted, while the last one made enough contact to startle him, jar him fractionally off course and make him spend the last rounds in his MP-5's magazine to neutralize the threat.

The barn was burning when he got there, flames from the initial RPG round fueled by something stored inside. It smelled of chemicals, and Manning knew that he had found the opium-processing plant that turned out better than one-third of all the heroin shipped out by Kenan Bey. It would be death to venture in there, with the flames and poisonous, potentially explosive fumes. There could be Turks inside, but Manning reckoned they would soon be well beyond participating in the fight if not already dead.

The tall Canadian decided he would let them burn.

Manning was falling back when the explosion came. At first he heard the whoosh, as if someone had lit the burner on a giant gas range. Then the barn appeared to swell, as if a huge balloon were being rapidly inflated on the inside, bowing boards and straining rusty nails. A heartbeat later, when it blew apart with a titanic thunderclap, Manning was diving headlong for the turf to save himself. The shock wave struck him like a draft from hell, flames rushing overhead and sucking oxygen out of the air before they dissipated in the daylight. Blackened shards of lumber started raining down around him, falling to the earth with twisted bits and pieces of the smack lab and remnants of the building's occupants.

Manning was shaken, breathless, as he staggered to his feet. His ears were ringing, and he was nearly deafened by the blast. His skin felt sunburned, and his eardrums ached, as if he had been slapped by giant hands on each side of his head. The hair around his nape was singed, but it could have been much worse, he realized. If he'd been standing upright when the blast went off, he could have been transformed into a screaming human torch.

The lab was trashed beyond repair, but Phoenix Force still wasn't finished yet. The central target of the strike was Kenan Bey, with second-place honors reserved for his Russian sidekick, Vladimir Mikhasevich. They had no photos of the Russian, but the militia lieutenant, Gromylko, had assured them he would know the man on sight.

Which made no difference to Gary Manning at all.

The rule was simple: anything that moved, aside from other members of the Stony Man team, was marked for death. Manning assumed there were no innocent civilians in the compound, given its illicit operation and the circumstances that had driven Bey to make the plant his sanctuary. Any noncombatants on the property must have realized that they were in the wrong place at the worst time possible, but Manning didn't let the outside possibility deter him as he started moving toward the house.

There were a few outbuildings he could check along the way, to satisfy himself that none of Kenan Bey's hired guns was hiding there, preparing for an ambush when his back was turned. The first one proved to be a toolshed, with a power lawn mower inside, all kinds of shovels, rakes and other handheld implements in racks against the walls. He backed out into sunlight, checked his flanks and moved on to the next shed, where the door stood open several inches, beckoning into the dark beyond.

On impulse Manning braced the stock of his MP-5 against his hip and sprayed the shed with a four-second burst. When he edged forward, drawing back the door with one hand, while his other held the sub-gun steady, Manning glimpsed the muddy soles of gym shoes, denim cuffs, the dark shape of a stocky body farther back. The guy was down and out, no rise and fall of respiration underneath the bloody shirt he wore, and Manning wrote him off without a coup de grace to make the guarantee.

Scratch one more member of the home team, and the odds were getting better by the moment, but they weren't done yet. The big fish were still out there, swimming free, as far as Manning knew.

And if he played his cards right, he could be the one to find them first.

GROMYLKO SPOTTED a familiar face when he was still some thirty paces from the house, approaching from the east. Although he was expecting Vladimir Mikhasevich, it still took him by surprise to see the mobster appearing in the flesh like that, with Turks on either side of him. The three men hesitated for a moment, just outside the doorway that had been their exit from the burning house, then began to move toward the Porsche convertible parked several yards away.

Gromylko saw his chance and snapped the AK-47 to his shoulder, sighting hastily before he pulled the trigger. He'd rushed it, and his first rounds ripped into the taller of the Turks, a young man with a thick mustache. The bullets tore into his chest and slammed him sideways, jostling the second Turk, both of them falling as Mikhasevich took off at a dead run.

Gromylko followed him, unmindful of the risk. It was the first time since his partner's murder that he had a member of the Chechen syndicate directly in his sights, and he didn't intend to let the golden opportunity slip through his fingers. Pounding after Vladimir Mikhasevich, he saw the mobster swerve around a corner of the house and disappear from view. Gromylko's bullets flayed the wall where he had been a heartbeat earlier, but it was wasted effort, wasted rounds.

Gromylko reached the corner where his man had vanished, poked his head around it for a hasty glance and jumped back instantly. But no bullets flew to meet him, and his brain held the impression of his quarry running all-out, racing for his life. Gromylko charged around the corner, breathing heavily and sweating like a marathoner, promising himself that his intended prey would not escape.

Between them, closing with Gromylko on a hard collision course, a pair of Turkish sentries clearly had another plan in mind. Gromylko opened fire with his Kalashnikov at forty paces from the nearest runner and cut the gunman's legs from under him. Any threat from that quarter ended as the tumbling body fell across his line of fire.

The second shooter was still advancing in a zigzag pattern, firing as he came with what appeared to be an Uzi SMG. That gave Gromylko an advantage, on both range and stopping power, though an Uzi hit could be the death of him. In this competition the lieutenant proved a better shot. A 5-round burst from the hip went home on target, left a dazed expression on the Turkish gunner's face as he collapsed onto the lawn.

He still had to deal with Mikhasevich.

Despite Gromylko's constant forward motion, he had slowed while he dealt with Bey's guards, and now he saw that his quarry had gained an extra six or seven yards. Mikhasevich had seemingly abandoned any hope of picking up a car. He bypassed two without a glance to see if there were keys in the ignition, and his course would take him to the tree line if Gromylko let him get that far.

It was a judgment call, and the lieutenant made it in the length of time it takes to formulate coherent thought. Gromylko stopped dead in his tracks, chest heaving from the sprint, and brought the AK-47 to his shoulder one more time. Mind closed to any other threat, he sighted down the barrel, found Mikhasevich and locked on to a point between his shoulder blades. He stroked the trigger once, twice, three times, knowing it was overkill but not caring in the least.

At least some of his bullets found Mikhasevich. Gromylko saw the fabric of his jacket ripple with the impact. Crimson spouted from the entry wounds as the Chechen pitched forward, arms stretched out to catch himself.

It didn't work.

The mobster went down on his face. Gromylko glanced around to satisfy himself that he wouldn't come under fire within the next few seconds, then he moved to check the body out for signs of life.

It was a wasted effort. As Gromylko turned the

body over, he recognized the eerie, boneless feeling of it, as if he could take this giant puppet home and pose it to his heart's content.

This much is done at least, he told himself. If only one of them could do the same for Kenan Bey, they could pull back with the knowledge of a job well done. But they would have to find the mobster first.

The truth hit home with Leonid Gromylko, and he cursed himself. Of course! Who else would be escaping with Mikhasevich, deserting those who served him under fire? The face, glimpsed only in a fleeting profile, suddenly came back to him.

It had been Kenan Bey, and he'd missed his chance for a clean sweep, taking out another member of the Turkish syndicate while concentrating on the end of Vladimir Mikhasevich. Meanwhile, Bey had managed to escape.

Or maybe not.

Gromylko left his Russian adversary stretched out on the grass and ran back toward the place where he had first glimpsed Mikhasevich, together with the two armed Turks.

Was it too late?

Gromylko blanked the thought out of his mind, stayed focused on his mission as he strove for greater speed.

THE GUNNER THRASHED and squirmed on the ground as blood flowed from his mortal wounds, and Bolan spent a mercy round to finish him. The Executioner was on his feet and moving toward the southeast corner of the house when he heard noises of an engine revving, drawing closer by the moment, gaining speed.

He stood his ground and waited as a bright red Fiat came around the corner, spewing gravel from its tires as it fishtailed, nearly running onto the grass. The driver's face was nothing but a blur behind the windshield, and in that moment instinct cautioned Bolan that he shouldn't let the man escape.

Instead of trying to avoid the sports car, Bolan stepped into the middle of the driveway and hoisted his Kalashnikov to draw a bead. A moment later, as the Fiat straightened out and started gaining speed, he had his first clear vision of the driver's face. The lower part of it was still obscured behind the steering wheel, but Bolan made the eyes and knew that he was facing Kenan Bey.

He held the AK-47's trigger down and swung the muzzle back and forth, in short, flat arcs. His bullets swarmed across the Fiat's windshield, drilling glass, then blowing it away. Behind that flimsy screen, the Turkish mobster's face became a bloody fright mask, bits and pieces of it airborne as the hot rounds tore into his flesh and skull.

The Fiat swerved to starboard, back in the direction of the house, as Bey's deadweight hauled on the steering wheel. Bolan held his fire and watched it pass him by, rolling on with a lifeless foot on the accelerator, crashing into the wall at some forty-five miles per hour.

The front end of the Fiat buckled, and momentum did the rest, propelling Kenan Bey out through the shattered windshield, slamming him headfirst into the wall, so that his body draped the crumpled hood like a morbid hunting trophy. Seconds later, when the leakage from a ruptured fuel line blossomed into flame and started racing for the gas tank, Bolan knew his job was done.

He palmed the compact walkie-talkie he carried on his belt and thumbed down the transmitter button, beaming out the signal to withdraw, alerting every member of his strike force that their mission was fulfilled. He was already moving toward the tree line as the confirmations started coming in, and he didn't relax until all were present and accounted for.

So far.

Before they started popping any champagne corks, however, they would have to find a safe way out of Turkey and complete the next phase of their task.

And there was still no guarantee that all—or any— of them would be going home alive when it was done.

CHAPTER NINE

Tbilisi, Georgia

Entering the Republic of Georgia, Leonid Gromylko didn't feel that he was coming home. Never a willing part of Russia, the territory had been annexed in 1801, touching off a nine-year war between the Russian czar and Persia. Absorbed by the Soviet Union in 1922 and granted the status of a constituent republic in 1936, Georgia had been the sight of a violent independence movement in 1989, finally winning its freedom when the USSR disbanded two years later. Even then, fighting continued, much of it spawned by ethnic Abkhazians, allegedly supported from Russia, who had seized most of the republic's territory by late 1993. Peace of a sort was restored the following year, with agreements granting Russian "peacekeepers" free access to the territory, and Georgia had accepted membership in the Russian-dominated Commonwealth of Independent States.

Crime-wise, Georgia had produced her own crop of native gangsters, known for ruthless violence in their everyday affairs. The small republic was a seller's market for military hardware, and homegrown criminals had turned up on the presidential staff as key advisers to the fledgling government. Georgia's position on the Turkish border made it a natural point of entry for heroin shipments, despite repeated assertions that most Georgians were devout Christians who shunned the narco trade as mortal sin. On those occasions when the locals did get squeamish, there were always Chechen mobsters waiting in the wings to take up any momentary slack.

Ivan Storzhenko was the Chechen front man in Tbilisi, watching out for Gregori Vasiliev's financial interests in the area. He had managed heroin imports with Vladimir Mikhasevich and Kenan Bey in Turkey. He also sold weapons stolen from a list of military arsenals in Russia, quoting prices that depended on his customers and their ability to pay. A local peasant might pay two or three months' salary for a Kalashnikov in working order, while a better price on bulk orders was readily negotiated with the likes of Arab terrorists or left-wing "freedom fighters" dropping by from sub-Saharan Africa.

Gromylko knew the major names and faces, both in crime and Georgian law enforcement, but his rank in the *militsiya* would do him no good here. If anything, it might increase the risk he faced if his official link to Moscow was revealed. The officers he served had no authority in Georgia, and any effort to invoke their names would no doubt spawn resentment from the locals. Worse, there was no way to know which Georgian officers to trust and which had been paid off by members of the *mafiya* to file reports on any strangers seeking information on the Thieves' Society.

Besides, the sort of no-holds-barred campaign Gromylko was pursuing with the six Americans broke every major law he could think of, whether in the Georgian state or back at home in Moscow. Noble aims aside, Gromylko was a criminal for the duration, and he must begin to think as such if he intended to survive.

The border crossing was no problem. The Americans had first-rate forged travel documents, and Gromylko did the talking. It required a minor bribe to keep their cars from being searched, but that was routine. It would have been embarrassing to have the weapons found, but no one at the border checkpoint cared enough to look once the *militsiya* lieutenant greased their palms.

It was no wonder that narcotics flowed through Georgia like an endless poisoned river, moving northward into Russia proper and the nations of the former Eastern Bloc. Some of that flow had been replaced with China white in recent months, but it would never stop entirely, not while poppies bloomed across the Turkish countryside. The deaths of Kenan Bey and Vladimir Mikhasevich would slow the trade, but only for a little while. Gromylko knew that there would always be new dealers waiting in the wings, prepared to take up where the dead left off. The narco business fed upon itself, and it was never satisfied.

It gave him cause to wonder whether he was really doing any good, with Mike Belasko and the rest. No matter whom or how many they killed, the moment they stopped firing, other predators would take up the slack. It was an endless struggle, and the men who fought for law and order always seemed to lose out in the end.

But he wouldn't stop fighting. Not while life and will remained. If nothing else, Gromylko still had debts to pay, and would see them settled yet.

In blood.

"So FAR SO GOOD," said Aaron Kurtzman as he finished scanning the report from Ankara. "They did all right."

"They're barely getting started," Barbara Price reminded him.

"What's on your mind?"

"Nothing specific. You want to know the truth, the whole damn thing smells bad to me."

"That's pretty vague."

They sat together in the dining area, with a table in between them, topped by mugs of steaming coffee. Price glanced around the empty room and shrugged.

"It's nothing I can put my finger on," she said. "I mean, just look at the big picture. Where they're going, leaders of the syndicate aren't satisfied with bribing politicians. Over there *they* run for office, and they win. If someone blows the whistle on their mob connections, they actually get more votes than they would have otherwise. It makes Chicago in the twenties look like some kind of Utopia."

"Well, it's a challenge, I agree," said Kurtzman.

"Challenge, right." The blond mission controller shook her head. "Another thing I don't like is this guy from the militia, this Gromylko. Who's to say he isn't really working for the other side?"

"You mean the mob?"

"Why not? We know they've got a major in with the militia, right? Payoffs don't cover it. Some of the ranking officers are *members* of the Thieves' Society, for God's sake."

"It's a gamble, I admit," said Kurtzman, "but we checked this joker out the best we could."

"Which means we read the file they sent us, plus some clippings from the newspaper that they provided, telling how his partner got rubbed out."

"You think they faked all that?"

"My point is, we don't know. Assuming this Gromylko's partner did get murdered on a drug raid, are we sure that means he's clean? Hell, we've known cops here in the States to take their partners out for stepping on a juicy deal, or just because they wouldn't look the other way."

"You're reaching, Barbara."

"I get paid to reach," she said. "We both do, right?"

"May I assume you raised these points with Hal?"

"Damn right I did. He recognizes all the problems, but he's under pressure from the Man. This Russian *mafiya* invasion has the Bureau going nuts right now. They're sending experts off to Moscow when we can't control the problem here at home. They haven't had much help from Interpol so far, and anytime they ask the Company for information, they get tied up in red tape."

"The same old song and dance," Kurtzman commented.

"With a major difference," Barbara said. "When

the Colombians rang up for help, the government was under siege. All kinds of violence in the street, with car bombs going off and judges being shot, mass prison breaks, the whole nine yards. I always had a feeling that the politicians at the top—or most of them, at least—were being honest when they said they wanted the cartels to go away.''

''But you think something's hinky with the Russians?''

''Think? I *know* it's hinky. So do you. They've got known members of the syndicate drawing paychecks on the president's staff in Georgia, and more in the Russian legislature. I could make an argument that the government *is* the mob, and vice versa.''

''I understand your feelings, but we're in it now.''

''Some of us are.''

''You think that it would help if you were in the field?''

''I didn't say that.''

''So, I'm psychic.''

''Right.''

''We're doing everything we can,'' he told her. ''If you think of something else, let's try it on for size.''

''There's nothing else,'' she said. ''Not yet.''

''Well, then, you may as well relax.''

''How does that work exactly?'' Price asked.

The Bear was frowning as he shook his head. ''I wouldn't know.''

She sat and watched the steam rise from her coffee as she said, ''One thing I'll do—speak to Hal to make sure we have all and any backup on hand in case they need to extract fast.'' She nodded to herself. ''It's not much, but more than nothing.''

IVAN STORZHENKO LIT his first cigar of the day and blew a stream of smoke toward the sluggish ceiling fan. His office was equipped with air-conditioning, but fans were something of a fetish with the Balkan contractors and decorators who did everything within their power to make several thousand offices look just the same. Storzhenko didn't mind the architectural monotony so much—he was a Russian native, after all, and had known nothing else from childhood—but there was a part of him that hated waste. There was no reason for a ceiling fan in air-conditioned rooms, and that meant someone had been paid good money to perform unnecessary work. If it had been Storzhenko's call, his money, he would happily have tracked the planner down and smashed his kneecaps with a length of pipe.

Storzhenko was a man of action, and despised the deskbound side of his assignment in the Georgian republic. He almost wished for trouble from competing syndicates so that he might enjoy the process of chastising those who lost their wits and tried to undermine him, frustrate his intentions. He had thrived on conflict in the past, a trait that led in large part to the choice that put him where he was today. A man who had the knack for settling problems swiftly, even brutally, with no expensive comebacks for the family.

And now it seemed that he might see some action after all. The very thought of it improved the taste of his cigar and made Storzhenko smile.

The call had come from Gregori Vasiliev in Moscow. How he got the news was anybody's guess; Storzhenko didn't care. It was enough to know that Vasiliev would not have called unless the facts were verified and double-checked, unless he thought there was a reasonable chance that Storzhenko's people would be called upon to fight.

The basic facts were simple: Gregori's brother and some of his men had been killed in the United States, by enemies unknown. Now, mere days later, Vladimir Mikhasevich was dead in Turkey, along with Kenan Bey and several dozen Turkish gunmen whom the godfather of Istanbul had trusted to preserve his life.

So much for trust.

Vasiliev's assumption, based on simple logic, was that enemies from Turkey might be tempted to attack the family's interests in Georgia. Geographic proximity was part of it, and Ivan Storzhenko was willing to admit that any number of people knew about the heroin pipeline through Georgia and his connection to Mikhasevich and Bey. The police knew, of course, on both sides of the border, but they were paid *not* to know, *not* to see. It was the kind of system that facilitated business, but it also raised the possibility of leaks and unpredictable reactions on the part of some unknowns who might acquire the information secondhand.

The Vorovskoi Mir was powerful, well-known for its policy of exacting revenge against enemies at any cost, but there was always one more out there who enjoyed the danger, thrived on risk, cared less for winning than the game itself. A psychopath, perhaps, or some of the punks who were too young and stupid to believe that they would ever die. These days, with all the drugs around, the Western influence from films and television, every teenage idiot thought he was a gangster if he stole a knife or gun and robbed old ladies in the street. They ran in packs, spun violent fantasies based on smoke and celluloid. Some managed to convince themselves that they were brilliant, indestructible. The fact that they were plainly wrong on both counts was no barrier to attempting wild, outrageous things. Drug burns and daylight robberies that turned into a Wild West shooting spree. Kidnappings with demands for ransom, which predictably wound up with murdered hostages and empty pockets. Some of the punks actively aspired to places in the *mafiya,* while others tried to beat the system, showed their lunatic bravado by going into business for themselves.

Storzhenko didn't think punks were responsible for the events in Turkey, much less the United States. If the assassinations of Mikhail Vasiliev and Vladimir Mikhasevich were linked, it meant an international conspiracy, with weapons, cash and expert personnel available at need. He ruled out Yakuza and Triads automatically, since no one had reported seeing any Orientals near the murder scenes in Turkey. That left the Italians, Corsicans, perhaps one of the South American cartels…or someone else.

He would consider it a challenge to identify the men responsible if they invaded Georgia. Privately Storzhenko thought there was no better than a fifty-fifty chance of that occurring, but he meant to be prepared in any case. His men were on alert, well armed, all holidays suspended until further notice. If and when the enemy revealed himself, Storzhenko and his people would be ready.

He would crush them like so many insects underfoot.

The prospect made Ivan Storzhenko smile.

BOLAN REMEMBERED RUSSIA from the old days, when it was the heartland of the Evil Empire, seeking domination of the globe. His introduction to the subject came from civics classes, newspapers, the television in his parents' living room. When he had gone away to war, against another race of Communists, the specter of the Russian bear was always present, lurking in the background, limiting the military options he and other soldiers like him could employ to wrestle victory from chaos. Later, on his own, the Soviet shadow had fallen many times across his path, the KGB supporting terrorists and "liberation armies" anywhere a crackpot leader reared his head and babbled out the rudiments of a coherent cause.

It was a different world these days, and Bolan still had trouble believing it sometimes. The KGB had changed its name, if not its mind-set, and the Russian Communists were banished to the sidelines. He wondered often if the effort had been more successful than the halfhearted attempt to "de-Nazify" Germany after the Second World War. In that case, as in the farcical attempt of Howard Hughes to run the mob out of Las Vegas in the 1960s, well-known criminals remained in place, their power intact, for one specific reason: they knew how to get things done. Most of the judges and policemen who had served Hitler had died off eventually, but relatively few had been removed from office by Allied authorities. And Bolan had a sneaking suspicion that much the same game had been played in Moscow. Armed dissidents had been suppressed, of course—their leaders had committed "suicide" or suffered lethal "accidents"—but even that was business as usual in the former Soviet Union. While the Balkan provinces seethed with revolt, Mother Russia still depended on the tried and tested ruling class of the former "classless" society to make the system work.

After seventy-four years of Communist rule, who else knew how to do the job?

The *mafiya* was glad to help, of course. There had been outlaw syndicates in the USSR, as in every other nation on earth, cooperating and corrupting, but the collapse of communism had brought a definite change in the Russian pecking order. It was perhaps one of the greatest and most revolutionary changes seen in Russia since those hectic days of 1991. Organized crime was out of the closet in Russia today, as nowhere else on the planet. Corruption might be rife in Bangkok or Palermo, while intimidation was the rule in Bogotá and Port-au-Prince, but nowhere outside Russia had known members of the syndicate been voted into legislative office by the public, nowhere else were they appointed to positions on the state police or presidential cabinets.

It was a new world, right, and Bolan wasn't altogether thrilled with the direction that new world was taking. He would never be mistaken for a prude or a reactionary, but he did cling stolidly to certain values in his life. One of which demanded that the human predators among us should be punished rather than rewarded. Men and women of authority who helped the savages prey on society at large were traitors to the human race, and they deserved no mercy. Bolan drew the line at firing on police, no matter how corrupt or brutal they might be, but he had dropped some politicians in his time and might again.

It all depended on what happened in the next few days.

He thought about Gromylko, wondering to what extent the Russian could be trusted. It had been all right so far, with Gromylko's baptism by fire—and Bolan gave him credit for eliminating Vladimir Mikhasevich—but they were no longer in Turkey. Georgia had been part of the Soviet Union for almost sixty years before the great collapse, and some would say that it was under Russian domination even now. They were returning to Gromylko's native turf, where his superiors might well have an agenda of their own, and Bolan had to wonder if their ally of the moment had his own personal ax to grind.

When they were done in Georgia, if they lived that long, the Stony Man warriors were scheduled to proceed against the syndicate and Gregori Vasiliev in Moscow. Hal Brognola had discussed the possibility of fall-back options if things got rocky, but the plan was vague, deliberately ill defined. The FBI had men in Moscow, working from the U.S. Embassy, but they could hardly be expected to support a group of vigilantes who were violating every major statute on the books. In fact, Bolan knew that if anything at all went wrong in Russia, they would all be up Shit Creek in a leaky canoe, with no paddle in sight.

Bolan derailed the train of thought before it took him any farther down the line toward self-doubt and despair. One of the basic weapons in a frontline soldier's arsenal was confidence that he could do the job. Self-confidence was not confused with arrogance or egotism—either one of which could drive a man to foolish or suicidal risks with no real prospect of success. A soldier who had faith in his ability and training also knew when he was overmatched, and would respond accordingly. He knew when it was time to save himself and fight another day.

But they hadn't reached that point yet with Leonid Gromylko. So far they were on a roll, and Bolan's apprehension was the product of a cautious mind. He made a habit of expecting trouble and was rarely disappointed; when his expectations let him down, it was always a pleasant surprise.

And he expected trouble from the *mafiya* in Georgia. Such men wouldn't turn tail and run simply because their adversaries made a little noise. Their honor would demand that they stand up and fight.

The Executioner wouldn't have had it any other way.

Moscow

THERE IS A TIME FOR GRIEF, thought Gregori Vasiliev, but not today. He knew his brother would have understood and approved his choice to put the business first. One death, or several dozen, mattered less than what befell the family at large. Vasiliev had known that when he won the rank of *vor v zakonye* in the Thieves' Society. He would avenge his brother's murder in due time, but not until he had secured the future of the larger enterprise.

The recent events in Turkey were disturbing. Vladimir Mikhasevich had been a friend for many years, and Kenan Bey—while rude and troublesome at times—had been a valuable associate. It would take time and a substantial expenditure of cash to reestablish the heroin pipeline from Turkey once the locals finished sorting out their problems and appointed a new leader for the syndicate.

Vasiliev considered breaking off relations with the Turks entirely, but it wouldn't do to burn his bridges yet. He didn't trust the Chinese Triads well enough to give them a monopoly on heroin shipped into Russia. It might come to that eventually, but he hadn't become a godfather by rushing into things, taking unnecessary risks. The Turkish product was a staple, and a bit of trouble on that front was not enough to scare a Chechen off the scent of money.

He was naturally concerned about the possibility of links between his brother's death in the United States and the unpleasantness in Turkey. It defied coincidence for two such outbursts to occur within a few days of each other. Nothing in Vasiliev's experience accounted for such happenstance, except the knowledge that sometimes, especially in his domain, there really *were* conspiracies.

Which meant that he would have to take steps to defend himself and everything that he had worked for through the years. It wasn't his style to be a sitting target for some enemy he did not even recognize. Before one of his adversaries bragged about defeating Gregori Vasiliev, the stupid upstart would have a grim fight on his hands.

He had been planning for this moment all his life, convinced that he would someday stand atop the pinnacle of power, knowing others would be anxious to depose him, steal his treasures, strip his life of everything he valued. He had never known exactly what form the assault would take or how much loot he would be called on to defend, how many men would stand behind him when the moment came. Now, with an army at his back and a vast empire at his feet, Vasiliev would give the battle everything he had.

The Georgian outpost was defended by Storzhenko and could not have been in better hands, unless Vasiliev had taken up the cause himself. There was a chance his nameless enemies would bypass the republic, but its close proximity to Turkey would be tempting, with the transit routes for heroin well-known on both sides of the law. If he was lucky, his assailants might bog down in Georgia, waste their strength and let themselves be cut off by Storzhenko's men. It would make matters so much simpler, but Vasiliev wasn't prepared to count on luck alone.

His life so far had called for effort, guile and careful strategy in every move he made. Vasiliev hadn't survived this long or risen to his present rank within the syndicate by giving in to circumstance, leaving his progress up to fate. Each man made his own luck, Vasiliev believed, and those who failed in life were simply less efficient, less ambitious than their brothers who succeeded over time.

Less ruthless, too.

The first time he had killed a man, at seventeen, Vasiliev had been surprised by the emotions it produced, the heady sense of power and accomplishment. Three decades later he had known that feeling more than a dozen times, and it had never paled. Perhaps, before the latest war was over, he would have a chance to know that rush again.

But it could wait.

For now, a wise commander would remain behind the lines and let his troops absorb the shocks of combat while he came to know his enemy. When he was educated perfectly in that regard, it would be time for him to strike—but only then.

Vasiliev took solace in the thought that it would not be long before that moment finally arrived.

CHAPTER TEN

It was a whole new game in Georgia, where they couldn't even sound the street signs out phonetically, but every member of the Stony Man team had come prepared with maps printed in English, and they took directions from Gromylko as they separated, moving toward their several targets. Bolan, teamed with T. J. Hawkins, sent Gromylko off with Calvin James and Rafael Encizo, on the theory that a Cuban and a black American would be the two most likely members of the team to hit a glitch in this particular arena. Mc-Carter and Manning formed the third team, though their targets were outside the city.

Now, as he climbed up the rickety fire escape attached to the back wall of the old hotel that was his target, Bolan wished they had more Russians standing by to help each two-man Stony Man team in case of language problems on the street. Security had trimmed the number down to one, however, and that one could be too many if the game went sour down the line.

At some point in its checkered past, the aging edifice had been a small but comfortable hotel. It had gone out of business years before, and squatters had infested it until the army and police came in to rout them. These days it was officially abandoned, but the property was owned by Ivan Storzhenko, front man for the Chechen *mafiya* in Georgia, and smart money had it that the building was employed as a narcotics depot, sometimes also as a hideaway for *gastrolyor*—the visiting shooters, or "guest artists," who were imported for specific, high-priority killings. Whatever, it was part of Gregori Vasiliev's beachhead in Georgia, and the place was coming down if Bolan had his way.

The canvas satchel slung across his back held twenty pounds of Semtex, sliced up into four-pound charges, each one with a timer and a blasting cap attached. The charges were secure until he armed the detonators and set the timers ticking down to doomsday.

He could have set the charges from outside and brought the building down that way, but Bolan meant to have a look around inside before it blew. With Hawkins standing watch across the street, he gave himself ten minutes, in and out, to get it done. Much longer, Bolan realized, and he would have a major problem on his hands.

The neighborhood was sparsely populated, with more than a few condemned buildings on both sides of the street. That minimized the risk of harming innocent civilians or of the police showing up and interfering with Bolan's plan, but it increased the risk of lookouts in surrounding windows. They had scouted out the street before he parked and left the car, but beyond that, it was all a gamble.

He used a glass cutter to enter through a fourth-floor window, moving with the darkness, dim lights waiting for him on the far side of a door that stood ajar. The room he chose had obviously been unoccupied for months, with thick dust over everything, no furniture except a shabby chest of drawers that stood against one wall.

Outside, a hallway branched to left and right. The light was to his left, in the direction of another open doorway, with the stairs beyond. He went that way, his MP-5 SD-3 submachine gun leading him along the murky corridor. A muttered sound of voices told him there were at least two men inside the room that had become his first stop on the tour.

Bolan glanced through the doorway, saw two chunky hoodlum types sitting in their undershirts and jeans, handguns tucked into the waistbands, smoking something pungent. There were weapons on the floor, and a wooden crate served as a makeshift table before the swaybacked sofa they occupied. On the crate was a plastic bag filled with hash, a box of matches and some rolling papers.

Bolan shot them where they sat, eliminating some extra gunners from the equation. The business of eradicating predators couldn't be that selective, and there was no time to weigh if they were small-time crooks or sharks still growing teeth.

He found no more wildlife awaiting him on the fourth floor, and made his way one level down cautiously, eyes and ears working in concert, while his nostrils flared, alert to any scent that would betray a human presence. Bolan met one shooter stepping from another shabby room and waxed him where he stood, his body sprawling across the threshold to prevent the door from closing on its own.

Three down. How many left?

The numbers game in this instance went in his favor for a change. All the rest—he counted seven, peering from the stairs—were gathered in the ground-floor lobby. An argument was going on that had irritated several to the point of shaking fists at no one in particular. Five of the seven sported side arms worn in plain sight, three shoulder holsters with no jackets and a couple who preferred guns tucked inside their belts.

He had expended roughly one-third of the submachine gun's 30-round box magazine, which meant he had approximately three slugs left for each of the assailants he could see, before he had to stop to reload. Instead, he palmed a Russian frag grenade and placed it with an underhanded toss, then ducked under cover of an intervening wall. With an alarmed yell, a couple of the shooters recognized the object, but none was quick enough to outrun the explosive charge or shrapnel.

Some of them were still alive but not far from the end. Once Bolan was satisfied that none of them would rise again without substantial help, he checked his watch and made a hasty circuit of the ground floor, planting charges here and there for maximum effect, arming the detonators as he went. That done, he made a beeline for the door and took himself away from there, felt Hawkins watching him as he approached the waiting vehicle.

They were a half block out and rolling when the charges blew, and the decrepit building gracefully collapsed, the upper stories dropping to entomb whatever lay below.

A HUNDRED DIFFERENT things could still go wrong, Gromylko thought, but he had planned ahead as best he could. A hasty survey of the target area had marked the lookouts and pedestrian approaches to the target, while the three-man raiding team was unobserved.

It had been fairly easy, covering the Cuban. He could pass without much difficulty as a swarthy Slav, provided that he kept his mouth shut, but his partner was a real concern. Black faces weren't unknown in Georgia, but they were unusual enough to attract attention on the street. Gromylko solved the problem, after a fashion, by dressing the black warrior as an Arab. The costume had three selling points: it helped explain the curiosity of a black man in Tbilisi; it allowed the Phoenix warrior to conceal a portion of his face at will; and the outfit provided ample room for hidden weapons.

The target was a clothing store that did no business with the public. There were shabby suits and dresses hanging in the window, tagged with prices that would be discouraging in any economic climate, and the rare potential customers who crossed the threshold were politely intercepted by a ''greeter'' who informed them that the shop was closed, or there was nothing in the patron's size—whatever it required to see the stranger out and on his way. This afternoon the presence of armed guards outside the shop informed Gromylko that Ivan Storzhenko was on full alert.

He approached the shop with his ''Arab'' partner,

their heads together, muttering in tones the sentries couldn't overhear. He trusted that the Cuban had them covered from his rooftop sniper's nest across the street and two floors up. Once they were inside the shop, that cover would not help them, but getting in and out were moments critical to any raid.

Both warriors carried semiautomatic pistols fitted out with silencers, which came in handy as the outside gunners moved to intercept them at the door. Two muffled coughing sounds, and the invaders pushed their way inside the shop, past fresh corpses huddled on the doorstep.

Leonid Gromylko didn't know the man behind the counter, but he recognized the type. A hoodlum, reaching underneath for what might prove to be a panic button or a hidden gun. It made no difference either way. More popping sounds, and he was flung into oblivion, collapsing from his metal stool.

They rushed into the back room of the shop together and caught three men unpacking leather suitcases. The floor was strewn with clothes, and two of the surprised men held penknives, each working on the stitches that secured false bottoms in the suitcases. The third had finished and was busily unloading plastic bags of powdered heroin. If they were kilo bags, as usual, each suitcase would contain approximately fifteen bags of uncut skag.

The three goons froze, gaping at the new arrivals when Gromylko and his "Arab" sidekick opened fire. Three head shots, and the smugglers went down where they stood. James reached into his pocket and produced a handful of incendiary sticks, priming each with a twist as he dropped one into each false-bottomed suitcase, saving one for the plastic bags stacked up on the table. It was overkill, but there was no point leaving anything to chance.

The fire would spread if it had time, and so Gromylko spent a moment on the sidewalk, looking for the nearest fire alarm. He spotted it on a lamppost, crossed the street and yanked the handle prior to moving back in the direction of their car. They drove around the block and found Encizo waiting for them on the next street over, with his folding-stock Kalashnikov concealed inside a bulky shopping bag.

"We have ignition," James informed the Cuban as he slid into the car's back seat.

STORZHENKO DID HIS BEST to keep from roaring through the telephone as he received the news. It was the third call in the space of half an hour, all from different sections of the city, each unique and yet depressingly alike. Two bombings and a fire so far, and he had already lost twenty men. There were no wounded, as Storzhenko normally expected in a clash of armed combatants, and as far as he could tell, his nameless enemy had yet to suffer any casualties. The bastards seemed to strike at will, throughout Tbilisi, as if daring him to hunt them down.

It was a challenge he intended to accept.

There was no way to keep the bad news from Vasiliev in Moscow, but Storzhenko didn't have to make the call right now. He could use his own best judgment, as the recognized commander on the scene, and wait until he had some good reports to mitigate the bad. Once he had found out who the bastards were and started whittling down their numbers, it wouldn't be so embarrassing to call back home.

Unfortunately there was still one major problem with his plan. Storzhenko was in the dark, without a clue to the identity of his assailants, nor had anyone suggested a reliable technique for him to use in breaking down that wall of secrecy. Storzhenko had already reached out to his men on the police force, but the brass was clueless. They had no idea who was responsible for the attacks, had no clear fix on how more raids could be prevented. Even with patrols out on the street, Storzhenko had no reason to believe that any Georgian officer would solve the case. They were a simpleminded lot, and even more corrupt than the *militsiya* in Moscow. It wouldn't have shocked Storzhenko to discover that his enemies were also paying off the local *musor,* purchasing a license to assassinate his men.

If that turned out to be the case, he would take pleasure in exacting sweet revenge, but it would have to wait until he solved the larger problem and fulfilled his mission on behalf of the Vorovskoi Mir.

But he needed a place to start.

Storzhenko had informers at all levels in the city, from addicts on the street to taxi drivers, hotel porters, nurses, waitresses, bartenders, prostitutes and pimps, sneak thieves and muggers. At his command, they had been known to locate men and women who didn't wish to be found, sometimes within an hour or less. But so far, in the present case, his extra eyes were blind.

It was a galling situation, but he wasn't ready to give up. Defeat was unprecedented for Storzhenko and totally unthinkable. If he couldn't control the action in Tbilisi, then he would be worthless to the family. Vasiliev would remove him from command, and there would be no second chance. Demotion, in such circumstances, meant a bullet in the head if you were lucky. Otherwise, if the disposal team had time to spare, the punishment for failure could be days of screaming agony.

The one and only way to save himself, Storzhenko realized, would be to locate and exterminate the enemy before Vasiliev started getting nervous. There was still a chance to pull it off, but he had no more time to waste, and he could ill afford another string of raids that cost the family soldiers, merchandise and money.

It was past time for him to seize the initiative, no simple task when he was fighting shadows. Still, he had an opportunity to strengthen his defenses even now. It was never too late to beef up the line, put more soldiers into the trenches. If his adversaries kept encountering resistance each and every time they struck, the law of averages dictated that they must sustain some casualties. There were no supermen, no ghosts.

He took a pistol from his top desk drawer and slipped it down into the waistband of his slacks. It made him feel more warlike, helped him get into the mood for what was coming. There would be more bloodshed in Tbilisi, but the city was already used to that. Its people were accustomed to the sights and sounds of war.

It was just as well, Ivan Storzhenko thought, because the killing wasn't finished yet.

Batumi

MCCARTER AND MANNING had drawn the short straw on assignments this time. It was a three-hour drive from Tbilisi to the largest Georgian seaport, at Batumi. They had targets there, along the waterfront and elsewhere, relevant to drugs and other smuggled merchandise that didn't travel overland. Some of the heroin from Turkey came by ship, instead of risking customs checkpoints at the several border crossings, and Batumi was also the port of departure for various items, including military hardware shipped to terrorists in Europe and the Middle East. Authorities occasionally seized contraband along the docks, mostly from independent operators, but they never made a dent in the illicit traffic flowing through Batumi's busy port.

The Phoenix warriors meant to change all that, at least to some extent. They couldn't hope to close the port, of course, nor would their efforts wholly block the east-west pipeline for narcotics. They could make the trade more costly, though, and that they meant to do, beginning with a Turkish freighter called the *Meme Gürültülü*.

Finding the ship was easy, since it was moored against the dock, but the approach was something else. They could have damaged it with RPGs, but there was no clear vantage point for firing, short of standing in the middle of the busy street and blasting at the freighter with their rocket launchers. They could have tried to walk on board with satchel charges, but the *Meme Gürültülü* had two crewmen posted on the gangplank to discourage uninvited visitors, and dropping them would only bring the others out to fight.

That left Plan C, which called for one of them to swim in from a distance, plant a Semtex charge against the freighter's hull and get the hell away from there before the detonator blew.

The water was a lukewarm seventy degrees, but it felt chilly to Manning when he first submerged, heat draining from his body through the skin. No one had thought to purchase diving gear when they were choosing their equipment for the mission, so he swam in jockey shorts, no wet suit, fins or face mask. The heavy satchel slung across his chest tended to pull him down, but he was stronger, swimming powerfully, remaining close beneath the piers whenever possible to keep from being seen.

It was a hundred yards or better from the point where McCarter waited with their car and all the guns, due north along the shore from where the *Meme Gürültülü* was docked. Swimming southward, laboring against the satchel's weight and the demand that he remain close to the surface, rising constantly to breathe, Manning felt his muscles straining, burning, even as his flesh began to chill.

There was no immediate danger from hypothermia; he would need several hours in the water at that temperature before he was at risk. Still, it was wearing on him, and it made him wish that he were dressed for diving, anything to give his body insulation from the chill.

Exertion was the key, he told himself, and concentrated on each kick, each long stroke of his arms. It took him twenty minutes, fighting currents underneath the docks, but then he saw the dark hull of the freighter looming to his right. He jackknifed underneath the scummy surface, salt water stinging his eyes as he felt his way along the hull and chose a point below the waterline, where his Sembex would do the most harm.

He had to surface twice for air before he finished up the job and set the timer counting backward toward the holocaust. He gave himself half an hour for getaway time, counting on fatigue to slow him down on the return trip to his starting point. Manning scowled as swarms of pinpricks tortured muscles in his shoulders, arms and legs. He couldn't linger near the freighter, resting, while his time ran out.

The swim back seemed to take him twice as long. In fact, he barely reached the pier where McCarter waited for him, scrambling up a knotted rope to clear the water in the shadow of an old, decrepit warehouse, when the Semtex blew.

He faced due south and watched an oily geyser spout beside the wounded freighter, while the *Meme Gürültülü* started rolling over on her side, to port. The water rushing through the jagged wound to fill her hold would soon consign her to the bottom.

He took the towel from McCarter's hand as they moved back in the direction of the car.

"That's one," McCarter said.

"And counting," Manning added as he slid into the rental's shotgun seat and reached back for his clothes.

HAWKINS HAD his AK-47 ready when the first truck came around the corner, moving slowly down the narrow street. There was another close behind it, two men in each cab, four gunners in a black sedan behind the second truck to watch the tail end of the little convoy.

If their information was correct, the trucks were hauling military-surplus weapons, ammunition and grenades that had been stolen from an arsenal near Stavropol. The hardware would be stockpiled in Tbilisi or a suburb, while the word went out to various prospective buyers that another shipment had arrived. From there the bidding would begin, with Palestinians, Iranians, perhaps even some Eastern European radicals competing for the prize.

Except that there would be no merchandise to bid on if the Executioner and Hawkins had their way.

When it was clear that there were no more vehicles behind the black sedan, Hawk reached beneath his jacket and took out a frag grenade. He thumbed the pin free, let it drop and stepped out of the alleyway where he had hidden, waiting for his enemies to show themselves. The pavement sloped a little from the point where he was standing, and Hawk had to use a little extra force with the grenade to send it wobbling toward the target. By the time the driver saw him, tried to figure out exactly what was happening, it was too late.

The hand grenade exploded underneath the lead truck's bumper. Shrapnel ripped into belts and hoses, punctured the radiator, spilled gasoline that instantly caught fire, flames racing back along the undercarriage. The driver and his shotgun rider hurried to bail out, but Hawk was waiting for them, peering through the sights of his Kalashnikov.

His first shots nailed the gunner who was riding shotgun, slammed him back against the dusty fender of the truck and dropped him in a heap amid the spreading flames. The driver was apparently unarmed and running for his life. Hawk let him go and concentrated on the second truck in line, while yet another blast told him that Bolan had the chase car nailed.

The street became a shooting gallery. There were at least two gunmen still alive in the sedan, both firing wildly, up and down the sidewalk, seeking targets neither one of them could clearly see. The shooter in the second truck was stepping down, unloading with a compact submachine gun, fanning slugs in Hawk's direction as he hit the pavement running.

Hawkins stood his ground and squinted through a haze of brick dust as the hostile rounds swept past him. He stroked a short burst from his AK-47, saw the runner jerk, then lurch toward a doorway he would never reach in life. The man fell six feet short from safety, fresh blood streaming out across the sidewalk where he lay.

The second driver had more fight in him than his predecessor, emerging from the truck's cab with a pistol in his hand. He managed two quick shots before Hawk nailed him with a tight burst to the chest and slammed him backward, out of sight behind his rig.

Hawk turned to face the black sedan, but it was over by the time he found a target. Bolan used a second frag grenade to silence his opponents, and the car went up in flames, more fuel splashed on the street, spreading fingers of liquid fire. In seconds flat the middle vehicle was burning, helped along by an incendiary stick that Bolan pitched across the tailgate.

Another job well done, and it was time to go.

CHAPTER ELEVEN

Rafael Encizo watched the gunmen come and go, still counting heads and wishing he were somewhere in the Western Hemisphere, where he could speak to strangers without involving an interpreter. It wasn't even that so much as that they only had the one guy to depend on, and no one really knew how solid he would be if things went wrong.

Gromylko had been straight enough when they were up against the Turks and then the Georgians, but he wasn't really *home*. Not yet. Encizo couldn't stop one portion of his brain from wondering, despite himself, if maybe it would all turn out to be a setup, someone with a grudge hung over from the bad old days, hoping to settle the score. It was improbable, he realized, with all the various security precautions they employed, but stranger things had happened. Bolan and the rest of them had dealt with more than one unhappy ghost before, and this would be the wrong place and the worst of times for another drop-in from the past.

Encizo brought his mind back to the moment, adding two more gunners to the head count. That made seventeen who had gone in while he was watching, versus three entirely different faces that had left. He would assume a bedrock minimum of twenty guns inside, and pray it didn't turn out double or even triple that.

The place was large enough, and then some. A dilapidated theater, long closed, it would have seated better than three hundred in its day. That day was long since past, however, and the Chechen mob had bought the property for next to nothing, left the theater intact and used it for occasional meetings when Ivan Storzhenko had to lay down the law.

There was no sign yet of Storzhenko tonight, and a glance at his watch told Encizo it was almost time to move. He brought the little two-way out from under cover, thumbed the button down and told the night, "We're clear out front. I make it seventeen arrivals, but there must be more inside. Three others bailed. Can't say if they'll be coming back."

"I heard that." James's voice was small and scratchy, coming from the little two-way's speaker.

"We should go ahead as planned," Gromylko said.

"Affirmative," James replied.

"I'm there," Encizo added.

The Cuban switched the two-way off and stashed it in an outside pocket of his trench coat, reaching back inside to find the Uzi SMG with its foot-long silencer attached. Encizo flicked the safety off, leaving a live round in the chamber as he made his way across the street.

He didn't have a clue as to the kind of gathering that had drawn twenty-odd Storzhenko soldiers to one place while they were very obviously needed elsewhere, and he didn't care. It was an opportunity to hit

Storzhenko's private army in a major way, and they weren't about to pass on that without compelling reasons.

Do or die, the Cuban told himself, and kept a firm grip on the Uzi as he closed in on the theater. Assigned to watch the front door, he was also going in that way unless somebody stopped him cold—as in stone dead. James would take the back door, while Gromylko used an alley entrance on the east side of the building. That would cover all the exits they could see and trap their targets in a killing pen...but things could still go wrong.

Encizo found that out as he was reaching for the handle on one set of double doors in front. A few feet to his right, the other set of doors swung open, and a pair of husky shooters came outside. The nearer of them spotted Encizo at once and muttered something that didn't require translation as he reached for his piece.

Encizo slid the Uzi underneath his outstretched arm and hosed them with a stream of parabellum shockers. His assailants did a jerky little dance along the sidewalk, reeling from the impact of the bullets, sprawling to the pavement when he let the trigger go.

No time to waste.

Encizo shouldered through the door, went in behind his SMG, prepared to deal with anybody who got in his way.

THE RPG WAS too flamboyant for a drive-by and might actually set the car on fire, so Bolan opted for grenades. It meant that he would have to walk up to

the target, but he didn't mind. Most of the patrons
would be regular civilians, and he had a feeling that
between himself and Hawkins, he could take care of
the rest.

The café had a doorman who was big enough to
double as a bouncer if the need arose. It wouldn't happen often, given the sort of clientele who patronized
the place, but something in the Executioner's de-
meanor made the man rise to his full height, sticking
out his chest and sucking in his gut. The whole act
fell apart as Bolan showed him the Beretta 93-R and
thumbed the hammer back, *click-clack*.

The slugger raised his hands and closed his eyes, as
if he didn't want to see it coming. Bolan swung his
left fist up and over, slamming right into the bouncer's
nose with force enough to crunch his skull against the
brick wall at his back. The bouncer's eyelids fluttered,
showing white, and then he melted to the sidewalk,
ending in a heap at Bolan's feet.

As Bolan crossed the threshold, he was busy reaching back inside his jacket for a stun grenade. He
wouldn't use a frag bomb with so many innocent civilians in the way, but giving them a headache
wouldn't trouble him at all. When the effects wore off,
they would have something new to talk about, and in
the meantime Bolan would have dealt with those who
carried arms and served Ivan Storzhenko for their
daily bread.

Storzhenko—or his Russian backers—owned the
restaurant where many of Tbilisi's "better" citizens
turned out to see and let themselves be seen. It wasn't
21 or Planet Hollywood by any means, but this was

not the States. What passed for high society in Georgia was a group of leading businessmen and politicians, some holdovers from the Communist regime and the trophy wives or mistresses they brought along to give the place some color.

Bolan had the safety pin out of his stun grenade before the hostess came to greet him, losing her smile as she saw the hardware in his hands. The proper phrase eluded him, so Bolan simply pointed toward the street with his Beretta, and kept on moving toward the main room of the restaurant. He pitched the canister overhand, well toward the back of the room, and sidestepped to put a wall between himself and the explosion, raising hands to cup his ears, eyes closed. Despite those measures, Bolan felt the jolt of the concussion, heard the screams of patrons as they toppled from their chairs, some dragging tablecloths and dishes with them when they fell.

There should be no real injuries so far, maybe some scrapes and bruises, Bolan calculated. When he moved back toward the open doorway of the dining room, he stayed to one side, knowing that the rush for daylight would begin as soon as people started lurching to their feet. A few were on the move already, visibly disoriented, but he wasn't focused on the diners now. Eyes tracking, he was seeking out the soldiers who were bound to be somewhere around the premises.

Almost immediately he spotted two of them off to his left. Both men had pistols in their hands, one weaving slightly on his feet, his free hand pressed against his forehead. Bolan leveled the Beretta, slammed a bullet through that hand and watched the gunner's head snap back, eyes rolling upward as he died, still on his feet. The pistol was unsilenced, and its sharp report cut through the wailing of the frightened customers, increasing panic, prompting more of them to stampede for the exits. Bolan pressed himself against the wall and got a shot off at the second gunman while he still had time, rewarded with a splash of crimson on the stucco as his target fell.

A handgun answered from his right, a startled woman shrieking as the wild shot pierced her thigh and dropped her, squalling, on her backside. Bolan spun to face his adversary, saw a short man weaving through the crowd and knew it would be dangerous to risk a shot. The gunner didn't seem to care about the café's patrons, though, still taking wild shots as he closed the gap between them, wounding two more innocents before the crowd cleared out in front of him.

It was a one-time-only opportunity, and Bolan didn't waste it. Squeezing off two shots, he nailed the little man through the jaw and larynx, spinning him around with such force that his head and shoulders struck the floor before his hips and legs. The body shivered once, and then lay still.

The crowd was frozen now, paralyzed by their fear of the explosion on the far side of the room and Bolan's pistol at the nearest exit. Bolan could see no more shooters in the crowd, so he retreated, breaking for the street, and heard the café patrons rushing after him. He hit the sidewalk running, the Beretta out of sight, and turned back toward the car where Hawkins waited for him with the engine running. Frightened diners poured out of the restaurant and scattered, running off in all directions, many of them screaming for police.

"A little something unexpected on the menu," Hawkins said.

Bolan responded with a smile.

THE *KEFFIYEH* HE WORE made Calvin James feel like an extra in a cheap Biblical epic, but he kept it on as he pushed through the back door of the one-time theater, aware that it would alter the perception of any survivors who glimpsed him in action. Leaving witnesses wasn't part of the plan, but shit happens, and enemies are sometimes overlooked in war.

Especially those who run away and hide.

The Skorpion machine pistol he carried had a silencer attached to the muzzle, nearly doubling the length of the gun, but its bulk gave him something to hold on to with his left hand for stability, and the rig still fit easily beneath his bulky jacket. But it was in his hands now, cocked and ready, as he moved along a murky corridor and homed in on the murmuring of voices somewhere up ahead.

James would have been backstage, except there was no stage, as such, in movie theaters. Back*screen* was closer to the truth, with curtained doorways leading off to either side, into the main part of the theater. James peered out through a crack between the curtain and the wall, saw twenty-odd thug types already lounging in the seats or standing in the aisle, some of them smoking, several conversations going on at once. Their voices reached him loud and clear, but all of them were speaking in what may as well have been Chinese.

He didn't need to understand them, though; that was the beauty of it. All he had to do was *find* them, and that task had been accomplished. Now, as he stood waiting for the others to arrive, James raised the silenced Skorpion until its muzzle pressed against the curtain fabric, aiming at the mobsters in the nearest row of seats.

He was expecting Leonid Gromylko to begin the party when he got into position, and the sudden uproar from the lobby startled James. The street approach was Encizo's, and all that yelling had to mean someone had spotted him. Which accelerated the pace for sure.

There were a few stray pistol shots, and then more yelling, coupled with what sounded like a cry of pain. *That* voice wasn't Encizo's, which meant that he was fighting back and scoring hits. It also meant that their precision plan had sprung a leak, and James couldn't postpone his entry to the fray while waiting for Gromylko to jump in.

Okay.

He whipped the curtain back and strafed the front-row gunners just as they were lurching to their feet. His spray of bullets toppled three before they fully gained their balance or had time to reach their guns. Thanks to the silencer, most of the thugs, already turning toward the lobby doors behind them, missed his entrance to the theater while they were focused on the sounds of combat from the general direction of the street.

Most, but not all.

A couple of the Russian mafiosi, seated near his early kills, had seen their comrades fall and marked the source of gunfire that had cut them down. They both had pistols out and were blasting as James lunged into the theater, their first shots high and wide, but getting closer all the time. James answered them with short bursts from the Skorpion and dived for cover behind the nearest seats, with bodies sprawled around him, leaking crimson on the floor.

The rest of the Storzhenko soldiers had a fix on what was happening by now, although they had no way of knowing who was on their case or why. That added up to what James liked to call the "rattle factor," anything that could unhinge the opposition, make them jump at shadows, give them second thoughts to slow down their reaction time.

Not that it helped a great deal when the odds were twenty-some to one, and he was pinned down under fire, with barely enough cover to absorb the first few hostile rounds. It would be suicide to pop up and return fire at the moment. If he didn't catch a break within the next few seconds, James knew he was on a fast track to the grave.

The break came when he needed it the most and least expected it. At first he almost missed the different sound of gunfire, with so many pistols barking at him, but a warrior with experience on modern battlefields never forgets the sound of a Kalashnikov. James didn't miss the cries of pain and anger from his adversaries, either, as the automatic fire ripped through their ranks.

Gromylko!

James didn't care if he was early, late or right on

time. The only thing that mattered was that he was there and doing what he had to do, against the odds.

And making all the difference in the world.

James braced himself on knees and elbows, took a breath and gripped the Skorpion in both hands, letting out a bellow as he rose to face his enemies.

GRAY DUSK WAS FALLING on the two-lane road that linked Batumi, on the Black Sea, with Tbilisi, to the east. It felt to Gary Manning as if they were running from the last warm rays of sunshine, racing into darkness with a vengeance, but he uttered no complaint. The dark road was familiar to him, from experience, and he could find his way around that territory without getting lost.

He was relieved to have the seaport well behind them, with Bolan and his other comrades drawing closer, mile by mile. McCarter had the wheel, and he was focused on a silent contemplation of the highway, flicking glances now and then at the speedometer and rearview mirror. They couldn't afford a traffic stop right now, much less a high-speed chase with the police, but every passing moment wore on Manning's nerves like sandpaper on sunburned flesh.

And they weren't even finished yet.

Midway between Batumi and Tbilisi was another target on their list, a farm owned by Storzhenko, where a local peasant crew went through the motions—planting, waiting, harvesting—while others used the place for a drop. It was one more depot on the Russian *mafiya*'s underground railroad of poison, rolling east and north from the Turkish poppy fields and processing plants, through makeshift labs where it was "stepped on," to the veins and nostrils of an estimated one million addicts in Mother Russia. And that was a conservative estimate, in a country where addicts committed sixty percent of all property crime and forty percent of all violent assaults.

The farm was settling down to rest when they arrived and parked their car well out on the perimeter, lights off, unloading gear and changing quickly into camouflage fatigues of NATO style. Their rifles were Russian AK-47s, their pistols Italian Berettas. If one or both of them got killed, it would be virtually impossible for anyone to establish an ID on the body. Any record of their fingerprints had been expunged outside the files at Stony Man, while military-service records and the like had been rerouted and strictly classified.

It made Gary Manning feel a bit like a ghost sometimes, when he suited up for battle. Not that it troubled him particularly, but he wondered on occasion what his mother and his sister would be told, what explanation would be offered when his luck ran out.

The wheat field was a safe bet to be clear of any high-tech security paraphernalia, what with hired hands and their farm machinery around. It also offered good concealment as the Phoenix warriors made their long trek toward the house and barn. It took ten minutes, but they got there, pausing at the edge of cultivated land to check the target out, up close and personal.

Two men cannot surround a house, nor would they try. There were no sentries posted on the property as far as Manning could make out, perhaps because the farm was deemed secure or remote enough to miss out on the action lately breaking in Batumi and Tbilisi. In either case, their strategy remained the same. They opted for a more direct approach, ignored the darkened barn and split up only as they neared the house, McCarter jogging toward the front, while Manning slipped around in back.

There were no standard porches on the house, as is the rule in rural North America. As Manning peered in through a window at the back, he found himself no more than six or seven feet from half a dozen bullet-headed types whose bulging muscles might denote a lifetime working on the farm or pumping iron in prison. Checking out the pistols on their hips or slung in shoulder holsters, Manning guessed the verdict could go either way.

The goons were hunched around a wooden table, spooning stew into their faces, chasing it with some clear beverage that could have been water, but was probably vodka. One of them would speak from time to time, still chewing, and produce a comment or a bray of laughter from his comrades.

With so much house between them, there had been no way for Manning and McCarter to arrange a signal. Rather, Manning checked his watch and saw that he had fifteen seconds left before the stuff hit the fan. No matter what else happened then, he would assume McCarter to be kicking in the front door on the stroke of 6:05 p.m., and he would move accordingly.

Ten seconds.

Five.

On one, he stepped up to the door, reared back and gave a solid kick to slam it open, barging through with his Kalashnikov while the six gunners at the table whipped their bullet heads around to face him, slack-jawed, gaping in surprise. A burst of automatic fire from the direction of the parlor told him that McCarter had arrived on time, and Manning held the trigger of his AK-47 down, raking the table with a deadly stream of bullets. Left to right and back again.

A couple of his targets tried to rise and draw their guns, but none got very far. He had them at a lethal disadvantage, and their legs tangled up with chairs, knees banging underneath the table, dishes flying, swept away by angry hands or flying bullets. One of them went over backward in his chair, flipping the table away from him, on top of another gunman. Before the last one toppled, Manning heard the sound of footsteps coming toward him, down a hallway leading from the front part of the house.

He swiveled, bringing the Kalashnikov around, and tried to guess how many rounds were still left in his magazine. No more than five or six, he thought, but it could be enough. A start, at least, to buy a little time.

"It's me," McCarter warned him, standing well back from the open doorway.

"Come ahead," said Manning as he let himself relax. "We're done in here."

GROMYLKO CAUGHT one of the Chechens breaking for an exit and dropped him with a short burst from his folding-stock Kalashnikov. Two other gunmen opened fire with pistols in response, and he ducked back into the alcove that had sheltered him since he engaged the enemy brief moments earlier.

It seemed like hours, but time's passage was deceptive in a crisis situation, sometimes lagging in slow motion, otherwise racing impossibly fast. Whichever way it felt, though, Gromylko knew that they were swiftly running out of time. It wouldn't be long before one of their adversaries scored a lucky hit or the police arrived to cut off their retreat.

There would be hell to pay in that case, on the off chance that Gromylko managed to survive. He could forget about explaining to the Georgian cops about how a *militsiya* lieutenant wound up several hundred miles from home, without his badge or any vestige of authority, assassinating Chechen gangsters in Tbilisi. They would laugh and beat him senseless, then sit down and list the charges he would have to answer at his murder trial.

No, thank you very much.

Gromylko reached into an outside pocket of his coat and found one of the frag grenades he carried for insurance. As he pulled the pin, he called a warning to his comrades, speaking English.

"Hand grenade!"

If any of the Chechens understood him, that was fine. He lobbed the fat green egg and ducked back under cover, bullets humming in the air around him, chipping plaster inches from his face. He had no special target marked for the grenade, cared little where it fell, as long as there was noise, confusion, something that would give Gromylko and his friends an edge they needed to survive.

He waited for the blast, then came out firing, even while the jagged bits of shrapnel were still airborne, ripping flesh or tearing into theater seats and gouging divots in the walls. He was in time to see a pair of Chechen gunners tumbling through the air, twisting awkwardly as they crashed among the rows of seats. No problem from those two, he guessed, and concentrated on the living.

Calvin James and Rafael Encizo both responded to his warning cry, quickly diving for cover, coming back with weapons blazing while their enemies were still disoriented from the blast. Triangulated fire swept through the theater, two silenced weapons joining with Gromylko's loud Kalashnikov, selecting targets as they tried to duck and hide or break out toward the exits. The lieutenant estimated they had cut the number of their enemies by more than half, and it was falling steadily, as were the jerking, lurching bodies, torn by bullets, sprawling over seats and in the aisles.

It was a massacre, and in another moment it was done.

Gromylko fed another magazine into his AK-47, watching as the others moved to join him, on the west side of the theater that had become a charnel house. The *keffiyeh* James wore had come undone, and he was cursing as he fumbled to replace it, working at the job one-handed, while his other kept a firm grip on the Skorpion he carried. Encizo had a grim expression on his face, as if the slaughter didn't suit his taste, but he had done his work efficiently and uttered no complaint.

"You have the Semtex?" the Cuban asked.

"Yes," Gromylko said. "Let's finish this. We haven't got much time."

Six minutes later they were on the street and rolling, turning left, then left again, to put some ground between themselves and what would soon become a heap of smoking rubble. Riding in the back, Gromylko tried to clear his mind, look forward to the next stop on their list.

And found that he could hardly wait.

CHAPTER TWELVE

The last report was finally too much, with the slaughter of twenty men, their meeting place destroyed by Semtex charges, burying their corpses in the rubble. Two or three more days would pass before the search teams had recovered all the bodies, but Ivan Storzhenko was preoccupied with what might happen in the next two hours. There was nothing he could do to help the dead, but he must think of those who served him and were still alive.

Above all else, he had to save himself.

He knew that it was time to ask for help, but the very act of reaching out to Moscow must be done in such a way that it would minimize his damage. He couldn't tell Gregori Vasiliev that nearly half his soldiers had been killed within a span of several hours, while he still had no idea who was doing it or why. Such an admission of incompetence would be his death warrant, Storzhenko realized, and he had no desire to die. Not yet. Not in Tbilisi.

He would twist the facts around a bit, not lying outright to the godfather, but using just enough discretion that he didn't come off sounding like a total idiot. And if Vasiliev somehow got the notion that

Storzhenko was about to solve the problem, could eradicate the family's nightmare if he only had a few more men and guns on hand...well, it was only for the good of all concerned.

How would it benefit the Thieves' Society to have its leader thinking, falsely, that the Georgian outpost had been lost? There was no telling what Vasiliev might do in such a case, since his mind and nerves were already tested to the limit by his brother's death and the events in Turkey. It was only good, sound strategy for Storzhenko to accentuate the positive, let Vasiliev believe that everything would be all right, if only Storzhenko had sufficient troops to do a proper job.

It was, Storzhenko told himself, the simple truth.

If he somehow failed against all odds, the extra time he purchased for himself would help to save his life. Ivan Storzhenko was no fool. He had been planning for the worst, preparing for it, from the day he was assigned to man the outpost in Tbilisi. With the Georgians in a constant uproar over politics, religion and whatever else it was that peasants fought about, he couldn't guarantee from one day to the next what would become of syndicate investments in the unstable republic. Nor, in the event of a disaster, was Storzhenko ready to accept responsibility for someone else's failure. He didn't intend to play the role of sacrificial victim for anyone.

There was a limit to his loyalty, after all. A wise man always plans ahead, prepares himself for all eventualities.

Storzhenko drank another glass of vodka, straight,

before he sat behind his desk and reached out for the telephone. Vasiliev should still be wide-awake, in Moscow. It was early yet, and no conscientious godfather would sleep while his family was under fire from unknown enemies.

Storzhenko had no fear of the authorities in Georgia, since he had been paying most of them quite handsomely since his arrival in Tbilisi, but he had a scrambler on his private line as extra insurance. Vasiliev had one just like it on his telephone at home, and in the downtown Moscow office where he spent three afternoons a week, in normal times.

These times were far from normal, and the news Storzhenko had to share would still be grim enough to make his boss hit the roof. But Storzhenko would remind the godfather of his first duty to the family: the presentation of a calm and self-assured exterior, to reassure the troops that everything was still under control and running smoothly in their outlaw world.

No matter if that self-assurance was exaggerated or an outright lie. The truth had little or nothing to do with daily life in the Vorovskoi Mir. A mobster's life was based on falsehood and deception, after all. Why should the godfather be any different in dealings with his various subordinates? God knew he himself had been lied to frequently enough throughout the years. Now he was simply going to return the favor.

He was doing it to save himself.

And that, he thought, was still the most important cause of all.

Moscow

GREGORI VASILIEV was no one's fool. He didn't have to read Storzhenko's mind to understand his game: self-preservation was the first law of the jungle, and he couldn't blame his underling for trying to obtain some extra time. It showed that he was on his toes, still thinking, but it would have been more gratifying to Vasiliev if Storzhenko could have put a finger on their common enemy.

There were still more soldiers he could send to Georgia, though he planned to keep the best at home to watch his own back in this troubled time. Storzhenko might indeed be able to destroy their adversaries with a bit more help, but if he failed, there would be bloody work to do in Moscow, and soon.

Vasiliev had tapped his source with Interpol to see if there was any indication of official moves against his family, from the United States or Britain, but there was no information that would help him either way. It was predictable, to some extent: a covert movement by some hostile government wouldn't be telegraphed to Interpol, which had no real enforcement powers anyway and was known throughout the world for glaring breaches of security.

Right now he needed men and information he could trust. If trouble came to him at home, it would be useful if he had something beyond his own bodyguards. All the better if he could rely on the police to do his killing for him, and avoid all personal involvement in a shooting war. It would be difficult, he realized, to stand outside the action and remain aloof, but he would do his best. He had more than one reputation to protect: the image of a thriving businessman, among his friends in high society, together with his image as a ruthless killer on the streets.

He didn't fear a threat from those around him, although clearly there were individuals within the family who wouldn't mourn his passing. Still, if one of them had found the nerve to move against Vasiliev, the move would almost certainly have come in Russia, not in the United States or Turkey, not even in Georgia. To Vasiliev that meant an enemy from somewhere else, and it was galling him that he couldn't discover who was after him or where the bastards came from.

It was curiosity verging on desperation, then, that made Vasiliev reach out for his top man in the *militsiya.* In normal circumstances they avoided any contact; even phone calls were relayed through trusted intermediaries, generally in code. The past five years Vasiliev could remember only two occasions when the officer had met him face-to-face.

Tonight would be the third.

Vasiliev couldn't meet with the officer in his penthouse apartment, nor could they be seen together at his dacha northwest of Moscow. The continued usefulness of an employee at that level meant that more than the illusion of security must be maintained. Should their connection be revealed in public, it would mean more than a trifling embarrassment for all concerned. The officer would certainly be ruined, hounded from his post, while some "reformer" in the new regime might even have some questions for Vasiliev. Bad business all around, but easily avoided if he only thought about it for a moment, used his wits as he had always done when there were obstacles before him.

It was simple when he thought about it. They would meet at a hotel Vasiliev had purchased from its one-time owners after they were driven into bankruptcy by labor problems. Two adjoining suites with a connecting door would do the trick. Vasiliev would make sure to arrive at least an hour early, just in case his contact had an unexpected tail, and he would let the officer leave first. Bring up a prostitute to occupy the soldier's empty room and watch TV, all for appearances, while they were talking in the suite next door. When they were done, if Vasiliev's companion wanted her, she would be paid for in advance. A touch of realism, that, but he would make sure that his contact was long gone before he ventured out of the hotel.

It was decided, then. Once Gregori Vasiliev made up his mind, there were no arguments, no second-guessing.

Satisfied, he reached out for the telephone.

Washington, D.C.

EIGHT HOURS BEHIND MOSCOW, Hal Brognola sat behind his desk and wondered if he ought to go for lunch. He had no appetite to speak of, but experience had taught him that it sometimes helped just to go through the motions of a normal day. He could go out, pick up a chili dog, pile on the onions, maybe crack a beer to wash it down and...

Jesus!

Brognola could feel his stomach rolling at the thought of it, and then his mind snapped back to the reports he had been catching out of Georgia, via Stony

Man. They had their ears on at the Farm, and kept him up to date, although he could have done without the running body count right now.

Brognola had resisted the idea of sending Bolan and the Phoenix warriors into Russian territory at the present time. It wouldn't be their first incursion into what was once Iron Curtain territory, but for all its danger, things had been more stable under the old Soviet regime. In those days you could readily identify the players, give or take a double agent here and there. Since the collapse of communism, though, with all the geographic and political divisions that had come to pass, you had more two- and three-faced characters in Russia than between the covers of a Batman comic. There were cops and politicians working for the mob, die-hard Communists who would do anything within their power to subvert the new regime, a growing fringe of right-wing loonies who made neo-Nazis in the States look like the very soul of moderation and a whole crop of religious players—ranging from the orthodox to weird black-magic cults—so long suppressed that they were making up for lost time with a vengeance, launching into business, education, politics as if there were no tomorrow.

Which, Brognola thought, there might not be.

Some of his friends at the State Department had been predicting civil war since it was first announced the ruling party was dissolved. The one attempted coup, so far, had been aborted, those who planned it shuffled off to mental institutions, prison cells or shallow graves, but there was no such thing as coup insurance for the Russians, not when you had bloody insurrections raging in the Balkan states. That kind of atmosphere was tailor made for opportunists like the Russian *mafiya*, the kind of parasites that could infest a not altogether healthy body, leaving it functional from all outward appearances, while they were boring from within, sapping the organism's raw vitality. They never killed the host outright, since the parasite couldn't survive outside, in broad daylight, but what remained was never healthy, never vital.

Never clean.

Brognola threw a mental switch and sent his train of thought off on a siding. He wasn't concerned about the state of Russian politics or economics at the moment. That was someone else's problem, and had no more impact on his daily life than, say, the price of caviar. What *did* concern Brognola, though, was the increased potential danger that his men in Georgia were facing now, thanks to the unstable situation with regard to politics and crime, the military and police.

Brognola understood the threat to U.S. interests from the Russian *mafiya*. The FBI had been concerned enough to open up a branch office in Moscow, and there had been no refusing when the Man gave Brognola a mission no one else could handle. Hell, it was a mission no one else would *touch*, because it was illegal all the way. In these days of congressional oversight and spot audits by the General Accounting Office, veteran officers of the FBI, CIA, NSA and military intelligence were walking on eggshells, looking over their shoulders every time they had an impure thought. Between the budget cuts and imposition of political correctness from the top, covert activities were often doomed before they started. In the old days any number of competing agencies would have been standing by to deal with someone like Vasiliev, fair means or foul, but times had changed. Brognola and his team at Stony Man were now the secret court of last resort.

Which meant that Brognola couldn't reject the dirty jobs, no matter how they troubled him or went against his own best instincts. Bolan could have turned him down, as he had done on rare occasions in the past, but the big Fed would have sent Phoenix Force regardless. There was work to do, and it was his job, come what may. It was the only reason Stony Man existed in the first place, to take out the trash and handle any dirty work that could not be reported on the public record.

Nothing in the tidy rationale could stop his mind from working overtime, however, looking for the weak point in their plan and trying to anticipate the enemy. The problem this time was that there were too damn many weak points: distance, language, numbers, local politics that fluctuated like the weather, their reliance on a single officer from the militia who might still turn out to be some kind of killer mole.

And if they failed...

Brognola stopped himself right there. It was unthinkable, no matter that he had to think about it anyway. He would postpone that morbid chore until he knew that it was absolutely necessary. And with any luck at all, it never would be.

But if anything went wrong...

In that case, he decided, a lot of heads would roll.

"YOU LIKE THE WOMAN, Yuri?"

Colonel Renko shrugged, indifference personified. "I have a wife at home," he said.

"We all do," Gregori Vasiliev replied. "A little something extra never hurts, though, eh?"

"You called me here on business, I believe."

And that was what galled Renko more than anything. Vasiliev had summoned him, as if he were a lowly private from the ranks, or one of the *bandity* who owed his allegiance to the Thieves' Society. It was not fitting for a full colonel to be treated in that fashion, even if the money he received from Gregori Vasiliev each year was more then double his official salary. There were proprieties to be observed, a certain minimum of courtesy.

"There is no reason why we can't enjoy our business, Yuri, eh?"

Another shrug. The last thing Renko planned to do was bow and scrape before the man who pulled his strings. Vasiliev might be the boss, might own his very soul, but Renko still had to live with himself, face himself in the mirror each morning and night.

"I would prefer to just get on with it," the colonel said.

"Of course." Vasiliev didn't appear insulted. He still wore the plastic smile that was his trademark, like a politician's brain-dead grin. "You weren't followed, I presume?"

"Of course not!"

Vasiliev was wasting time with foolish small talk now. He knew that Renko was the one with more to lose if anyone found out about their business dealings.

He would certainly be court-martialed, might possibly wind up in prison if the secret was revealed. As far as Renko knew, he was the highest-ranking officer in the *militsiya* who drew a secret paycheck from Vasiliev, but even if there were some others higher up the ladder, they would not step in to help him. It would be each man for himself, and some would certainly be glad to see him go, a vacancy in rank leaving hope for a promotion.

"Very well." Vasiliev seemed satisfied at last. "You've heard what happened to my brother in America?"

A nod from Renko. "*Da.* You have my sympathy."

"*Spaseeba,* Yuri. I'm afraid that it was not an isolated incident, however."

"No?"

Vasiliev had lost his smile, replaced with an expression that was neutral, solemn, stopping just short of a frown. "There have been incidents in Turkey," he continued. "Vladimir Mikhasevich is dead, along with Kenan Bey and a considerable number of his men."

"And you believe the incidents are linked?"

"I'm sure of it," Vasiliev replied, "since the attacks began in Georgia earlier today."

Renko could only frown at that. The *militsiya* no longer had any jurisdiction in the Balkan republics, but he tried to keep track of their criminal trends, on the theory that problems from one district were likely to infect others. He had been unaware of the events Vasiliev described, and Renko didn't enjoy being the last one to know.

"Attacks?"

"Assassinations, bombings, arson." There was no animation in Vasiliev's voice. He could have been discussing items on a grocery list, instead of violent acts directed at his own subordinates. "Ivan had asked for help."

That made it serious, thought Renko. If Ivan Storzhenko needed help to crush an enemy, the man—or men—involved must be a prodigious fighter.

"You believe the trouble may be on its way to Moscow," he suggested, cutting to the chase.

"If Ivan fails to stop it in Tbilisi, anything is possible." Vasiliev was frowning now, the effort carving furrows in his cheeks beneath the sunlamp tan. "In that event I'll need your full cooperation to contain and minimize the damage."

"It would help," said Renko, "if I knew who was responsible."

"Indeed! I'm hoping you may be of some assistance with that aspect of the problem," said Vasiliev.

"You don't know who it is?" Renko felt laughter rising in his throat, but swallowed it before it could escape.

"Unfortunately, no. From the techniques employed, the range involved, it may be an official effort."

"The Americans?"

Vasiliev considered that, then shook his head. "Not CIA," he said. "It's not their style. Frankly I doubt they could coordinate this kind of effort with their present capabilities."

"Then who?"

"Yuri, I'd hoped that something might occur to

you. There may be someone you can ask, some avenue
of exploration that is closed to me.''

A notion came to Renko, tugging at the corners of
his mouth, but he was quick enough to hide the smile.
''There may be something I can do,'' he said at last.

''I hope so. It would naturally mean a bonus.''

''I will do my best.''

''As always,'' said Vasiliev, recapturing his smile.
''I shall look forward to hearing from you. And,
please, take your time with the girl. Consider her a
token of my friendship.''

''Very well,'' the colonel said. ''If you insist.''

''YOU'VE CONFIRMED the reinforcements?'' Bolan
asked.

Gromylko nodded, sipped his coffee, sat back in one
of the hotel room's straight-backed wooden chairs.
David McCarter occupied the other, while other members of the team sat on the bed or on the floor.

''It's definite,'' Gromylko said. ''A charter flight
from Moscow landed half an hour ago. There were
eighteen men on board, with luggage. As a private
charter flight, their baggage was checked through
without the usual security precautions.''

''Meaning they brought hardware,'' Gary Manning
said.

''I am inclined to think so, yes.''

''We must have hurt Storzhenko, if he's called the
cavalry,'' said Calvin James.

''One way to look at it,'' said Bolan. ''On the flip
side, if he's got reserves up the wazoo, there's only
so much damage we can do.''

"Unless we wrap it up and take him out right now," McCarter said. "He won't be calling anybody then."

"We'll have to pin him down," said Bolan.

"I believe I've done that," Gromylko interjected.

"Oh?"

"Ivan Storzhenko owns a small block of apartments in the northwest corner of Tbilisi. One whole floor is his—the top floor, I believe—with the remaining flats reserved for his security detachment. They'll be doubling up now, with the Muscovites in town...unless they've lost so many men that they have vacancies to spare."

The Executioner considered it. He shared the sense of urgency his comrades felt, a need to finish up the Georgian end of their campaign and take the war where it belonged, directly to the doorstep of Vasiliev and company in Moscow. It would call for one last push, and with Storzhenko's army reinforced by new, fresh guns, but he could think of no good reason to delay the move.

"How many soldiers does this give Storzhenko, with the new bunch?" Bolan asked Gromylko.

The lieutenant shrugged. "I've only seen the basic numbers estimated, anywhere from sixty-five to eighty," he replied. "Assume that we've eliminated roughly half the men he started with, then add back the eighteen. He should have fifty soldiers, maybe sixty."

"Damn." Encizo's smile wasn't reflected in his tone of voice. "And here I thought we had been making progress."

"You were right," Bolan said. "Sixty soldiers

doesn't mean he's got them all together. Even granting that he'll have a solid force around his digs, Storzhenko still has other enterprises in the city he'll be wanting to protect. We haven't swept the list yet, and he'll have to spread the guns around, unless he plans on sacrificing everything he has.''

"We'd better do it while we can," Gary Manning commented. "If he thinks about it long enough, there may be more planes on the way."

"Agreed," said Bolan. "Anybody think we ought to try some other way?"

He had expected no dissenting votes, and got none. Bolan knew that no one on his team was thrilled by the idea of storming yet another hardsite, facing killer odds again, but Manning was correct in saying that delays might only make things worse. Another couple planeloads of imported mercenaries, and they might lose any chance they had of taking out Storzhenko. He might even slip away while they were busy hitting peripheral targets around Tbilisi.

It was time to finish what they started, and move on.

"All right," Bolan said, "let's get it done."

CHAPTER THIRTEEN

Ivan Storzhenko lit a Turkish cigarette and inhaled deeply, savoring the taste. The nicotine should soothe him, but he wasn't convinced that it would be enough. He needed alcohol to speed the process up, but that could be a fatal error. There was every chance that he would need his wits about him in the next few hours, and if that meant suffering anxiety along the way, so be it.

It was better now that he had troops from Moscow. They wouldn't entirely replace the men that he had lost, but another eighteen guns was bound to help. He had assigned the new men to key pieces of his property around Tbilisi, using them to free up more familiar veterans of his own brigade for palace duty, to protect himself. It was a selfish act, of course, but what else was there? He hadn't been working, fighting all these years, to sacrifice himself without good reason, to an unknown enemy. The rest of it could be replaced—the cars and buildings, contraband, even the soldiers—but without a leader, it was all in vain, a total waste.

The old apartment block wasn't a large one. It had fifteen units, with a ground-floor laundry room and slide. He had two other guards outside, downstairs, with one in front and one in back. Eliminating them was but the first step in dismantling his defenses and getting to the man himself.

Hawk lay beside Bolan in the darkness, watching as the sentry walked his beat around the broad, flat roof. There was an air-conditioning unit up there, along with a satellite dish and a small, shedlike structure that would offer access to the stairs and floors below. The sentry walked and smoked and kept his eyes wide open, carrying an AK-47 in the crook of one arm. If he was bored or sleepy, he concealed it well.

Each pass the sentry made brought him within ten paces of the Executioner and Hawkins. They were stretched out prone on the adjacent roof, due west of the apartment block Storzhenko had appropriated for himself. Both men were dressed in black, their hands and faces darkened with combat cosmetics, their weapons, extra magazines and hand grenades secured by military webbing. Bolan's wristwatch showed they still had forty seconds left before the others would begin their probe downstairs.

And that meant it was time to go.

"My treat," Hawk whispered, drawing a Beretta autoloader from the tied-down holster on his thigh. It had a chunky silencer attached, and since it was a double-action weapon, Hawkins didn't have to risk the sharp metallic sound of drawing back the hammer with his thumb.

He waited for the sentry to complete another round and move back into easy range. The shooter's cigarette glowed like an ember in the darkness, but his face seemed blurred and gray, almost devoid of human features as he walked his lonely beat. They couldn't see the eyes dart back and forth, in search of enemies that he would never see in time to save himself.

There was no more than twenty feet between them when the black Beretta snorted once, its pop reminding Bolan of an air gun. The parabellum round went in on target, snapped the soldier's head back, staggered him, before his legs gave out and dumped him on his back. The AK-47 spun away from lifeless fingers, clattering across the roof.

Would that noise have been audible downstairs? It was unlikely, with the intervening layers of stucco, wood, tar paper, metal, insulation, but there was an outside chance that someone may have heard it. What if this sentry had been scheduled for replacement? His relief could be approaching, climbing up the stairs right now, this very minute.

Bolan was moving by the time the thought took shape, Hawk right beside him as they dropped onto the lower roof and scuttled past the sentry's corpse. It was a waste of time and energy to check for vital signs. Downstairs the others would be moving in, a three-man team out front, another team in the back, their watches synchronized. Delays were more than risky now—they were potentially disastrous.

Bolan wore his AK-47 on a shoulder sling, braced in a tight one-handed grip as he reached out to find the doorknob. It turned at once, a small convenience that would come back to haunt Storzhenko now. If Bolan had been placed in charge of site security, he would have had that door secured from the inside.

There was no outer keyhole, and the metal door was fairly solid. By the time they blasted through it, everyone downstairs would be on full alert.

Unless someone forgot to lock it, right.

The door swung back on well-oiled hinges, granting access to the stairs. There was a dim light down below, but it did little to relieve the darkness of the staircase. Bolan led the way, with one hand on the metal railing bolted to the wall beside him, while the other gripped his weapon. Hawkins followed cautiously, a few steps back, prepared for anything. The light below seemed brighter once they were within the deeper darkness of the stairwell, but it was a matter of degree. The cast of shadows placed it somewhere off to Bolan's left, with only darkness to the right. He didn't know if there were lookouts down there waiting for him, but the only way to find out was to move ahead and check it out.

The stairs were made of concrete, with lateral strips of some substance that felt like sandpaper added for better traction. Bolan walked on the balls of his feet to avoid scraping sounds, still sliding one hand down the banister as he progressed. He didn't check on Hawkins, knowing T. J. would be right behind him all the way.

When he was nearly at the bottom, Bolan's ears picked up the muted sound of voices coming from his left, in the direction of the light. He paused, glanced back at Hawkins, and the Phoenix warrior nodded, indicating he heard them, too.

Bolan released the metal banister and gripped his AK-47 in both hands. Another three steps down, and he would be exposed to anyone who occupied the corridor. His only hope, from that point on, was the advantage of surprise.

He took a breath and walked into the light.

McCARTER STEPPED ACROSS the prostrate body of the gunman who had been detailed to watch the rear of the apartment house. A neat hole in the middle of the dead man's forehead made it look almost as if he had three eyes, all staring blankly at the dark sky overhead. McCarter slipped his silent pistol back into its armpit holster and continued toward the back door, their point of entry to the building.

It was locked, but Manning beat it in ten seconds flat, a poor lock that surrendered quickly to his picks. Storzhenko seemingly put more faith in his soldiers than in hardware when it came down to security. McCarter waited for the tall Canadian to enter first, then followed him inside.

The laundry room was on their left, unoccupied, four washers and two dryers standing silently against the stucco walls. McCarter double-checked the room to make sure no one had been overlooked, a lurker who would pop out and surprise them when their backs were turned. That done, they moved along a corridor that took them past a smallish recreation room, a billiard table standing unattended, with the lights off. There was noise ahead of them, a radio or television set, male voices talking over it, as if in the midst of some friendly dispute.

McCarter was shoulder-to-shoulder with Manning as they closed in on their targets, moving silently along the corridor. No need to check his watch again to know that it was time—the others would be in the house by now and ready to begin their sweep. If something had delayed them, it was still McCarter's duty to proceed on schedule, get the action rolling and nail as many of the Russian gunners as he could.

Ahead of them, on Manning's left, a door stood open, spilling light into the hallway. From the looks of it, the glimpse McCarter had, it may have been the rental office at one time, converted into security central when Storzhenko took over the flats. Two men were standing in the room, a third one seated, watching a karate tournament on a portable TV. They took turns jeering at the tiny fighters, sometimes striking poses, demonstrating how they would have handled this or that maneuver if *they* had been battling in the ring. McCarter couldn't understand their words, but their clumsy gestures told him they were talking crap.

The former SAS man cleared his throat and tapped the muzzle of his AK-47 twice against the doorjamb, grinning broadly as the three heads snapped around. Both rifles stuttered, rattling off short bursts that crossed, diverged and then came back again to drop the jerking, twitching soldiers where they stood. Spent casings pattered on the carpeting around McCarter's feet, while the reports of gunfire echoed in his ears.

McCarter turned to face the sound of running feet, Manning beside him, and they met another pair of gunmen bursting from the door of an apartment two doors farther down the hallway, on the right. Both men had slacks on, one bare-chested, running in his socks, the other with a long-sleeved shirt unbuttoned, flapping, barefoot on the carpet.

Mr. Topless had an Uzi, cocking it as he came into view, while Barefoot pumped the slide on what appeared to be a sawed-off 12-gauge shotgun. Both of them stopped short as they caught sight of the intruders, breaking off to either side and lowering their weapons into target acquisition as they tried to save themselves.

McCarter went down firing, braced on knees and elbows as he hit the carpet in a prone position, while the shotgun hammered at him, buckshot swarming overhead like angry bees. His bullets stitched the barefoot gunner in a ragged line from groin to solar plexus, slammed him over backward in a lifeless sprawl.

The topless gunner got a short burst off at Manning, but his haste resulted in the bullets going high and wide, etching a zigzag pattern on the wall. Before the shooter could correct his faulty aim, a burst from the Canadian's AK tore through his chest and dropped him to his knees. He toppled slowly forward, leaning on the Uzi like a stubby walking stick and firing half a magazine into the floor as he collapsed.

The corridor smelled powerfully of cordite and was littered with spent casings as McCarter scrambled to his feet. The old, familiar sights and smells were energizing, driving him to hurry. With Manning at his side, he stepped around the sprawling bodies and ignored the squelching sound his own feet made on blood-soaked carpeting. Explosive sounds of gunfire reached his ears from the direction of the street in front, and muffled noise from somewhere overhead told him the other members of his team were on the job, engaging hostile troops.

McCarter checked his rifle's magazine, replaced it with a fresh one and went off to find the war.

STORZHENKO CROUCHED behind the sofa, wincing as the pistol in his pocket gouged him through the fabric of his slacks. He held the AK-47 with its muzzle braced across the low back of the couch, aimed toward the door of his apartment, where his enemies would have to enter if they wanted him. No matter what went on outside the flat, no matter how many of his defenders were cut down, Storzhenko's adversaries had to see him face-to-face if they meant to finish it.

Unless they used explosive charges or set the place on fire. Tear gas could flush him out, or maybe smoke grenades.

Whatever happened, he wasn't about to make it easy for them. They would have to kill his bodyguards, then force their way into his flat and deal with him. Storzhenko would admit that he was out of practice when it came to killing, but the act itself was much like making love or pedaling a bicycle: once you learned how to do it, no one ever really lost the knack. It came back in a flash, with all the old self-confidence that seemed to make the years melt from his shoulders, just like that.

Storzhenko squinted over gun sights, covering the door, and wondered what was keeping them. Perhaps his men were better than he thought, and they were winning, driving the invaders back. It seemed too much to hope for, after all the damage he had suffered lately, since the faceless enemies began the raids around Tbilisi. It had come to this, Storzhenko cornered in his own apartment, while the soldiers he had begged from Moscow sat around a warehouse and the office of a trucking company he had suspected would be tempting targets for his enemies. But then, they had made their own plans.

Storzhenko grimaced at the smell of smoke, afraid the house was burning, but he recognized the stench of cordite in another moment, welcoming the recognition with a measure of relief. At least he didn't have to flee his hiding place just yet. The battle was not finished. There was still a chance his chosen bodyguards might earn the bonus he had promised to the ones who laid the lifeless bodies of his enemies before him.

It might not be enough, of course. His men were mostly peasant bullies, if he thought about it seriously. They were killers, certainly, but they had grown accustomed to confronting others like themselves or spineless hustlers who had stolen from the family. But those situations required more brawn than brains. If they were matched against trained soldiers now, or the equivalent, Storzhenko couldn't be assured of victory.

Or of survival.

When he realized that he was frightened, it enraged Ivan Storzhenko. He hadn't acknowledged fear since he was nine or ten years old, the first time he had fought a larger, older boy with knives. Fear was a weakness, sometimes fatal in its consequences. If he gave in to it now, Storzhenko knew he might not live to see another day.

The shock wave of a powerful explosion shook the building, brought a large oil portrait crashing down behind Storzhenko, while the smell of cordite from the hallway mixed with something else—a similar aroma but distinct. Not Semtex, he decided; that would smell like marzipan. Perhaps a hand grenade or dynamite.

Outside his flat someone was hitting high notes, crying out in agony. He was certain his troops were not armed with hand grenades or other explosives, since he didn't want them bringing down the house or bringing in police if it could possibly be helped. That meant the blast had been touched off by one of his assailants, that the enemy was better armed than his defenders.

And it meant they didn't give a damn what happened with the cops as long as they wreaked havoc on Storzhenko and his men. They would do anything to reach him, anything to bring him down.

Ivan Storzhenko almost panicked in that moment, but he caught himself before the fear could run amok and send him racing out of the apartment. It was time for him to flee—no doubt about it. But he couldn't rush madly through the hallways, down the stairs, much less stand waiting for the elevator like a stationary target. He would need a plan, and he admitted that his options were distinctly limited if he intended to survive.

At that moment survival was the most important thing on earth to Ivan Storzhenko. He didn't think about Vasiliev or his duty to the Thieves' Society. Self-preservation was the only problem on his mind. He mustn't let himself be killed or captured by his faceless enemies.

Step one was getting out, but he would have to do it carefully, no slipups. One false step, Storzhenko realized, and he was dead.

Reluctantly he stood up from behind the couch and started moving toward the door.

FOUR SENTRIES on the front, all armed with automatic weapons, but Calvin James had the feeling none of them really believed they would be called upon to fight, much less to die. He saw it in their attitudes, when they first glimpsed him barging through the door, with Rafael Encizo and Gromylko close behind him, recognition of their sudden danger wiping smug grins off their faces as they grappled with their weapons, trying to defend themselves.

Too late.

Converging streams of fire from three Kalashnikovs ripped through them, tossed their bodies left and right like crash-test dummies. Blood was spattered on the walls in a random pattern around the lobby.

"That tears it," James remarked. He was clad in a nightsuit and his military webbing, all in black.

As if in answer to his words, he heard rough, excited voices drawing swiftly closer. Five or six men, by the sound of it, though he couldn't be sure until they showed themselves. James turned to face a hallway running straight back from the lobby, toward the rear part of the building, where he knew that Manning and McCarter should have made their way inside by now. Upstairs the last two members of their team should have penetrated to the interior, unless stopped by resistance.

No time to think about the others, as the enemy came into view. He counted seven guns before they all cut loose at once, and he was forced to dive for cover near the bank of mailboxes and hunched down behind a potted palm.

The racket in the lobby almost deafened him, with ten guns blasting all at once. It seemed miraculous that anyone survived the first five seconds of that roaring fusillade, but everyone appeared to be intact when Calvin James poked his head around the stout base of the palm to look for targets.

The defenders had already recognized their weakness, having charged into the lobby with no thought for cover, trusting speed and firepower to sweep their enemies before them. When it failed and bullets started flying back the other way, they found themselves exposed, like lizards sunning on a rock. The lobby had been long since stripped of furniture, and there was nowhere they could hide unless they drew back through the corridor that had delivered them to danger in the first place.

Picking out his mark, James fired a short burst from his AK-47, feeling hasty, doubting he would score until he saw the burst of scarlet from the gunman's hip and watched him fall. Cursing and sobbing with the pain, his target tried to drag himself across the floor, back toward the hallway and the only hope he had of getting out alive. James aimed this time, and sent another 3-round burst to finish it. The wounded soldier shuddered on impact, then collapsed like an empty suit of clothes.

Incoming bullets clipped palm fronds above James's head and rattled on the wall behind him, pale dust streaming down from divots in the stucco. Ducking low, he let loose a burst, and heard Gromylko call out a warning as he cocked his arm to pitch a hand grenade. James ducked back under cover, tried to brace himself in preparation for the blast and still felt as if someone had slapped cupped palms over both his ears with stunning force.

He knew the screams that followed were not coming from a distance, but they sounded that way to his ringing ears. He risked a glance around the smoky wasteland of the lobby first, then rose from cover, following the muzzle of his AK-47 toward the point where bodies thrashed and wriggled on the floor.

They might be dying—there was blood enough for him to think so—but he couldn't take the chance. If even one of them survived, came up behind him when he was distracted, fighting someone else, he would be finished. *All* of them could die if he showed any mercy to the wounded now.

James started firing at those bodies on the floor, saw bullets striking flesh, dark blood exploding from the wounds. The sound of his own weapon was remote and muffled, but he felt its lethal power pulsing through his arms and shoulders. Someone else was at his side now, also firing, but he didn't look to see who it might be. Encizo or Gromylko, maybe both of them together, helping with the brutal, heartless task of making sure.

A cautious adversary could have killed James then, but there was none to try it. Moments later they

sighted figures moving down the hallway through a
haze of gun smoke, drawing closer. It was Manning
and McCarter, finished with their bloody work out
back. Grim faces smeared with greasepaint, none of
them was inclined to smile. And when James sought
out the Russian's face, he saw Gromylko looking
blood-weary but determined.

No words were necessary as James turned and
moved in the direction of the stairs.

THE FRAG GRENADE OPENED jagged holes in the hallway walls and ceiling, shrapnel ripping into plaster
and flesh with abandon at ground zero. Bolan heard
one of the gunners wail as he was airborne, flung
against a wall by the concussion of the blast. The Executioner was moving out before the echoes died
away, his AK-47 seeking targets, Hawkins coming up
to join him from the far side of the corridor.

They had shot three men before the reinforcements
started charging up the stairwell at the far end of the
hall, unloading aimlessly with everything they had.
Now Bolan counted seven bodies in the hallway, three
of them still moving fitfully, despite their ghastly
wounds.

One slumped against a wall, legs folded under him
at awkward angles, kneeling in a pool of blood. He
still clung to a lightweight submachine gun, though,
and he was trying desperately to lift it from the floor
beside him as he saw his enemies approaching through
the haze of smoke. His muscles weren't responding,
and his time ran out as Hawkins fired a short burst

from the hip, a stream of bullets ripping through the shirt already stained with blood and ending it.

The other two who still showed signs of life were both on Bolan's side: one on all fours, head hanging like a wounded animal, and the other lying on his side, braced up on one elbow, reaching for a pistol several feet in front of him.

A short burst from the AK-47 nailed the gunner, slapped him over on his back and left him there. The other looked up through a screen of blood that streamed from ragged wounds along his hairline, finding strength and guts enough to snarl before he died.

The way was open. Bolan headed for the one apartment door that he could see, with Hawk beside him all the way. He didn't try the knob, but hosed it down with automatic fire and watched it swing open. Charging forward, Bolan went in low and fast, expecting hostile fire and feeling bullets fan the air above him as he powered through a shoulder roll, came up behind a heavy easy chair. He was aware of Hawkins entering, a short burst from his friend's Kalashnikov responding to the fire that emanated from behind a long, plush sofa.

There was no point trying to communicate with the godfather of Tbilisi. Language barriers aside, he had no information Bolan needed, and their time was running short. The task was to root out Storzhenko in the time they had, instead of letting him delay them while police rushed to the scene. It took about a quarter of a second for the Executioner to make his choice.

"Grenade," he said.

Hawk crouched behind a matching easy chair, some

twenty feet away from Bolan and to his right. "Let's make it two," he said.

They made the pitch in unison, hunched down behind their makeshift barriers and waited through the countdown, heard Storzhenko give a cry of panic as he vaulted to his feet and tried to reach the nearby bedroom door.

He almost made it.

Then twin blasts hit like a massive one-two punch, upending and smashing him against the nearest wall. Storzhenko's body left a crimson imprint before he slithered to the floor. With all that blood, the way his head was cocked at a crazy angle, Bolan didn't have to check his pulse to see if he was done.

Scratch one gorilla.

"Is everyone okay in there?"

McCarter's voice came through the open doorway to the corridor. His face appeared seconds later, after Bolan's, "All clear."

"Storzhenko?" Gromylko asked.

"He's wallpaper," answered Hawkins.

"We should probably be going, then," McCarter said.

And he was right. It was a long way to Moscow, and they weren't finished with their job. In fact, if Bolan didn't miss his guess, the worst of it was yet to come.

CHAPTER FOURTEEN

The phone call from Tbilisi awakened Gregori Vasiliev at 3:15 a.m. He didn't bother cursing at the young man on the other end for the delay. There had apparently been much for him to do, and he was still disoriented by Storzhenko's murder. Overall, Vasiliev considered it a wonder he was notified before he read about it in the morning newspaper.

Storzhenko's death depressed Vasiliev. They weren't friends, in any normal sense of the word, but he had been counting on Storzhenko to prevent their common enemies from penetrating Russia if they took the Georgian route. Now he had failed and lost his life—along with close to thirty soldiers—in the process. That left more than sixty dead in Georgia, adding to the carnage that Vasiliev had suffered since the morning when his brother died.

But his losses looked bad, and those who doubted his ability to lead would start to talk among themselves before much longer, if they hadn't already. He would have to watch his back, henceforth, as well as hunt for the strangers who had come to stalk him from outside.

The last thing that he needed was a two-front war. It would be best if he could trace his adversaries now and wipe them out, before the shock waves from Storzhenko's death emboldened his so-called comrades to take some hostile action of their own. He had an edge, a few more hours, but it was foolish to believe that he could track the strangers down in that amount of time, when they had managed to elude him for this long.

They would be on their way to Russia; that was obvious. They hadn't gone to all this trouble, traveled this far from America, to kill Ivan Storzhenko and his men, then turn around and go back home. But if Vasiliev couldn't prevent them from coming after him, at least he could be ready for the sons of whores when they arrived. His troops would be on full alert, and so would his confederates in the *militsiya.*

He trusted Yuri Renko just as far as he could see the colonel, which was anywhere in Russia, if he wanted to. The *mafiya* had eyes and ears throughout the country and beyond. If Renko tried to trick him—hold back crucial information, for example—then Vasiliev would soon find out, and Yuri would regret the day he was born. An officer who kept his nose clean and opposed the Thieves' Society was one thing, an expected risk of doing business, but one who took cash from Vasiliev and then failed to deliver on demand was asking for a one-way ticket to the slaughterhouse.

In fact, Vasiliev wasn't concerned that Renko might betray him. Rather, he was worried that the information he required might lie beyond the colonel's reach. If Renko tried his best and still came up with nothing, he was useless, and the problem of defending Moscow would become that much more complicated.

Vasiliev would count on the *militsiya* to do its best

when trouble started, but the force had no real training in guerrilla warfare. Their elite strike force was patterned on the SWAT teams in America, recruiting officers with military training, preferably with Spetsnaz, but they were primarily employed against drug labs and houses or in neighborhoods where gangs terrorized the old people. Vasiliev had no idea how they would fare in confrontation with committed, well trained soldiers, mercenaries or whatever else his adversaries might turn out to be.

Of course, it could be helpful if a few young officers were killed. That made it personal, and it would drive the rest into a frenzy, while he could sit back and watch the fun.

Still, it would be better for his reputation if he could solve the problem on his own, present the heads of his assailants to the Thieves' Society at large. There would be no doubt of his competence when that was done, and any bastard who attempted to depose him would be doomed before he started.

Either way, though, Gregori Vasiliev intended to survive. Whatever it required, he would not let malicious strangers rob him of his life or of the empire he had built from nothing with his own two hands. They had already killed his brother, along with Ivan Storzhenko and a rising number of his soldiers.

It was time—past time—for them to pay.

IT TOOK SOME DIGGING, but the facts were there just waiting for him. All he had to do was ask the proper questions in the proper way, and give a twist to certain arms when no one else was looking. Yuri Renko was a master at coercion, whether it was physical or the subtle, office-politics variety. His years in the *militsiya* had taught him which toes he could step on with impunity and which he must avoid. He only needed ninety minutes of concerted effort to discover Leonid Gromylko's mission.

He had been curious at first, when the lieutenant was dispatched to Turkey, but it was a sweet relief to have him gone, if only for a few short days. Renko assumed that the special assignment had been busywork to keep Gromylko occupied and help him cope with his partner's death. Of course, that was before the violence had broken out in Istanbul.

It could have been coincidence, but then came Georgia. Quite by accident, Renko had seen a copy of a memo to the general in charge of his division, lying on the general's desk while Renko was reporting progress on another case. One of the tricks he had acquired through years of practice was the art of reading upside down.

The memo said that Gromylko was in transit to Tbilisi.

That had been two days ago, and Renko had dismissed the matter from his mind...until Vasiliev had briefed him on the raids in Georgia and Storzhenko's death. It seemed to Renko more than mere coincidence that Gromylko should be in two countries where a sudden rash of violence wiped out local operations of the Chechen *mafiya*. That kind of circumstance smelled of conspiracy, and with pressure from Vasiliev to urge him on, Renko had begun to sniff around headquarters, looking for a weak point where he could apply the necessary leverage to prove his theory either right or wrong.

As luck would have it, an assistant to the general's private secretary had a dirty little secret that he didn't care to advertise. The facts were known to Renko, but he reassured the corporal that they would be known to no one else…as long as he cooperated in a search for certain information vital to the maintenance of state security. The young man had been happy to oblige, and thus Renko had learned of Gromylko's mission to collaborate with the Americans in an attack upon the Thieves' Society.

Renko still had no ID on the Americans, but he knew the link must be official. The *militsiya* was working with the FBI these days, and while this kind of operation didn't fit the Bureau's style, there was no end of secret agencies controlled from Washington. The colonel knew that much from what he had been taught before the Russian system fell apart and communism was declared obsolete. If things had changed in Russia, though, it didn't follow automatically that the Americans had changed *their* stripes. The only difference was that the Russian state was opening its doors to Western gunmen in an effort to control the *mafiya*.

In other circumstances Renko might have welcomed the assistance, even cheered them on, but he had taken too much money from Vasiliev and his associates to sneak by with a posture of neutrality. The godfather demanded information he could use to stop the hit team, and now Renko had enough to get him started. It would cost his life if he couldn't deliver on demand.

The bright side of the situation was that he could be rid of Gromylko once and for all. Renko was sick of the man's holier-than-thou approach to fighting crime, the pretense that he never felt temptation in his dealings with the syndicate, the easy money that confronted ranking officers of the *militsiya* from day to day. Before his partner died, the two of them had been insufferable, always trying to outdo the rest of the division with their drug arrests and harassing businessmen who would be better left alone. There had been no way to restrain them, short of taking action that would leave Renko exposed for what he was, but he had celebrated in his heart the night Alexei Churbanov was killed.

Gromylko had been different since it happened, more reserved, as if uncertain what he should do next. Now Renko understood his strategy: the bastard had been waiting for his chance to pull out all the stops, and it had been delivered to him on a silver platter, courtesy of the Americans.

But he wasn't done yet.

If Yuri Renko had his way, Gromylko's triumph would be brief.

The maverick lieutenant was an accident waiting to happen, and it was about to happen.

Soon.

Voroshilovgrad

THE LONG DRIVE NORTH was a concession to security. There had been too much paperwork involved in chartering a plane, with customs waiting when they got to

Moscow, and the hardware they were hauling would defy explanation. The result was a trip that would have taken them three hours tops by air was taking them two days. Over a thousand miles from Georgia north to Moscow, three men per car, and all of them alert to any sign of trouble on the road.

They found a take-out restaurant in Voroshilovgrad and sent Gromylko in to order. He came back with roasted chicken, potatoes, steaming cups of coffee and a pint of medicinal vodka. They pulled over at a rest stop on the edge of town, and wolfed the meal while talking over plans for Moscow and sipping coffee.

The basic plan was simple: find their marks in Moscow and start kicking ass till someone squealed. They had cooperation of a sort from the militia, through Gromylko and the brass behind him, but the state police couldn't be seen to stand aloof while blood was flowing in the streets. They would be going through the motions of preventing further violence, and since no more than a handful of the ranking officers had any clue to what was happening, it stood to reason that the street cops Bolan and his people met in Moscow would be deadly serious about their jobs.

Which meant that it was not so simple after all.

Police aside, they knew that Gregori Vasiliev had been aware of trouble since his brother bought the farm more than a week ago. The hits in Turkey and in Georgia gave the Chechen godfather a fair idea where his enemies were coming from, and their long drive to Moscow gave him two more days in which to strengthen his defenses, batten down his hatches for the coming storm. He had dispatched a squad of reinforcements to Tbilisi, indicating that the Moscow mob had men and guns to spare. Whatever happened once they hit the Russian capital, there was no question of an easy victory.

The Phoenix team was clear on Bolan's absolute refusal to use deadly force against police, regardless of their nationality, political philosophy or their involvement in corrupt activities. Another time and place, he might have made a personal exception for Gestapo agents, but the rule was carved in stone as far as Bolan was concerned.

As for the others, they were free to make the rules up as they went along.

"What kind of heat can we expect from the militia?" Manning asked when he was finished with his meal.

Gromylko frowned. "I'm acting under orders," he replied, "but they are strictly confidential. It would be a grave mistake to look for help from the authorities."

"More plausible deniability," McCarter said, and sipped his coffee.

"Hell, you can't expect the government to 'fess up on a deal like this," Calvin James added. "*Ours* damn sure wouldn't, if the shoe was on the other foot."

"I still don't fancy getting shot down by the same blokes who invited us," McCarter said.

"Consider it a challenge." Hawk was grinning as he spoke.

"I will," McCarter acknowledged. "It's enough to make one nervous, though. I don't like being nervous."

"I'd like to keep this job as clean as possible,"

Bolan remarked, "if we get the chance. Our target's still the Chechen mob and Gregori Vasiliev."

"Your comrade has a point, of course," Gromylko said. "It's well-known that the Thieves' Society has paid off some *militsiya* officers to look the other way, or worse. Those who oppose us may be acting in accordance with their oath of duty, or they may have other motives."

"And there's no quick way to tell the two apart," McCarter said.

"Unfortunately, no." Gromylko stared into his coffee for a moment, then went on. "I would expect you to protect yourselves at any cost."

That silenced everyone for several seconds while they thought about his words and what it must have cost him, as an officer of the militia, just to say that much.

"Thanks for the warning," Bolan said. "And now we should get a move on. We've still got at least nine hours on the road."

"And miles to go before we sleep," McCarter said. "I'll drive the next bit, if no one objects."

"That makes it my turn," Calvin James said, speaking for the second car.

"You need your *keffiyeh*," Encizo reminded him, putting on a grin.

"I've got your *keffiyeh* right here," James answered, smiling back.

The sour mood was broken for the moment, but it left the basic problem unresolved. When they were on the spot in Moscow, and push came to shove, each man would have a choice to make.

And as always, on the killing ground it would come down to each man for himself.

"NO WORD?" Barbara Price asked.

"Still on the road," Kurtzman replied. A touch of the controls brought his wheelchair around to face her. Kurtzman recognized the worry written on her face, and knew she would prefer that he not see it. "We'll hear something when they get to Moscow," he concluded.

"It was pretty clean in Georgia."

"Clean, and then some," he agreed. "The big fish won't be easy to replace. I had the sat-link up with Interpol this morning. They were pleasantly surprised, to say the least. Storzhenko was the number-four man on their Top Ten list of narco dealers for the European theater, but they could never catch him out of the country. They'll be popping corks on this one—unofficially, of course."

That won a fleeting smile, but it was gone almost before it had a chance to register. "I wish we had a better in with the militia," Price said.

"Me, too," Kurtzman agreed, "but they're all hung up on rank. You know their man will only talk to Hal."

"Their man," she said. "That's just the problem. Any time you get this kind of covert action, where the left and right hands are completely out of sync, it's flirting with disaster."

She was right, of course, but it was nothing new. In fact, considering the kind of operations run from Stony Man, Kurtzman would have called it SOP.

"Their man's a general, remember," Kurtzman said. "If he can't pull it off—"

"We're screwed," she finished for him. "I'd feel better if the Russian outfit wasn't so well integrated with the government and cops."

"They wouldn't need us, otherwise," he said.

"My point exactly."

"What's the word on Able Team?" asked Kurtzman, hoping to distract her.

"What? Oh, nothing new since last night's check-in. Still in Guatemala City, waiting for their contact. He's twelve hours overdue."

The Able warriors had a job as dicey, in its own way, as the mission that had drawn Mack Bolan and the men of Phoenix Force to Russia, hunting right-wing *narcotraficantes* with a taste for terrorism that included strikes at U.S. diplomats and tourists. They were counting on assistance from a disaffected member of the group, but he was running late for contact now, and Kurtzman had a sneaking hunch that he was history.

"How long until their next check-in?" he asked.

"They're coming up at 0900 hours," Price said. "I'll take it if you want."

He checked his watch. Another sixteen minutes.

"'Kay. I'll grab some coffee or whatever, and come back in half an hour."

"Fine."

It was the waiting that could get you, Kurtzman reflected as he wheeled himself past banks of monitors and terminals, heading for the exit that would lead him to the dining area. Working at the Farm, you didn't face much risk of being killed in action—not these days, at least—but there were other perils. Such as watching from behind the lines as old friends put themselves directly in harm's way, time after time, when there was little you could do to help beyond processing and coordinating information, answering their questions from the field and manning sat-links for intelligence around the clock. Sometimes you lost one, but the war went on.

The damn war had a way of always going on.

Like now, for instance, putting his best friends in the world out on the firing line.

God keep, he thought, and then said it aloud.

"God keep."

Voronezh

THEY HAD FINISHED nearly two-thirds of the drive to Moscow, and the trip was wearing painfully on Gromylko's nerves. It had been all right up to now—a strange, cathartic marathon of violence—but the closer they approached to Moscow and his headquarters, the more Gromylko felt that he had crossed a line.

Perhaps it was the point of no return.

All of his training, from the early days of childhood to the military and his years with the *militsiya*, ran counter to the orgy of destruction he had witnessed and assisted in the past few days.

And yet he felt no guilt. The feeling that kept nagging at him was apprehension. He was worried about what would happen when they got to Moscow, whether the Americans or he would be compelled to fire upon *militsiya* officers in the performance of their duty.

Granted, there were certain officers he knew, more than a handful, who had sold their souls to Gregori Vasiliev and company. Gromylko would not mind if some of them were forcibly removed from office, but the notion ran against his grain, for its implied insult to the authority and the respectability of the *militsiya*. No matter that the men in question brought dishonor on themselves. They had defiled their uniform, as well, and that brought shame on every honest man or woman who was working overtime each day to help restore the rule of law in Mother Russia.

Gromylko had already made his mind up that he wouldn't interfere if one of the Americans were forced to shoot an officer in self-defense. He hoped it wouldn't come to that, but his instructions from the general had come with no proviso for abandoning the mission if it started getting rough. The nature of the struggle had presumably been understood before he was dispatched to Istanbul. Accordingly it stood to reason that his own superiors must know what to expect when he and his companions got to Moscow.

They were counting on a fireworks show, but that didn't mean he would be immune to criticism if the game got out of hand. From long experience he knew that the bureaucracy—in Russia, as in any other nation—had an infinite capacity for shifting with the tide of public sentiment, while politicians scrambled for their lifeboats at the first sign of a storm cloud in the sky. Someone had voted to approve the plan that put him where he was, and someone else could just as easily rescind it if the danger of embarrassment became too great. In that case, the lieutenant knew, his own life and the others' would be forfeit.

Would they go so far as to eliminate the general?

It was doubtful, in the modern day, though he wouldn't have said so a few years earlier, before the big changes.

Someone had written that the more things change, the more they stay the same. A Western author, and the name eluded him, but he could still appreciate the truth behind the words.

Gromylko closed his eyes and tried to push the grim thoughts from his mind. There would be time enough to worry when they got to Moscow. For the moment they were still together, still alive.

But he was moved to wonder how much longer it would last.

CHAPTER FIFTEEN

The main streets in the Russian capital are laid out in concentric, if somewhat uneven, rings. A bird's-eye view presents the image of a giant pond, with ripples spreading from the epicenter where a stone has dropped. There used to be a standing joke with pilots serving the Strategic Air Command, back in the 1950s, that Americans should thank the Russians for their thoughtfulness in painting a bull's-eye on Moscow.

The Cold War history meant nothing to Mack Bolan at the moment, and geography was simply one more tool to use in the destruction of his enemies. They were on Gromylko's home turf now, and he expected full cooperation from the Russian officer, no matter what it cost in terms of second thoughts, misgivings, guilty spasms in the middle of some dark and stormy night a year from now.

Assuming any of them lived that long.

They had split into teams again, which left them right back at the language barrier, but Gromylko had spent a goodly portion of the long drive drilling them on basic Russian phrases, with a lightning course in Russian profanity that no Berlitz instructor would have recognized. It wouldn't win them entry to a cocktail party at the Kremlin, but it ought to see them through if one of them should be pulled over by a traffic cop or have to stop for gas along the way.

Right now, though, Bolan's mind was miles away from studies in vocabulary. His first target was a seedy building in a neighborhood that may have been appealing once, around the time when Josef Stalin was in power. Years had passed since anyone took pride in where they lived; the place was run-down and filthy and graffiti scarred. It could have been some portions of New York, Chicago, or Detroit, except for street signs in Cyrillic and an almost total absence of black faces on the street.

The building was, at least ostensibly, a rooming house. In fact, despite Moscow's growing homeless problem, there were only three rooms in the building occupied by persons who would pass for normal tenants. All of those were gunmen serving Gregori Vasiliev. Their mission—watch the place and keep up tight security.

Above all else, Vasiliev didn't want strangers peeking at the upstairs lab he used to process and cut heroin prior to distribution on the street. The pure shit would be mixed with everything from baby laxatives to baking soda—anything, in fact, to give it the appearance and approximate consistency of first-rate skag.

Hawk took the roof this time, while Bolan went in through the front. The mini-Uzi in his hand was fitted with a silencer, to keep the noise down while he found his way around and got to know the home team.

Two of them were waiting for him when he breezed in off the street, tall bruisers, built like Russian bears and wearing fur, enough to round out the illusion. Bears don't carry leather blackjacks, though—or drop them in a hurry when they glimpse a weapon, reaching underneath their coats for hardware that was obviously tucked away too well for a fast draw.

Bolan killed them where they stood, one sweeping burst to tag them both and slam them back against the wall behind them, pinned them there for just an instant, then allowed their bulky forms to settle with the draw of gravity.

There seemed to be no elevator, so he used the stairway the dead men had been guarding. If Gromylko's information was correct, the drug lab was on the fourth floor, perhaps with more security on two and three, plus lots of empty storage space on five. At this rate Hawk should reach the lab before he did, unless that attic storage area turned out to hold surprises for the uninvited visitor.

The sound of an explosion overhead told him Hawk was on his way. Bolan slipped his face mask on in case the skag dust blew downstairs or started dribbling down through shrapnel holes.

On the stairs between the third and second floors, he heard a rush of footsteps from behind: two or three men, coming on the run. He turned and waited for them, balancing the Uzi in his hands, around waist level. They stopped short, three faces gaping at his mask, his jet black overcoat, the automatic weapon in his hands. All three were packing, two side arms and a Kalashnikov, but by the time they thought of using all that hardware, it was too damn late.

The Uzi whispered to them, blowing lethal kisses

from a range of twelve to fourteen feet. There was no question of a miss; he didn't really even have to aim. Their bodies jerked and reeled on impact, finally tumbling backward down the staircase.

He was proceeding cautiously upstairs, toward four, when Hawkins stepped out on the landing just above him. Bolan could tell that he was smiling from his eyes, despite the mask that hid his nose and mouth.

"All done?"

"Except the blowout," Hawkins told him, glancing at his watch. "Five minutes to go."

They were outside and almost to their waiting car before the Semtex charges blew. With any luck at all, the smoke and flame would wipe out any drifting cloud of heroin that otherwise might settle on the slowly dying neighborhood.

THE TRUCKING COMPANY was situated south of downtown Moscow, in the Cer'omuski district. Driving out there, Gary Manning took his time. McCarter rode in the shotgun seat, and their RPGs were stowed in back, beneath a thrift-shop blanket. Watching out for landmarks rather than the street signs that he couldn't read, the tall Canadian asked questions now and then, McCarter coming up with answers from the English-language city map he had unfolded on his lap.

"We're almost there," McCarter said.

"It's about time," Manning commented, consciously relaxing his white-knuckled grip on the steering wheel.

In fact, the trucking plant was exactly where it should have been, from listening to Gromylko plot their route ahead of time. There was an eight-foot chain-link fence around the property, with coils of shiny razor wire on top. The warning signs, hung every twenty feet or so along the fence, were all in Russian, but the lightning-bolt design conveyed their message loud and clear: no trespassing, unless you want to fry.

Well, that was fine.

The Phoenix warriors didn't plan to set foot on the property. They had a clear view of the warehouse and garage from where they sat across the street, and Manning counted seven semi rigs lined up and waiting for the order to depart with shipments of God knew what. The cargo might not be illicit each and every time they left the lot, but Manning didn't care if they ran only one load of narcotics in a thousand trips. The trucks and property were owned by Gregori Vasiliev, and that was all he had to know.

"Let's do it," McCarter said, opening his door and stepping out. Manning was right behind him, checking up and down the two-lane access road for witnesses before he opened up the back door on the driver's side.

The RPGs were ready; it had been risky business driving with them loaded, but at least they had engaged the safety on each launcher. McCarter joined him on the driver's side of the car, shouldering his launcher, both men resting their elbows on the roof of the car for support and stability while they were aiming.

It was difficult to miss at that distance, about one-third of the effective range for stationary targets with an RPG. A man would have to shut his eyes and stagger like a drunkard if he meant to miss at that range, and the chain-link fence would be no obstacle at all, too frail to set the rockets off or even spoil their aim.

"I'll take the first truck on the left," Manning said.

"Loading dock," McCarter added. "Come back and meet you in the middle."

"Right."

He sighted quickly, didn't wait to hear the loud whoosh from McCarter's launcher, squeezing off a heartbeat in advance of his companion. It was still exciting, after all that he had seen and done, to watch the rocket sail downrange, fire streaming out behind it, punching through the tall fence like a bullet through a hair net, detonating with a smoky thunderclap as it ripped through the big truck's grille.

McCarter's round went home an instant later, opening a new doorway between the loading dock and warehouse proper as it blew a great hole in the concrete wall. A cloud of smoke and dust rolled out of there, reminding Manning of those Western movies where the silver mine caves in and miners rush out coughing, gagging, running for their lives.

Except that no one was emerging from McCarter's man-made cave.

Reloading as his partner reached out for his second rocket, Manning worried that it all seemed just a bit too easy. Where were all the sentries, set to pounce on anyone who posed a threat to Gregori Vasiliev? Had they withdrawn to more-strategic sites, or had the Russian godfather evacuated Moscow altogether, thereby giving them the slip.

I'll think about that later, Manning told himself, and

concentrated on his aim. Next truck in line, a trailer with no tractor rig in front. Most likely empty, but it still had cost Vasiliev a pretty ruble, all the same.

It had to go.

Manning was smiling as he squeezed the trigger and his rocket sizzled off downrange.

IT HAD BEGUN.

There was no doubt of that, no matter how Vasiliev attempted to deceive himself, pretend that the initial incidents were unrelated to the recent massacres in Turkey and Tbilisi. Even with his best men and the eyes of the *militsiya* watching, his elusive enemies had found their way to Moscow, and they felt secure enough on his own turf to launch a new round of attacks.

Gregori Vasiliev wasn't some teenage punk from the streets, who could be frightened off by fireworks. He had killed men with his own two hands and felt their warm blood splatter on his face. He had seen comrades cut down while they stood beside him, close enough to touch, and he was still alive. His courage was a combination of self-confidence, experience in dealing death and a determination formed in adolescence that it was a true man's lot to stand and die, if necessary, while the yellow-livered cowards ran away.

Whatever happened in the next few hours or days, he wouldn't let himself be driven out of Moscow like some *stelat kozyol,* one of the bitches used by stronger, abler men in prison. If the game went badly for him, if he lost, the pigs would find him where he fell in battle, with an empty weapon in his hand.

It was the only fitting way for a *vor v zakonye* to die.

But he wasn't conceding victory to his opponents yet, by any means. Vasiliev still had a few tricks up his sleeve, still had an army to defend him, with some help from the *militsiya*. As far as anyone could prove in court, he was a law-abiding citizen, deserving of the same protection as any nine-to-five drone, and he wouldn't be shy about demanding his due. After all, he had paid more police salaries in his time than any other taxpayer in Russia.

And he reckoned it was time to see what he was paying for.

He had already lost commercial property worth several hundred million rubles, not to mention soldiers gunned down like so many cutout targets on a shooting range. For all the good those men had done him, Vasiliev may as well have killed them himself.

At least, he thought, their deaths might serve as an example to the others, keep the scared survivors on their toes. He didn't grieve for those who died—they were employees, after all, not friends, and easily replaced—but he regretted that it was beyond his power to punish those who failed him.

An opening skirmish or two did not predict the outcome of the war. If that were true, the last two generations of Americans would all be speaking Japanese.

Vasiliev had time, but he would have to use it wisely.

Starting now.

GROMYLKO HAD BEEN dreading the telephone call for hours, before they ever got to Moscow. He knew it was inevitable, but that made the task no less onerous. Risking his own life was one thing, but it was something else entirely when he started risking other lives in the cause.

Besides, there weren't that many people he could trust these days, and even fewer whom he would count as friends. Sergeant Vanya Dobrinin was one such, and it weighed heavily on Gromylko's mind that he was placing a friend in mortal danger. It brought back grim memories of his partner, sprawled dead on the ground.

Still, duty called, and Dobrinin was an officer in the *militsiya*, sworn to pursue the enemies of justice. More to the point, as Gromylko's friend, he would have been insulted—even furious—if he was arbitrarily excluded from the last phase of the plan.

Gromylko could have reached out for the general personally, but he knew how sensitive the campaign would become. There were already special bulletins on radio and television, airing details of the early strikes in Moscow, guessing at the motives or fabricating them from thin air. The handful of command-grade officers involved in the campaign would be walking on eggshells and jumping at shadows until it was finished, desperate to present the appearance of policemen doing their jobs by the book, while covertly supporting the crime wave. Gromylko knew he must avoid contact with the general at all cost, except in the most extreme emergency.

But Dobrinin could assist him, had agreed before Gromylko left for Turkey. It had been a violation of his orders and a flagrant breach of operational security to tell Dobrinin anything about his mission, even withholding the fact that he was working with Americans. Dobrinin might not understand the full extent of what was happening—indeed, he probably wouldn't believe the things Gromylko had been up to in the past four days—but he knew enough to understand that any help he offered to Gromylko must be strictly unofficial, and provided at the risk of his career.

The telephone rang twice before Dobrinin's gruff, familiar voice came on the line. *"Anno!"*

"It's me," Gromylko said.

The brusque tone hardly changed, but Gromylko could tell the difference. His friend was worried, maybe even frightened. "Ah," Dobrinin said, "so there you are."

"Is this line safe?" Gromylko asked.

"Who knows these days? Are *you* safe?"

"More or less," Gromylko said. "I need your help, though, and it can't wait long."

"We live to serve." The note of sarcasm made Dobrinin sound a bit more normal, as if he was starting to recover his composure. "What exactly did you have in mind?"

"I need a copy of the file on Gregori Vasiliev," he said. "Specifically the details on his business interests, personal connections—names and addresses."

He knew the basics, but there had been too much in the file for him to memorize. If they were going to destroy the Thieves' Society or make a decent try at it, Gromylko wanted all the major targets at his fingertips.

"That's quite an order," Dobrinin said, but he didn't seem put off by the task. "It can't just disappear, you understand. I'll have to make some copies on the sly."

"How long?"

The sergeant thought about it for a moment. Finally he said, "We're into lunchtime now. Most of the brass is gone. If no one catches me, I should have what you need within the hour."

"I can't stop in there to pick it up."

"I didn't think so. Listen, by the time the rest of them get back, it will be my turn to go eat. They'll hear my stomach growling all the way to Gorky Park. I'll bring the stuff along, and we can meet."

"Meet where?" Gromylko asked.

"Let's see… I can't go far. There won't be time for me to drive all over town, and it would be suspicious if I took a car."

"Somewhere in walking distance, then," Gromylko said.

Another moment slipped away while Dobrinin thought about the problem, then he said, "Let's meet at the museum."

Gromylko didn't have to ask which one. Dobrinin had to mean the huge Museum of the Revolution, on Leningradski Prospekt. Even in these days, when communism was discredited with the majority of Russians and historical nostalgia had set in for some, the bold events of 1917 were still a point of pride, as if the Russian mind could seize on one event and somehow manage to forget the countless others it had brought to pass, the despotism that had sprung full-blown from a crusade to wipe out tyranny.

"What time?" Gromylko asked.

"Let's say two-thirty. If I'm not there by two forty-five," Dobrinin said, "you'll know I won't be coming."

Gromylko didn't like the sound of that, but he knew what Dobrinin meant. There were a hundred different things that could go wrong around the office, short of the sergeant being caught while he was copying the files. He might be swamped with paperwork when his superiors returned from lunch—especially if the Americans kept striking at their present rate and leaving bodies in their wake.

Our wake, Gromylko thought, correcting himself. He was as much a part of it as anyone. The blood was on his hands, as well.

"I'll see you then," he said. "Be careful."

"Always."

With a click the link was broken, and he left the phone booth, walking back to where the Americans waited for him in the car.

"We have a date at the museum," Gromylko told them, "but not just yet. With any luck we should have time for one more stop along the way."

"YOU MANAGED THAT quite well," Yuri Renko said, putting on a mirthless smile.

Vanya Dobrinin's answer was reluctant. "Thank you, Colonel."

"I'm aware of your regard for the lieutenant,"

Renko said. "It does you credit that you can distinguish between friendship and your duty."

"I can't think what must have driven him to this," Dobrinin said. "Perhaps when Churbanov—"

"In any case," Renko said, interrupting him, "we're forced to work with circumstances as they are, not as we wish they might have been. It's quite apparent that Lieutenant Gromylko has violated his oath of office. He is certainly involved in murder and a list of other crimes. He must be stopped before he can do further damage to the public or the reputation of this unit."

"Yes, sir."

"You will meet him at the museum, as arranged. You should have no great difficulty holding him in conversation while our officers move in. He will be taken quietly, assuming he doesn't resist. And as for you, your service to the unit will not be forgotten. I can personally guarantee that you will be rewarded for cooperating in this most unpleasant matter."

"Thank you, sir."

Dobrinin clearly wasn't happy with the thought of earning a reward for giving up his friend, but Renko didn't give a damn about the sergeant's tender sensibilities. He simply had to follow orders, and the trap would be successful.

"I won't need any papers, then, sir?"

"Papers?" Renko frowned, uncertain what the fool was babbling on about.

"The file on Gregori Vasiliev," Dobrinin said.

"Don't be ridiculous. It's foolish to believe that the *militsiya* would ever give approval for a vigilante action like the one Gromylko claims to be involved in. Anyone with half a brain can see what's happened— either he's become unbalanced from the grief of losing Churbanov, or he's sold out to some competing faction of the *mafiya* that wants Vasiliev destroyed. In either case we can't allow the madness to continue."

"No, sir."

"You will take a briefcase with you to allay suspicion, but we certainly won't send any confidential files outside the office on a job like this. Think of security."

"Yes, sir. I simply thought—"

"Don't think!" the colonel snapped. "It only gets you into trouble. Soldiers follow orders. Are we clear on that, *Lieutenant?*"

"Yes, sir. I—"

Dobrinin blinked twice rapidly, before a guilty-looking smile turned up the corners of his mouth.

"Yes, *sir,*" he said again with greater confidence.

"In that case go prepare yourself. You have a rendezvous to keep."

The colonel's smile turned predatory as he watched the office door close, leaving him alone. He reached out for the telephone, and was relieved to find his hand was steady as a rock.

CHAPTER SIXTEEN

Vanya Dobrinin walked to the museum, departing from his office at the stroke of two. He wore civilian clothes—an inexpensive suit and tie, blue polyester, with brown shoes. His fashion sense wasn't refined, and he cared nothing for his personal appearance at the moment. He had left his uniform behind to make the meeting less conspicuous, but he was armed, the Makarov's butt and hammer gouging into the small of his back with every other step he took. The simulated-leather briefcase he carried in his hand contained a folded newspaper.

Dobrinin was acutely conscious of his treachery as he moved north on Leningradski Prospekt toward the rendezvous with Leonid Gromylko. Years of friendship were about to be destroyed, a major portion of his life unraveled like a shoddy sweater. It was a conscious choice, and afterward he would never be able to look back on the moment with any hope of shirking personal responsibility.

He had been foolish, Dobrinin realized, to swallow the bizarre tale in the first place. Why would ranking officers of the *militsiya* select Gromylko for a secret one-man mission to destroy the Chechen *mafiya,* and how could his friend have hoped to see the mission through alive if it were true? Dobrinin realized that he had *wanted* to believe the fantasy, because it seemed in those few moments that he had his friend back, the Gromylko he had known before Alexei Churbanov was killed, and everything began to fall apart in Leonid's life. He had the old fire and determination back, without the nervous edge of paranoia that had come to feel like second nature.

Still, the whole thing was preposterous. In retrospect Dobrinin wanted to believe his friend was on a private vigilante mission, striking back at those who killed his partner, but in that case how had he survived this long? Assuming he possessed the skill and the equipment, somehow evading the hunters dispatched to cut him down, Gromylko still couldn't appear at two or three points simultaneously, as the Moscow raiders had been seen to do. The most determined zealot in the world couldn't ignore the laws of physics, time and space.

Which meant that he had allies, and since they were not from the militia, *that* meant he had found help somewhere else. Who better to assist Gromylko in a move against Vasiliev than someone on the wrong side of the law who wished the Chechens dead—or driven out of power? It could be one of the local Muscovite gangs, maybe the Ukrainians or even someone political perhaps. The details would come out once Gromylko was safely locked away and Colonel Renko had the time to question him at length.

Gromylko would blame Dobrinin, naturally, and that was only proper. Any act of personal betrayal had its price, regardless of the traitor's good intentions. It was something that Dobrinin would be forced to live with, something he would see etched on his features in the mirror every day until he died.

They hadn't specified a meeting place in the museum, because it was unnecessary. Dobrinin and Gromylko had used the museum for quiet meetings more than once in bygone days. There was an open courtyard at the center of the complex, trees and benches, with a smallish plot of grass to give the concrete some relief. Gromylko would be coming there to meet him, as he had before.

And Dobrinin would be waiting for his old friend with a briefcase full of newspapers. He would be waiting with the Judas kiss.

Dobrinin didn't know how many officers were detailed to surround the meeting place and keep Gromylko from escaping. He had seen none of them so far, but that simply meant that Renko had assigned surveillance experts to the job. If Dobrinin saw them coming, so would Gromylko, and that would ruin everything.

Dobrinin checked his watch. Another fifteen minutes, give or take, and it would all be over. He could walk back to the office with his briefcase and resume his paperwork, secure in the knowledge that he had performed his duty and betrayed a friend.

But it wasn't a total waste.

Lieutenant Dobrinin. Yes, he liked the sound of that.

In ten or fifteen years Dobrinin thought he might be able to forget what it had cost him, moving up the ladder of success.

GROMYLKO TOOK HIS TIME on the approach. His nerves were jangling, he was anxious to be gone, but there was no point in rushing it. He had to prepare for the eventuality that some last-minute delay might well keep Dobrinin from delivering the file on schedule. If that happened, he would have to call again, arrange another meeting at the sergeant's earliest convenience. And in the meantime his companions would be turning up the heat on Gregori Vasiliev.

The raids in Moscow had gone well enough. The godfather himself was nowhere to be seen, but that wasn't unusual. It was predictable that Vasiliev would go to ground, direct his army from a safe place, well back from the firing line. The trick would be to flush him out from cover—or alternatively, to find his hiding place and kill him there.

The six Americans appeared to be in no great hurry when it came to taking out the man in charge. Rather, they seemed intent on tearing down his empire, piece by piece, before they swept the dragon from his lair. It was a commonsense approach, in terms of doing major damage to the syndicate—a godfather could always be replaced, with no great inconvenience to the Thieves' Society—but Gromylko was worried that they might delay the final strike too long, allow their adversaries one too many chances to strike back.

They had been lucky so far, and he recognized that fact. Gromylko also understood that luck was transient, and could never last indefinitely. They were overdue for a reversal or a setback, and he wished something could be done to wrap the mission up before that came to pass.

Perhaps, he thought, the information Dobrinin brought to him would make the difference.

There were always people in the courtyard, a popular retreat for clerks and secretaries fleeing stuffy offices, to eat their lunches out of paper bags, surrounded by their nation's history. That stately aura still hung on, regardless of the fact that the museum was basically a monument to communism, now discredited and passed away. Gromylko felt it, passing through the tall, arched doorway, footsteps ringing on the marble floors as he proceeded to the courtyard.

Dobrinin sat there, waiting for him. They weren't alone, of course. As long as the museum was open, there would always be at least a few spectators lolling about, resting up between exhibits or waiting for a guided tour to begin. It made no difference to Gromylko if they had an audience. No one would overhear their conversation; there was no more KGB to watch and eavesdrop in such places—or, if so, at least the name and the initials had been changed, and presumably the mission, too.

He headed directly toward the bench where his friend sat, put on a smile, then almost lost it when he saw the way Dobrinin looked at him. His friend seemed nervous, almost to the point of flinching when he saw Gromylko, even though their meeting had been arranged. The short hairs on Gromylko's nape were bristling as he closed the gap between them, but he told himself that Dobrinin had good reason to be ill at ease. The information in the briefcase resting at his feet was classified; he could be punished with dismissal and a prison sentence for removing it from headquarters, even at the request of a superior officer.

Gromylko settled on the bench beside his friend, stuck out his hand and felt the sweat in Dobrinin's palm as they shook hands.

"You look well, all things considered," Dobrinin said.

"I'm still alive. You seem…uneasy."

"I'm fine," Dobrinin said hastily. "It was a close thing getting here, that's all. They have a flap on, with these raids against Vasiliev."

"I would imagine so. You have the information?"

"Yes, right here." Dobrinin's eyes flicked back and forth around the courtyard as he bent to lift the briefcase.

"Vanya?"

"*Da?*"

"Is something—?"

Wrong.

Before the word could pass Gromylko's lips, his friend lurched backward, gasping, eyes wide open in astonishment. A splotch of crimson blossomed on his shirt, immediately followed by a second, and Gromylko heard the bullets slapping home, although there was no sound of gunshots in the courtyard.

Instinct saved him, and he pushed off with his legs and vaulted backward, dropping on his side behind the bench. A third shot struck the painted wood and gouged a hole there as Gromylko palmed his Makarov.

Too late he realized the cause of Vanya's nervousness. The trap was sprung, and there was no way to be sure that he could wriggle out of it alive.

THE FIRST SHOT came as a surprise to Rafael Encizo, even though he had been ready for any kind of treachery. The major fear had been a tail from headquarters, in case Gromylko's friend was spotted photocopying the files. In that event, Encizo would have expected uniforms or a plainclothes team that would converge with badges, nabbing two suspects instead of one. He was prepared to intervene if that went down, but it had never crossed Encizo's mind, after Gromylko gave the buildup on his friend, that a hit team would show up at the museum.

But he was wrong.

The sergeant was already dead before Encizo got his pistol out and started scanning for the source of gunfire. From the corner of his eye, he glimpsed Gromylko diving under cover, flattening himself behind the heavy bench where his late associate was sprawled out in a crimson spill of blood. The third shot came from somewhere to Encizo's right, and he was quick enough to spot the two shooters—both average men in average clothes—as they advanced in the direction of the bench. Their pistols were equipped with silencers, but they were all done trying to be subtle and strode forward with the weapons plainly visible.

Encizo lined up on the nearer gunman, squeezing off the standard double tap to make it stick. The shooter lurched against his buddy as the slugs drilled through his chest, the impact rocking both of them before the dead man folded, sprawling in a heap and nearly taking his partner down with him.

Nearly but not quite.

The survivor swung around toward Encizo's position, no target clearly visible, but firing anyway on instinct. He came damn close. One bullet hissed past Encizo's ear, while the second sprayed chips of masonry into his face from the column beside him. Encizo ducked backward, crouching, cursing underneath his breath and hoping for another shot before the gunman broke and ran.

But his intended target wasn't going anywhere. The next incoming round hit so close to Encizo's knee that he initially believed his man was charging, but a hasty glance around the column showed the Russian standing fast. Two more rounds chipped the column near his head, but the gunner was facing toward Gromylko now, apparently intent on finishing his job.

Then who the hell was firing?

Encizo glimpsed movement on the far side of the courtyard. Two or three more bodies rushing toward him, though he couldn't be certain of the count. It may as well have been an army, in the circumstances. All they had to do was pin him down while their associate rubbed out Gromylko, and the Moscow strike was finished, even if Encizo managed to escape. Without Gromylko they were stranded.

They were well and truly screwed.

Encizo rolled from cover on the left side of the column, firing from a prone position, his Beretta steady in a two-handed grip. He blew the first shot, even so, but scored on one of his assailants with the second, saw a blur of crimson as the gunman staggered, then went down. The other two cut loose with silenced pistols from a range of forty feet or so, still rushing, daring the Cuban to stop them if he could.

Three rounds in rapid-fire reached out to catch the second shooter in midstride and spin him in a tight spiral. Before he hit the deck, Encizo was already tracking on the sole survivor of the trio, trading shots with him and praying he was better, quicker than the Russian—anything to give himself an edge before the shooter scored a hit.

Encizo saw his bullets strike their target: one, two, three red geysers spouting from the Russian's chest and throat before he toppled over backward, legs still pumping for a moment as his muscles tried to override the lethal message from a dying brain.

Encizo came up on his elbows just in time to catch the action as Gromylko dropped the second gunman who'd initiated the firefight, pumping two rounds underneath the bench at ankle height, then rising up to finish it with two more in the chest. It looked like victory, a short reach for the briefcase, and they could be out of there before the other museum visitors recovered from their shock sufficiently to summon the police.

He was halfway to his feet when automatic-weapons fire erupted in the courtyard, bullets chipping pavement as they flew from somewhere overhead. No silencer this time. No pretense of avoiding panic. All the shooter wanted was to do his job at any cost.

Encizo made a dive for cover, back behind the column, cursing bitterly and hoping Calvin James could make the save. If he was late—or already dead—then Encizo's future, and Gromylko's, would be very brief.

THEY HAD AGREED that James should take the second floor and check out the exhibits there, ready to observe the handoff from a balcony that overlooked the court-yard on all sides. No ambush was expected when they made the plan, but it was common sense to have a spotter on the high ground. It was supposed to be a milk run. Once the briefcase had been passed, James could retrace his steps and meet them at the exit for a short walk to the car.

But then the whole thing went to hell.

He missed the first shots, since he was drifting ca-sually along the rail and trying not to be obvious about surveillance on the courtyard. James saw Gromylko take his seat, then cruised back in the direction of the gallery to check for any spotters on that level. It was only when he heard a woman scream down below that he doubled back in time to see Encizo finish off his adversaries, while Gromylko popped up from behind the bench and dropped another in his tracks.

That should have been the end of it, but then an automatic weapon started firing from the balcony to James's left, halfway around the courtyard. Swiveling in that direction, he could see a bullnecked gunner leaning out across the rail and firing short bursts from a submachine gun, first at Encizo, then at Gromylko, pinning both men down.

James fired a quick shot to distract the gunner, rush-ing toward the corner that would put him on the same side of the balcony as his intended target. Running all out, he was nearly at the corner when a woman stepped in front of him and aimed a swift kick at his groin.

He sidestepped, felt her shoe slam solidly against

his thigh before he straight-armed her with force enough to send her sprawling. At the moment he was less concerned about what made her intervene, or whether she was injured, than with taking out the shooter on the north side of the balcony. Another burst of fire directed toward the courtyard added urgency to James's mission, so he shrugged off the cramped pain in his left leg as he ran.

The bullet coming from behind him nearly ended it. He heard the shot and ducked his head, already weaving, dodging to the side, before the slug struck metal on the railing, chipping paint and whining into space. James spun around in time to see the woman on her knees, a shiny autoloader in her right hand, lining up another shot. Her nose was bleeding from the impact of his open hand, her lips and chin dark crimson.

But she wasn't just some would-be vigilante, James realized. She had to be a kind of backup spotter for the hit team, standing by for situations just like this.

He crouched and squeezed off two quick shots, trusting instinct and the close range of his target. The lady's sweater rippled as the slugs went home, and she went over backward, triggering a last shot toward the ceiling as she fell.

He went around the corner belly-down in a long slide, as if the last run in a crucial baseball game depended on him stealing home. His enemy was facing him and firing from the hip, the bullets swarming over the Phoenix pro's head. Returning fire, he pumped off four rounds, watching as his target staggered, reeling, back against the rail. Another heartbeat, and the Russian toppled over, plummeting some twenty feet to strike the pavement in the courtyard.

Downstairs he saw Encizo and Gromylko up and running, headed for the nearest exit. James retreated past the crumpled figure of the woman, tucked his pistol out of sight but kept his fingers wrapped around the grip.

Someone had set them up, and there were questions that Gromylko ought to answer before they went ahead with any further strikes in Moscow. First, though, they would have to get the hell away from the museum, before they ended up as fresh exhibits. The police would be arriving any moment now, and there might still be other gunners skulking in the shadows.

Either way they had been lucky, more or less.

But luck would only stretch so far, and Calvin James could almost hear his ripping as he quickstepped toward the stairs.

"IT LOOKS LIKE your amigo set you up," Encizo said. His voice was flat, devoid of any emotion as he concentrated on his driving, watching out for squad cars or civilian hunters in the rearview mirror.

"That's impossible," Gromylko said, though with less than full conviction. "I saw his face before he died. Vanya was taken by surprise."

"I'll bet," James muttered from the seat behind Gromylko. "He was counting on *you* getting dusted, not himself."

"He wouldn't do that," the lieutenant said. "In all the years we worked together, Vanya never took a ruble from the *mafiya*. I'd stake my life on that."

"In case you didn't notice," James reminded him, "your life *is* riding on the line."

"How else do you explain the firing squad?" Encizo asked. "Unless your friend tipped someone off..."

"Impossible," Gromylko said again.

"So, check the briefcase out," James said. "If he delivered what you asked for, maybe we can work out some alternative to how the shooters found you. Otherwise, I'd say your man's on the hook."

Gromylko raised the briefcase from between his feet and placed it on his lap. He hesitated, with his thumbs pressed to the twin latch buttons, suddenly reluctant to find out what was inside. It wouldn't be a bomb, of course—that was ridiculous—but if the file on Gregori Vasiliev was missing from the case, it meant that he was wrong about Dobrinin.

He snapped the latches open, raised the lid and scowled at the newspaper lying neatly folded in the briefcase. With a whispered curse, he closed the case and latched it.

"So." There was no mocking irony in James's voice. It sounded more like sadness, tempered with fatigue.

"He scammed you, then," Encizo said. "If we assume he wasn't working for Vasiliev—"

"I won't believe that," Gromylko insisted stubbornly.

"Then who *could* talk him into breaking trust that way? There must be *someone* you can think of, some idea of why he'd set you up."

"Perhaps..."

"We're listening," James said.

"If he'd been convinced that I was working with the *mafiya*, that I had somehow lied to him," Gromylko said. "Vanya would not have brought assassins with him, but there is a chance he would have brought detectives. People whom he believed to be detectives, I should say."

"If we assume that's true," Encizo said, "who would have set it up?"

Gromylko puzzled over that one for a moment. It couldn't have been the general in charge of his division, since the plan had originated from his office. If he was anxious to betray Gromylko and the others for some unknown reason, he could easily have set a trap before they ever got to Moscow. That meant it was someone else, perhaps unaware of the general's role, the very details of the plan. Someone who sought to help Vasiliev and kill Gromylko in a single stroke. Someone with rank and close ties to the Chechen syndicate.

Someone like Yuri Renko.

"There may be someone...."

"So," James said, "let's have a name."

"I must be sure before I act," Gromylko said. "He is a well-respected officer of the *militsiya*."

"Sounds like the man needs to retire," James muttered.

"If I am correct, I will take care of it myself."

"That's risky business, comrade. You're already way across the line."

"Vanya Dobrinin was my friend, no matter what he

thought of me in his last days. I owe him this much, at the very least," Gromylko said.

"A sense of duty is noble," James said, "but don't forget what this is all about. Vasiliev and company, remember?"

"I will not forget," Gromylko promised him. "I owe Vasiliev too much already."

"Well, I hope you get the chance to pay him back real soon."

"I'm counting on it," Leonid Gromylko said.

CHAPTER SEVENTEEN

The worst thing about bad news, Yuri Renko thought, was when a circumstance demanded that it be passed on. He wasn't troubled by the usual emotional aspect of sharing morbid tidings, since emotions—barring lust and anger—were entirely foreign to his nature. Rather, it disturbed the colonel when he had to break bad news to someone who was both more powerful and potentially more destructive than himself.

As in the present case.

He had the word from his *militsiya* investigators on the scene at the museum. There was no doubt that eight persons were dead—Vanya Dobrinin and the seven members of the hit team sent by Gregori Vasiliev to finish Leonid Gromylko. One of those turned out to be a woman—not that Renko cared, but he was curious about the choice, what made Vasiliev decide that these particular incompetents should do the job.

It would be simple, Renko thought, for him to stall until the grim news reached Vasiliev by radio or television, even word of mouth, but it would also be bad form. His man had been the Judas goat; the plan, essentially, was his. It didn't matter that Vasiliev's hired guns had failed to carry out a simple hit-and-run. The

Chechen godfather wasn't a man who readily admitted errors in judgment, much less in a matter of such great importance that his whole empire—indeed, perhaps his very life—depended on a satisfactory result.

He would be looking for a scapegoat, someone he could scream at, blame and punish for the failure of his own subordinates. If Renko had to bear some measure of the heat, he was prepared to live with that, but he wasn't about to be the only one. In fact, if things went badly in the next few hours, he might be needing scapegoats and a sanctuary of his own.

Already Renko knew the briefcase that Dobrinin carried was not found at the museum. Since no one from the hit team had survived, and none of them would logically have grabbed the case, he assumed that Gromylko must have snatched it as he fled. And that, in turn, would verify Dobrinin's role in setting up the trap.

So what? the colonel asked himself. It would be better, with Dobrinin dead and gone, to let him bear the brunt of any anger on Gromylko's part. Unfortunately Renko knew Gromylko's style. He understood that the lieutenant wouldn't simply curse his late, lamented friend and let it go at that. He would be looking for whoever was *behind* Dobrinin, those who had the power and influence to make him sell a friend.

And how long would it take before Gromylko thought of Yuri Renko's name?

The question now, in Renko's mind, wasn't *if* Gromylko would make the link, but *when*. More to the point, once he made the connection in his mind, what would he do? In ordinary circumstances Renko wouldn't have been too concerned...but these were far from ordinary times. Gromylko wasn't entirely rational, if he believed that he could stand against the Thieves' Society. He might try anything.

More to the point, he wasn't operating by himself. The colonel still had no idea how many others were helping him, but there had been enough strength in numbers at the museum to kill seven of Vasiliev's hired guns. There had also been enough of them to take out Kenan Bey in Turkey, and Ivan Storzhenko with his private army down in Georgia.

For certain there would be enough to kill one ranking officer of the *militsiya*.

He needed help and couldn't count on his superiors this time. There was no explanation for his sudden fear, without a full confession of his ties to Gregori Vasiliev, his role in setting up the massacre at the museum. If he confessed all that, the general would "protect" him in a prison cell, and Renko would be lucky if he didn't end up with a death sentence. In Russia that meant something. There was no long-winded system of appeals, delays, postponements. The condemned had one chance to appeal, immediately after the conviction, and the judgment of the court was almost always negative. A few days after that, the inmate was escorted to a "shower room" that featured no amenities except a small drain in the middle of the floor, and he or she was rubbed out with a pistol bullet in the head.

It was a tidy and efficient system. Renko loved it, but he didn't plan to be on the receiving end. Not while he had a single trick left up his sleeve.

To *really* be protected from Gromylko, he would have to disappear, clean out his secret bank account in Liechtenstein and find another place to live. In fact, he had the false ID already, waiting for the day he could retire and start another life. Renko had counted on a few more years in uniform to fatten up that numbered bank account, but it was fat enough already for his needs. He could survive quite nicely for a decade, at the very least, on what he had already earned from Gregori Vasiliev.

And now Vasiliev would do him one more favor, a parting gift, as it were. But they couldn't discuss it on the telephone.

Which meant that Renko would be forced to break his news in person.

And he had to do it without delay.

"ARE WE ALL RIGHT without the files?" asked Bolan.

Gromylko nodded thoughtfully. "We still have all the major targets," he replied. "The list I sought from Vanya would have doubled, maybe tripled, what we have, but principally with smaller places, home addresses for a number of Vasiliev's associates. We should be fine."

"About that leak you've got back at the office—"

"That is my affair," Gromylko said. "I'll deal with him myself."

"I know the feeling," Bolan told him truthfully. "You're welcome to him, but that's not the problem I was thinking of."

"What, then?" Gromylko asked.

"It seems to me he's got a handle on the operation,'' Bolan explained. ''There's no way to predict how much he knows or where he got his information, but you could be compromised right to the top.''

''I don't believe that,'' the lieutenant said.

''You didn't think your friend would screw you, either,'' Calvin James reminded him.

''I still don't think he knew there would be shooting.''

''Say you're right,'' Bolan put in. ''That means you've got somebody in your office who's killed one militia officer and tried to make it two. My guess is that he won't be satisfied or feel secure until you're dead, along with everybody else connected to the operation. He's exposed right now. You come in from the cold, he's history.''

''Depends on who he is,'' said Gary Manning.

''What?'' Gromylko looked confused.

''Well, you've said there are just a few men at the top who know what you've been doing for the past few days.'' The tall Canadian was frowning now. ''Suppose that one or more of them are being paid off by Vasiliev. They slam the door behind you, and you can't come in.''

''That brings to mind a film I saw,'' McCarter said to no one in particular. ''A chap goes into prison undercover, and the only man who knows his true identity—''

''We've seen it,'' Manning interrupted.

''Bloody cheek.''

''You think the *general* is involved in this?'' Gromylko asked. His head was shaking even as he spoke, a grim, emphatic negative.

"He said 'what if,'" the Executioner replied. "It doesn't matter, from the angle of assistance, since you can't get help from any of your buddies anyway. But it could make a major difference in the way militia forces are deployed. They wind up covering Vasiliev, it multiplies our problems."

"No," Gromylko said again. "I don't believe that. There is one man—he's a colonel, my superior—who has been taking money from the *mafiya* for years."

"Just one?" McCarter sounded skeptical.

"One who despises me enough to want me gone by any means available. One who could find a way to raid the general's secret files and learn the truth."

"Which means Vasiliev would know," Calvin James said.

"He may know *what* and make a decent guess at *why*," Bolan argued, "but he can't know *who* or *where*. That still gives us an edge."

"So, what's the plan?" Encizo asked.

"We rock the town," said Bolan. "Turn it upside down, if necessary, till Vasiliev has no choice but to stand and fight or run for cover." He faced Gromylko. "Is there someplace he might go?"

"I know a place," Gromylko said.

"Then that's the plan."

"When do we start?" Gromylko asked.

"Right now."

Stony Man Farm

THE COM-SAT LINK was perfect, the reception loud and clear. Of course, you couldn't make out squat by listening to the transmission as it reached the farm. A high-pitched squeal, twelve-hundredths of a second long, it sounded like an insect buzzing past, perhaps a taste of feedback from the speakers, there and gone. You had to take the tape and slow it down, *way* down, before the words of the encrypted message were discernible, and then you had to know the daily code before those words made any kind of sense at all.

Technology.

A few years back it would have taken a transmitter with a dish some six or seven feet across to beam that message out of Russia, bounce it off a satellite in space and back down to the Blue Ridge Mountains of Virginia. The recording gear needed to compress a message and emit the high-speed pulse of sound would probably have weighed a hundred pounds and filled a good-sized suitcase. Nowadays the tape deck was the size of a transistor radio—a small one—and the folding dish looked like an average-sized umbrella, with the lining made of shiny foil. Assembly took two minutes, if the operator dragged his feet. The gear could be set up, a message broadcast and the rig dismantled in the time it took to smoke a cigarette.

Decoding was no problem, either, if you knew what you were doing. Aaron Kurtzman had a full year's worth of daily codes programmed into his IBM. A few keystrokes, and Bolan's message was replayed with no distortion of the sender's voice. He sounded fit enough.

The message was disturbing, though.

He listened to it twice before he buzzed for Barbara

Price and Yakov Katzenelenbogen, sitting through the tape twice more while they absorbed it.

"I don't like the sound of this," said Katz. "They've got a major problem if their man with the militia sold them out."

"He didn't say that," Kurtzman noted.

"Not exactly." Price's voice was grim. "That's what it sounds like, though."

"One way to look at this," Kurtzman said, "is that if the link *is* broken, they'll have trouble bailing out, the same as if they hang around."

"Depends on how you work the odds," Barbara Price stated. "If their militia man's rolled over, that could put another army on the street, besides Vasiliev's. You know Mack's problem with the cops."

"I don't think he regards it as a problem," Kurtzman said.

"Whatever. When they're shooting at you, and you won't shoot back, I'd say it stacks the odds."

"One thing," Katz said. "Regardless of what's going on with the militia link, the only Russian who can finger any member of the team is still connected. That's a plus. The brass hats know they're working with a team from the United States, but that's the limit. They've got nothing when it comes to faces, names, the rest of it."

"Small favors," Barbara said.

"And sometimes they're enough." The gruff Israeli's smile had years of grim experience behind it. "Keep in mind that Russia's not the closed society it used to be. Our people have been in there when it wasn't open to the public, and they made it back. It's not as easy spotting foreigners in Moscow as it used to be—much less a group of first-rate pros who're taking pains to keep a low profile."

"You call shooting up the capital a low profile?"

Katz didn't lose his smile. "They had an invitation, Barbara, remember?"

"Which may well have been revoked." She turned to Kurtzman. "Bear, how long before we have another contact window open?"

"Midnight through half-past." And he didn't need to add, If they can make it.

"Damn!"

"If anybody asked me," Kurtzman said, "I'd say they're doing the right thing. Pushing it this way, they keep Vasiliev disorganized. For all we know, he's on the run right now. On the militia end, it's even money. I'd be happier if they were in Bermuda, soaking up the sun, but I'm not ready to start playing taps."

Silence hung between them for a moment, broken finally when Price said, "We'd better patch this through to Hal. He'll have a cow if we don't clue him in."

"He'll have the whole damn herd," Kurtzman said. "I'll get on it right away."

There was a telephone within his reach, but Kurtzman turned his chair around and motored toward another console on the far side of the room. He sensed that Price could use some time with Katz, and Kurtzman hoped the ex-commando could provide some of the reassurances she craved.

That was the problem when it started getting personal, when you had friends and loved ones on the firing line. He could have warned her off, but what would be the point? A sterile life, without human connections, barely qualified as life at all. Sometimes you had to take your chances, reach out and touch someone to verify that you were still alive. And if it blew up in your face somewhere along the line, the pain was validation of another kind.

Life was a gamble, from the first breath to the last, with nothing certain but the final outcome of the game. There were no winners, in the sense of gaining youth eternal or the secrets of the universe, but you could rack up points along the way, depending on your style of play. The race was sometimes to the swift, and sometimes to the dogged runner who refused to stop for obstacles.

And sometimes, Kurtzman thought, it was enough to just keep kicking ass.

THE HEADACHE HAD BEGUN almost precisely on the stroke of noon, a grim reminder to Vasiliev that he was halfway through another day without identifying his persistent enemies. Each time the telephone demanded his attention, it was more bad news, another of his people dead, another piece of property destroyed.

And now he had to deal with Yuri Renko.

They had blown it with the trap at the museum. Seven guns should have been ample for the job, but something had gone wrong. Now the authorities were raging over the elimination of a sergeant who was no more than a secretary, shuffling paperwork and fetching coffee in the office. Seven to one, when they were finished counting bodies, and the pigs still wanted their revenge. Some of the officers Vasiliev had purchased years ago were shunning him this afternoon, as if he had the plague. It did no good for him to threaten them, since any leak about the bribes would implicate himself, as well.

But Renko was the worst of it.

There was no mystery to why the man would panic. Basically Vasiliev expected nothing less. In his estimation the kind of man who had to hide behind a badge and uniform had no real courage of his own. Exercise of authority went to a coward's head and made him reckless sometimes, but it didn't make him brave. It was one thing to throw your weight around when you were backed up by an army, quite another when you had to face the enemy alone. Vasiliev had seen both sides, and while he much preferred his present state, he didn't rank himself with men like Yuri Renko, who derived their strength from numbers and were lost if forced to stand alone.

He could have driven Renko out the moment he had finished spilling out the details of the massacre at the museum, but something stopped Vasiliev from sending him away. The man might still be useful in the proper circumstances. If his various superiors in the *militsiya* didn't know that he was running yet—and Renko swore that they did not—Vasiliev could picture situations where the colonel might assist him in the final contest with their enemy.

If only he could find out who the bastards were!

Americans, he thought, and shook his head disgustedly. That told him nothing as to whether they were mercenaries or clandestine agents of the government with an official sanction. In either case they had already proved that they were dangerous in the extreme, completely ruthless—worthy of his admiration if the circumstances had been different.

The only thing that mattered now was crushing them like insects, rapidly, before they had a chance to damage any more of Gregori Vasiliev's empire or reputation. There were mutterings already in the family— behind his back, but loud enough for him to hear— that said he might have lost his touch. It might be time for someone else to take the helm and lead the Thieves' Society in new directions, time to sacrifice Vasiliev before he brought them all down in defeat.

But he wasn't defeated yet. He still had better than a hundred of his Chechen soldiers spread throughout the city, some on guard at special properties, while others combed the streets for any information that would lead them to the enemy. He didn't trust his eyes in the *militsiya* just now, but knew the uniforms were out there looking, too. If they got lucky, it was all the same to him, as long as his assailants were removed from circulation—permanently.

Death was all that mattered in the end. Vasiliev wasn't concerned about who pulled the trigger, just as long as it was done effectively.

And soon.

Meanwhile he would provide the colonel with a place to hide, on the condition that his services were still available as needed. It was a good deal all around, and there was ample time to cut Renko loose when they had dealt with their opponents once and for all.

When that was done, the colonel would be expendable. Vasiliev would have to flip a coin and see if he should drop the colonel in a shallow grave or let him slink away and find himself another hiding place. Whatever he decided, there would be no trail to lead detectives to his doorstep.

Not this time.

The Chechen godfather was burning bridges with a vengeance, and the smell of smoke was sweet.

THE HOTEL ROOM was nearly small enough to qualify as claustrophobic, but Gromylko didn't care. He sat on one end of the double bed and checked his weapons, starting with the pistol, moving on to the Kalashnikov, spare magazines and finally the grenades. He didn't want the pins to stick in an emergency. It helped to loosen them a little, getting ready for the moment when he had no time to spare.

Around him his associates were doing likewise, barely speaking as they field-stripped weapons, reassembled them and loaded up. Gromylko watched them working, and he tried to understand why any one of them would take the risk of coming to Russia for a shot at Gregori Vasiliev. He knew the Russian *mafiya* had found its way to the United States, competing with the homegrown gangsters there, but that wasn't enough to bring these men so far from home. They were prepared to sacrifice their lives, if necessary, to complete the job, and that was more than he could say for many of the officers in Russia who were sworn to help enforce the laws.

Whatever motivated them, Gromylko thanked his

not-so-lucky stars that they were on his side. Without them, he might still have tried to break Vasiliev, but he had tried before, and it had cost his partner's life. Alone, he knew the odds against him would be insurmountable. Indeed, they *still* might be, but he no longer felt the helplessness of fighting on his own, while everyone around him talked about lost causes and attempted to divert him to some other course.

He thought of Yuri Renko, then—the bastard's smirking face—and knew that he couldn't live with himself until the colonel paid for Dobrinin's death. For all Gromylko knew, there might be some connection between Renko and Churbanov's murder, too, although it seemed unlikely that Vasiliev had been tipped off about their raid. In that case he would almost certainly have stayed away to spare himself the risk.

It was enough that Renko was responsible for Dobrinin's death, however. There was no hard proof, but the lieutenant wasn't working up a case for trial. He knew how Renko operated, understood the colonel's mind and realized that Dobrinin's life meant nothing to him in the scheme of things. Vasiliev would merely have to make a call, and Renko would perform like any other animal that has been trained to jump, play dead, sit up and beg.

The question nagging at Gromylko now was how the colonel could have known what he was up to. Reaching Dobrinin wouldn't have been a problem, but the *why* of it was still a riddle. Had the general, after all, decided he should share the details of their project with a fellow officer, perhaps to be prepared for the events in Moscow when they broke? Had Renko tapped the files himself, without the general's knowledge, and reported on Gromylko's mission to Vasiliev?

The latter option seemed more likely, but again Gromylko was not overly concerned with *how.* It was enough that he knew *who,* within a moral certainty, and that he had a chance to make it right, no matter what it cost him in the end.

Gromylko saw no way to salvage his career, with all that he had seen and done the past few days. He was prepared to find himself a quiet line of work, somewhere away from Moscow if he could, but not before he finished with the job that he had started.

Not until the Chechen godfather was crushed.

And Yuri Renko. He wouldn't forget the colonel if he lived to be a hundred.

Which, considering the way he planned to spend the next few hours, was a most unlikely prospect.

"I'm all done," he said to no one in particular.

The others were completing preparations even as he spoke. It took another moment to conceal their weapons in the suitcases and duffel bags that they would use to carry them downstairs.

"In that case," said the tall American who led the team, "let's hit the bricks."

CHAPTER EIGHTEEN

The repair shop in the Degunino district, north of downtown Moscow, was supposed to specialize in the repair of small appliances. It had been documented that the men in charge did some such work, though not enough to keep themselves in groceries. The shop closed down at least three days a week on average, and it wasn't uncommon for a housewife with a broken toaster to be told that she would have to wait a week or two before the item could be fixed. In Russia such delays were not unheard of, but in this case they had less to do with simple inefficiency than with the shop owner's preoccupation in another area.

Civilian ownership of firearms in Russia is restricted to the point of virtual nonexistence. In the past, exalted Communist Party members had been able to acquire the necessary permits for sporting rifles and shotguns, while pistols and paramilitary hardware were, at least in theory, the exclusive province of the state. Today permits are still required, and those with high positions in society are first to be approved by the *militsiya*. In practice, though, Moscow has turned into a full-scale arms bazaar, with military-surplus weapons readily available to anyone with ample cash on hand. In practice that means criminals and wealthy men who live in fear of crime. It is a thriving business for the Russian *mafiya* and shows no signs of fading in the stretch.

The small appliance shop in Degunino specialized in guns. Its three technicians removed serial numbers, shortened or replaced barrels, converted semiautomatic weapons to full-auto, fabricated silencers and threaded muzzles to receive them—in short, performed the full range of underworld gunsmithing. As an armorer himself, Bolan admired their enterprise and skill. As a committed enemy of those they served, he was prepared to wipe them off the map.

It sounded like a one-man job, so Hawkins waited in the car and kept the engine running. Bolan wore an Uzi underneath his topcoat, on a swivel sling, and flicked the safety off when he was several paces from the door of the appliance shop. He couldn't read the sign to see if they were closed or open, but he tried the door, found it unlocked and heard a small bell jingle overhead as he stepped through.

A stocky, crew-cut man in his late thirties stared at Bolan from behind a long display case, where assorted new and secondhand appliances had been arranged without much thought to visual appeal. The shop's proprietor spoke gruffly, but his words were lost on Bolan. Rather than attempt to answer him, the Executioner exposed his weapon, muzzle pointed at the Russian's chest.

In retrospect he had to give the fellow points for nerve. Confronted with a submachine gun, he still tried to reach a weapon underneath the register. He shouted something, a threat or a warning, and then his voice was silenced by a burst of parabellum manglers ripping through his chest and throat. The impact hurled him backward, smashing him into shelves with force enough to bring down an avalanche of ancient-looking appliances.

The Executioner kept moving, made his way around the near end of the counter, headed for an open doorway leading to the back, where shuffling sounds told him there was at least one other enemy to deal with. Instinct sent him through the doorway fast and low, a spray of bullets whipping through the empty space above his head.

It wasn't a Kalashnikov; the sound and muzzle-flashes told him that. Perhaps a Skorpion or something similar. In any case it would be big and bad enough to do the job, if Bolan gave the shooter time to find his mark.

But the next second he made target acquisition, and the Uzi stuttered, bullets flying in a zigzag pattern, rising from the floor, stitching the gunner from his ankles to his throat before he toppled over backward.

There seemed to be nobody else around the place, and that was fine with Bolan. Rising to his feet, he took a moment to reload the Uzi, then removed an incendiary grenade from one of his overcoat pockets and dropped the safety pin. Before he let it go, a glance around the workshop showed him racks of military hardware that would easily bring several billion rubles on the street, allowing for the current rate of exchange.

"And now it's garbage," Bolan told the dead man, tossing the grenade. When it went off, the white-hot chemicals would start a fire that water couldn't quench, a blaze that would consume concrete and steel, as well as flesh and bone.

Before that happened, he was on the sidewalk, moving swiftly toward the car. It rolled to meet him, Hawkins braking at the curb while Bolan slid into the shotgun seat. A glance back toward the shop showed eerie, dancing lights inside, intensifying by the moment.

"Looks like another careless smoker," Hawkins said, and put the car in gear.

GROMYLKO'S TARGET on the west side of the city, the Kuntsëvo district, was an automotive shop that handled both mechanical repairs and bodywork. Behind the scenes it doubled as a chop shop for disposal of hot cars, remodeled others so they met the special needs of smugglers or assassins and maintained the private vehicles of ranking members in the Thieves' Society. It was a Chechen operation, owned by Gregori Vasiliev, but the technicians would serve anyone who paid in cash and demonstrated an ability to keep a secret. They were very democratic that way, in the mold of Russia's new regime.

Encizo flipped a coin to see who would remain to watch the car. The Cuban lost and muttered something underneath his breath in Spanish as he slipped his pistol from its shoulder holster, hiding it beneath the newspaper that he had folded in his lap. Gromylko slid out of the car and waited in the street for Calvin James to join him.

It was dark by now, and lights were showing from inside the auto shop, through smallish windows at one end. Gromylko didn't try to hide the folding-stock Kalashnikov he carried, daring anyone who crossed his path to try to stop him from proceeding with his mission of the moment. Calvin James was left to scan the street in each direction, watching out for witnesses, but there was no one visible in this commercial neighborhood, where nearly all the shops had closed down for the day.

They passed the front door by and walked around to the rear, Gromylko leading. At the back door he stepped up close and knocked—three raps, a pause, two more, another pause, then two again. A step back from the door, and he was ready, with his AK-47 leveled from the waist, when it was opened by a porky man in grease-stained coveralls.

Gromylko shot the Chechen gangster three times in the chest and blew him backward, landing with a solid thump against the concrete floor. A heartbeat later Gromylko and James were both inside the auto shop and facing off with three more surly types in oily denim jumpsuits. They were grouped around a Zil sedan, hood raised, and while the wrenches in their hands might qualify as deadly weapons in a brawl, Gromylko was more conscious of the shotgun and four pistols spread out on the workbench several paces to the right.

One of the mob mechanics hurled his wrench at Calvin James as all three broke in the direction of the workbench arsenal. Gromylko tracked them with his AK-47, firing from the hip, while his companion cut loose from a crouch. Twin streams of automatic fire converged on the runners, tearing into them before they reached their guns. Another moment and they lay together on the floor of the garage, bright crimson pooled beneath them, beading on the oily concrete as it spread.

A smell of cordite filled Gromylko's nostrils as he moved among the dead and made sure they were finished. Checking out the car, he saw that they had been engaged in customizing the engine compartment, remodeling its interior to accommodate a fair amount of hidden contraband. Drugs could have filled the twin compartments fashioned there, perhaps handguns or stolen jewelry.

There was a single gasoline pump out in back. James stretched the hose out to its limit, stopping short some ten feet from the open door of the garage, and locked open the trigger on its nozzle, which was lying on the ground and aimed in the direction of the building. Pungent fuel came gushing out and quickly formed a river, some of which spread out along the back wall of the auto shop, while still more made its way inside. The warriors stood and watched it for a moment longer, then Gromylko unclipped an incendiary grenade from his belt, pulled the pin and tossed it through the open doorway with an underhanded pitch.

"Let's go," he said, and they retreated to the car in a hurry. When they got there, flames rushed through the shop and lit the stream of gasoline that led outside. The pump exploded, spewing flames like a volcano as it burned.

"Not bad," Calvin James remarked.

"How do you say it in America?" Gromylko asked,

then answered for himself. "You ain't seen nothing yet."

VASILIEV WAS IN A RAGE. He had been on the telephone almost nonstop for better than three hours now, relaying orders to his soldiers on the street, consulting with subordinates and trying to instill some courage in the weaker individuals, who wanted to evacuate while they were still in shape to travel. He had cowed them for the moment with his threats and promises, but each new word of some disaster from the streets increased the danger that his men would start to panic—worse, that some of them might soon start thinking for themselves.

Not that Vasiliev could blame them when he thought about it. He was on the verge of bailing out himself.

Evacuating Moscow would require a measure of finesse, however, if he didn't wish the other ranking members of the Thieves' Society to scorn him as a coward and unfit to lead. He must give a strong impression that he possessed a plan to trap and crush their enemies, and furthermore, that his departure from the city was a crucial aspect of the plan's success. He must present himself as living bait and make it seem that he was offering himself to those who hunted him, risking his life for the good of the order he served.

Meanwhile his troops in Moscow would be under orders to redouble their efforts, take any steps necessary to find and destroy the men responsible for his embarrassment. Vasiliev didn't really intend to sacrifice himself, any more than he intended to orbit the moon on a broomstick. But appearances were everything, and when his soldiers stopped the enemy in Moscow—*if* they did—the honors would accrue to Gregori Vasiliev.

Meanwhile he would be safe and sound, well out of danger at his dacha in the country. By tomorrow evening it would make no difference if his enemies burned Moscow to the ground. Assuming that his soldiers and the whole *militsiya* couldn't stop them, they would still have no clear shot at Gregori Vasiliev. The Chechen godfather would be long gone.

His change of heart concerning last-ditch stands in Moscow was an evolutionary process. Simply stated, he had watched so many of his soldiers die within the past few days, that he no longer thought himself invincible. The fact of personal mortality was driven home to him each time the phone rang, with another grim report of his subordinates blown up, gunned down, cremated in the string of raids that never seemed to end. Vasiliev, while still concerned about potential loss of face among his fellow mobsters, had begun to rank survival as his first priority.

He would be taking Yuri Renko with him when he left. It was distasteful, but Vasiliev still thought some situation might arise where it would serve him well to have the colonel close by. If nothing else, should the police come knocking on his door with questions, Renko could assure them that he had the matter well in hand. It was a flimsy stall and wouldn't last for long, but if it came to that, Vasiliev wasn't too proud to grasp at straws.

He thought about his brother, murdered in America,

and cursed the day their business had expanded to the States. It was the largest market for the Russian *mafiya* these days, and there had been no way to dodge the risky enterprise, but twenty-twenty hindsight made him wish that he had left the field to others. Not so much because Mikhail was lost to him, as for the danger he was now facing alone.

Throughout his life Vasiliev had taken pride in following his brain instead of acting on crude instinct. It was the difference that had kept him out of prison all these years and made him fabulously rich, while others were convicted, sometimes executed or else weeded out in gang wars, slaughtered by their own. No one had ever managed to intimidate Vasiliev.

Before today.

He told himself that leaving Moscow under fire wasn't the same as running. Wise men chose their battlegrounds and lived to fight another day, while fools rushed in and spilled their blood in clashes that were soon forgotten, wasting energy and lives. So many of his enemies had fallen, men whose balls were larger than their brains, who wouldn't hesitate to kill or be killed on the basis of a passing insult, eager for the smell of blood instead of taking time to think things through and find a way to gain both vengeance and a tidy profit on the side. Vasiliev had seen them come and go, the dinosaurs of crime, and he didn't intend to join them on the list of vanished species.

Not if he could find a way to save himself.

But he wasn't prepared to leave just yet. There were some final preparations to be made, an outside chance that he would catch a break and see his adversaries run to earth before he was required to flee. In that event Vasiliev would be prepared to welcome the congratulations of his colleagues in the Thieves' Society.

But he would still be on his feet and breathing when the smoke cleared, come what may. It was a promise to himself, the only person he could trust in life.

Whatever happened in the next few hours, he intended to survive.

HAWKINS THOUGHT the whorehouse could have passed for a hotel, perhaps a small but stylish convalescent home. Its placement in the upper-middle-class Chimki-Chovrino district was no accident, but rather a concession to the kind of clients who could well afford the services it offered, even in these days of runaway inflation. At that rate, classy whores—or *any* whores, for that matter—were well beyond the budget of the common workingman. You wouldn't get far on the stroll, with smiles and promises in lieu of cash, much less among the silk-and-satin set who plied their trade indoors.

It was traditional for customers to call ahead instead of simply dropping by, but Hawk and Bolan had no time for the niceties. Their schedule was a trifle cramped for setting up appointments...and they didn't speak the language.

To hell with it, Hawk thought as he approached the back door of the house. Sometimes the party crashers had more fun than those with invitations, anyway.

He checked his watch and saw that Bolan should be on the front step now, his finger on the bell. Hawk tried the back door and was pleasantly surprised to feel the knob turn at his touch. It was the kind of break-down in security that seldom preyed on a civilian's mind until it was too late.

He stepped inside and closed the door behind him softly, standing with his AK-47 braced against his hip, one-handed. There was no one to oppose him as he moved along a hallway decorated with erotic paintings that resembled outtakes from the *Kama Sutra,* with a Russian twist. The women tended toward a Ruben-esque ideal, except for the contorted faces, painted to appear as if they couldn't get enough, no matter what bizarre activities they were engaged in at the time.

Hawk smiled. I may not know much about art, he thought, but I know what I like.

He was still smiling when a door ten feet in front of him swung open, and a man stepped out into the hall. The guy wore two-thirds of a three-piece suit, without the jacket, so that Hawk could see his shoulder holster and the shiny autoloader slung beneath his arm. Perhaps two seconds ticked away before the shooter tried to reach it, dying for his trouble as a 3-round burst tore through his chest and slammed him back against the doorjamb, toppling awkwardly across the threshold back into the room behind him.

That tore it. Hawkins started double-timing toward the sound of startled voices, just about the time more gunfire echoed from the street side of the house. That led to women screaming and male voices shouting curses and questions, something Hawkins couldn't even start to understand.

He was on it, rolling, chopping down a gunner who came charging out in front of him from what was probably a bathroom, brandishing a pistol in his right hand, holding up his trousers with the left. He never saw death coming, but took it in the back and went down flopping, on his face.

To hell with chivalry.

The upstairs rooms had emptied by the time Hawk made it to the parlor. Bolan had four women and a couple of their johns lined up against one wall, another handful edging down the stairs, all eyes on his Kalashnikov. Behind him in the foyer lay the bodies of two gunmen who had failed to do their job. Blood soaked into the sky blue carpet, making purple splotches that would never wash away.

They didn't bother asking for a volunteer interpreter. Instead of trying to communicate in spoken language, Bolan stood aside and waved the muzzle of his AK-47 toward the open exit to the street. It took about three seconds for the girls to catch his drift and take off running, while the johns were slower on the uptake, huddling like a group of frightened schoolboys as they scuttled toward the door.

When they were gone, the Executioner turned back to Hawkins. "One more thing. We need a run-through of all the rooms, checking any wardrobes, under beds, any hiding places. Somebody may have crawled away, and we don't want them here for the fireworks."

Hawkins nodded and went off at a run to make a sweep of the place. When he came back to give the all clear, Bolan said, "Okay, let's do it."

Hawkins palmed a thermite canister and primed it, pitched it back in the direction he had come from, moving toward the street as Bolan lobbed a second firebomb toward the second-story landing. Smoke and flames were visible before they reached the curb, but none of those they had evicted from the whorehouse could be seen.

"You know, way we're going," Hawkins said, "someone's gonna be pissed off."

That brought a smile from Bolan, as he answered, "Hold that thought."

THE PRIVATE AIRFIELD on the outskirts of the Nikulino district, in southwestern Moscow, was another property controlled by Gregori Vasiliev. Since communism's fall it was permitted for selected wealthy businessmen to purchase private planes and helicopters, and to travel as they liked, without advance permission from the government. The new regime encouraged spending, capital investment, all the things its predecessors had presumably despised for some three-quarters of a century. Of course, with freedom came new risks, new opportunities to steal and smuggle, none of which was overlooked by Gregori Vasiliev and his blood brothers in the Russian *mafiya*.

It came as no surprise to Calvin James, therefore, when he was told that drugs and other contraband were frequently delivered or dispatched on flights arriving and departing from the Nikulino airfield. While Vasiliev maintained a staff to fake the necessary paperwork and keep the aircraft fit to fly, he also doled out bribes to the inspectors charged with making sure that private pilots carefully observed the letter of the law. For every ruble spent on bribes, he made a thousand back on dirty business operated from the airstrip, so that everyone was happy in the end.

Except for Calvin James and company.

The field was dark when they arrived, no evidence of any guards on duty. That was almost certainly because Vasiliev maintained the airfield through a paper corporation, with a pair of front men listed as proprietors of record. If he had to guess, James would have said the last thing on the Russian mobster's mind would be his adversaries sniffing out the airfield, taking steps to scratch it off the master list of targets they were carrying.

The rub was that he would have been dead wrong.

They left the car and fanned out in the darkness, checked the buildings first to verify that they were all alone. From there it was a short walk to the apron where Vasiliev had two planes parked: an Antonov An-28 fifteen-seat prop plane, and a larger Yakolev Yak-40 jet, with seating for twenty-seven, plus flight crew.

It took five minutes to rig up the Semtex charges on the planes, then they walked back to the office, set the timer on another fist-size charge and wedged it in the mail slot. One more block of plastic explosives for the twin fuel pumps that stood outside the hangar, after they had satisfied themselves that there were no more planes inside, and they were finished. James drove ninety yards before he stopped the car and waited, glancing back and forth between his wristwatch and the darkened airstrip, waiting for the fireworks to begin.

The timers had been set to blow in unison, and they

were right on time. Both planes, the office and the fuel pumps went together, fireballs leaping skyward in the night, while James grimaced, squinting at the sudden flare of brilliant light. The shock wave reached them next; it felt as if a giant hand had slapped the car just hard enough to capture their attention, without breaking anything. In seconds flat the smoke from burning oil and gasoline obscured the airstrip, blocking the view of the destruction they had caused.

"Not bad," James said. "Our boy has any travel plans, he'll have to wait in line for tickets, just like everybody else."

"He won't be flying where he needs to go," Gromylko declared.

"You've got it figured out already, then?"

The Russian smiled at James, his face pale in the dashboard light, and said, "I would not be surprised."

CHAPTER NINETEEN

The Ostankino smoking parlor, north of downtown Moscow, was the kind of dive where those enslaved by drugs gathered to do more ruin to their bodies. Depending on their choice of poisons—and the cash they managed to scrounge up or collect by begging, strong-arm robbery or fencing stolen goods—they could procure *anasha, mak* or *khimka* on the premises and smoke it to their hearts' content—or until their cash ran out. At that point they were on the street and on their own.

Police were paid to look the other way with regard to smoking parlors, as with so much else that happened in the new Russia. On occasion, when a raid was called for to promote some candidate's political campaign, a call from headquarters would warn the principals involved and give them time to clear the premises before police arrived. If some of their befuddled customers were carted off to jail, it made a dandy photo opportunity for the politicians.

There would be no warning call tonight, but Bolan felt quite certain that the clients in the place would have no interest in standing in his way. Their main concern would be to get away, and not have their escape to narco-heaven disrupted.

He went in through the front, an Uzi flat against his thigh until he cleared the threshold and the first strongman tried to stop him. Igor X was puffing out his chest and swaggering until he saw the submachine gun, then he made the worst choice of his miserable life and tried to reach a pistol holstered underneath his jacket. Bolan shot him in the heart, three parabellum rounds that painted abstract patterns on the wall.

The Uzi wasn't silenced, and there was no time to waste as Bolan moved on past the corpse in search of other targets. It was smoky in the main room of the building, but the real stench came from smaller rooms that opened off the large central chamber. There, he knew, the users would be segregated by their drug of choice, as many as a dozen in a room, to smoke their brains out—literally—while a team of Chechen thugs stood guard.

A couple of the heavies were advancing on him now, both drawing pistols as they lumbered into view. They must have heard the gunfire, but they didn't know quite what to make of it until they glimpsed the Executioner and realized their buddy on the door was history.

They broke in opposite directions. They were heavy on their feet, but quick enough to make it challenging. The one on Bolan's right was a greater threat, since he was aiming as he ran.

Bolan squeezed off another short burst from his Uzi, and he saw the gunman stagger, clutching at his stomach with his free hand, while he wasted two pathetic shots. Momentum and the pull of gravity took over, brought him down, and Bolan swiveled to confront the second gunner, dropping into a defensive crouch.

The Chechen's first shot sailed a foot above his head and struck the wall somewhere behind him. Number two was closer, but not close enough. The Uzi had a target fix by then, and it was hammering a stream of manglers into flesh and bone. The shooter reeled, then sprawled over backward in a lifeless heap.

A glance back toward the other gunman showed that he was still alive, if not exactly kicking. Down on hands and knees, blood streaming from the belly wounds that would eventually kill him, he was reaching for the pistol he had lost, his face a twisted study in determination. Bolan didn't feel like risking it, and so he stroked the submachine gun's trigger lightly, dropped the wounded shooter on the blood-slick floor.

A number of the parlor's clients had emerged from different rooms, all checking out the action, most of them recoiling from the sight and smell of death. But a handful hung in there, trying hard to stare the warrior down with bleary eyes. One of them found the nerve to come at Bolan from the left, a shiny cutthroat razor flashing in his hand as he advanced with lurching steps.

It would have been no trick to kill him where he stood, but Bolan exercised restraint. He ducked the first swing of the razor, hooked the Uzi's muzzle in below his adversary's ribs and heard the smoky breath explode from heaving lungs. Before the junkie could collapse, the Uzi whipped around and met his teeth on the upswing, with force enough to flip him over on his back, out cold.

It was enough to make the others do a rapid fade, back into smoke and shadows. Bolan had considered burning out the place, but now he thought there were enough burn-outs already on the scene, he left a military smoke grenade behind to flush them out of hiding once he'd gone, and put the place behind him, walking swiftly back to Hawkins and the waiting car.

"Smells like you found the party," Hawk remarked when they had covered half a block.

"It wasn't that much fun," said Bolan, staring out his window at the Russian night. "No snacks, no band."

"You take a chance on that shit when you're not invited."

"You ever think of doing comedy?" he asked the newest member of the Phoenix team.

"I might, at that," said Hawkins. "I'm a stand-up kinda guy."

THE STAUNCHLY middle-class Z'uzino district lies due south of downtown Moscow, a preserve of clerks and secretaries, public servants who will never head their own departments, but who keep the wheels in motion, even when it seems sometimes that Russian government must shudder to a halt. Z'uzino's kind of crime isn't the sort that leaves fresh bodies in the gutter every morning or places hookers on the corners of its residential streets, but there are always drugs around, as well as out-call services that deliver playmates of the gender specified to those with means to pay.

Z'uzino's four-year-old athletic club wasn't a place where local residents spent any time. In fact, it was a private operation, membership by invitation only, and as luck would have it, all the members were associated with the Chechen *mafiya*. Not thugs and bruisers, but the rough equivalent of middle management, who went about their business every day and kept a sharp eye on the men above them, waiting for a slipup that would make room on the next rung of the ladder. Dog eat dog.

In normal times the mobsters hung around the club to let their hair down and relax, work out with weights or take a swim, steam off a few pounds in the sauna. On a night like *this*—and they were rare these days— the club became a staging area, where phone calls were received and orders issued, teams dispatched to meet the latest threat or chase a lead on the elusive enemy.

There had been no real leads to speak of, though, since the attacks began in Moscow, and the club was operating with a skeleton crew when Rafael Encizo let himself in through the back door at 12:15 a.m. A pungent odor of cigar smoke helped him navigate along unlighted corridors until a spill of pale fluorescent lighting brought him to an office. The presence of several voices told him there were two or three men in the room, at least. Encizo held his AK-47 ready as he stepped up to the open door.

James and Gromylko would be waiting for him on the street out front to deal with any who got past him and escaped in that direction. Encizo didn't intend to give them any, but you never knew how something might play out once you were in the middle of the game. It wasn't as if they had a hard, fast rule of play, with everyone on both sides willing to abide by certain rules. Once the manure hit the fan, there was no telling which way it would blow.

He stepped into the office doorway, counting three gunners at a desk, all sitting down, two of them smoking, while the third used a penknife to clean underneath his fingernails. Encizo cleared his throat to capture their attention, giving them a chance to see death coming, even if they had no time to save themselves.

At that, one of the smokers kicked back in his chair, hand groping for a pistol on his belt, while his companions ducked for cover. Half a dozen rounds from the Cuban's Kalashnikov ripped through the smoking shooter's chest, his body slamming to the floor, still seated in his metal folding chair.

The others had nowhere to hide, but they were trying. Mr. Clean was desperate enough to fling his penknife at Encizo, but it flew on past him, out the door, and rattled in the hallway. Three rounds from the AK-47 hurled him against a watercooler in the corner, the spill of water helping to wash his blood away.

And that left one.

The guy behind the desk was on his knees and fumbling in the top drawer, looking for a weapon, when Encizo walked around to face him. He started babbling, then raised both hands as if he wanted to surrender on the spot.

"Too late," Encizo said, and flattened him with three rounds to the chest.

He was retreating from the office when a bullet

struck the wall six inches from his face. Encizo hit a fighting crouch and spun in the direction of the pistol shot. A naked fat man was standing in the middle of the hallway, dripping sweat, a shiny automatic wobbling in his left hand, while the right secured a terry towel around his waist.

Encizo didn't know if he was coming from the sauna or the swimming pool, nor did he care. The AK-47 stuttered as he found his target, stitching bloody vents across the mobster's bloated stomach, up across his chest, the last two rounds exploding in his face. The impact swept him off his feet and dropped him on his backside with a heavy thud.

Encizo took another moment checking out the place and making sure he was alone, then placed his Semtex charges, set the times, made his exit through the front door of the club. The car was waiting when he got there, James at the wheel, Gromylko in the shotgun seat.

"All clear. Let's roll," Encizo said.

VASILIEV WAS TROUBLED. He couldn't help but think that he was running out of luck. Until his brother's death, he would have said his life was charmed; at least it *had* been from the time he took control of it and climbed up from the gutter to command respect from those who made a business of devouring the weak and helpless. He wasn't a man to trifle with, by any means, but in the past two weeks his whole life had turned upside down. He wondered if his brother's death had been an omen of disaster for himself, as well.

Vasiliev knew nothing of religion. He had grown up under communism, educated by the state and on the streets, and while he was not a committed atheist, he had seen little to persuade him that a loving, caring deity had anything to do with men's affairs. If people did not live and die by chance, they had their wits to thank for anything they gained along the way. Strong men with brains inevitably prospered if they kept their guard up and didn't allow themselves to be cut down by cunning peasants.

Even without the prospect of reward and retribution in an afterlife, Vasiliev was forced to wonder if his late misfortunes might betray the hand of fate. Some of his cronies in the Thieves' Society were superstitious to the point that they would kill a black cat rather than allow the creature to cross their paths. They made a fetish of avoiding certain numbers, colors, anything at all they perceived to be bad luck. Vasiliev had spent a lifetime laughing at their peasant foolishness, but now he had to wonder if there might not be another guiding hand at work behind the scenes.

But then, he scoffed, if God was truly in His heaven, how could he allow the *mafiya* to flourish or create such crops as opium, cocaine and hashish for the drones to use and syndicates to sell?

Still, even lacking God, that did not rule out... something else. Some force that could decide, from time to time, to meddle in affairs of men and shift the balance just enough to topple empires, while the peasants had their day.

Vasiliev was tired of thinking. It was time for him to act, and all that he could think of at the moment was evacuation from the city that had turned into a smoking battleground. He hadn't been alive when German troops laid siege to Moscow during World War II, but he imagined that the residents must have felt similar to how he felt, this night. His dreams were going up in smoke around him, and cold logic told him he would die, if he didn't escape without delay.

Taking Yuri Renko with him was a mild annoyance, but Vasiliev would find a way around that problem when he did not need the colonel any longer. And the more he thought about it now, the more he told himself that Renko had no right to simply disappear, run off and live his life as if he were a normal man. He would be dangerous to Gregori Vasiliev and every other member of the Thieves' Society as long as he survived. Such risks were better dealt with swiftly and decisively rather than allowing them to linger, preying on the mind until something went wrong.

That settled, the godfather finished packing for his trip. He wouldn't carry luggage—that would be beneath him—but he always packed it for himself, without relying on his servants. No one else knew what he wanted on a trip; they would be guessing, drawing on their own preferences instead of his, and that was unacceptable.

He might be running, but Vasiliev would run in style. The limousine was parked downstairs, his soldiers waiting in the hall outside his suite, with more around the car. Another vehicle was on its way to fetch the colonel from his temporary hideout. No one knew where Renko was except Vasiliev, and if the enemy should find him somehow...well, he would have to let nature take its course.

The main thing now was getting out of town as rapidly as possible. His dacha was secure, more readily defended than the Moscow penthouse, safe from interference by authorities if he was called upon to fight. It wouldn't come to that, he told himself, but it was better to be safe than sorry. When he finished packing, in a few more moments, he would be away from Moscow, and his enemies could chase their tails forever—or until their luck ran out and they were killed by Chechen gunmen or police.

In either case they would be dead.

And Gregori Vasiliev would still be king.

He felt it in his bones.

PERVERSION NEVER SLEEPS. It plots and schemes around the clock, observes no holidays, takes no vacations. It is ravenous, insatiable. It cannot rest.

The house in Kuz'mink, east of central Moscow, had been renovated by the latest occupants, but they were less concerned with style than with security. Soundproofing had been added, double thick to guarantee the necessary privacy, and good-size trees had been trucked in and transplanted for the extra shelter they provided on the grounds. The neighbors were impressed at so much money being spent, at least in part to beautify their neighborhood, that few remarked on how the house had seemed to disappear, no longer visible to those who lived on either side of it, a bare glimpse possible from straight across the street or driving by.

The tenants needed privacy, in fact; their trade demanded it. If anyone in the exclusive neighborhood had seen through their facade, revulsion would have been immediately followed by a call to the *militsiya,* and someone would have gone to jail, regardless of the bribes that had been spread around downtown.

For there were children's lives at stake.

The tenants were no pedophiles themselves, but they were plugged into the network of "child lovers" and abusers—sometimes killers—who would pay hard currency to anyone who made their sick, perverted fantasies come true. Most of the customers were men—and women, too, a small but growing number— who could pass you on the street without a second glance, unless you were impressed by their apparent wealth, the cultivated air of high society that clung to them like the aroma of a sweet perfume. Their crimes against humanity were no more obvious, during a face-to-face encounter, than a virus coursing through their blood.

It had the same effect, though. They were incurable because they did not *want* a cure, immune to psychiatric treatment, threats of punishment—the whole nine yards.

McCarter knew the type, and he despised them even more than terrorists. With a religious or political fanatic, you could always tell yourself the bomber or the triggerman believed that he was doing good for someone—members of his race, religion, ethnic group, whatever. With the scum who preyed on children, though, it was a twisted sex-and-power trip, their brains wired so that nothing mattered but their own needs and desires. If someone else should suffer while they had their fun, so much the better.

He was looking forward to this strike with grim anticipation. Any adults in the house were guilty, simply by the fact of being there. He did not have to check ID or wait for someone to produce a gun.

No prisoners.

Gromylko had assisted with a phone call to arrange McCarter's "date," though he would not be with them on the raid. The language barrier meant nothing to McCarter as he rang the doorbell, hoping Gary Manning had had time to make his way around in back. Whatever, it was time to roll. He couldn't wait a moment longer.

Bigfoot's cousin opened up the door, huge body stuffed into a suit that seemed about to rip along the seams, his brute face frowning at McCarter. The expression changed immediately when McCarter shot him in the groin, his trousers smoking from the AK-47's point-black muzzle blast. The hulk lurched backward, gasping as he fought to keep his balance, but a second round zipped through one nostril, and the whole top of his head came off.

"Don't bother to announce me," McCarter said as he stepped across the corpse and made his way inside.

Another man was moving toward him, shoulder holster over shirtsleeves, reaching for the pistol as he came. McCarter shot him in the chest with the Kalashnikov, three rounds in semiauto mode, conserving ammunition, moving on without a moment's hesitation as the shooter sprawled out on the floor.

It would have been a beautiful two-story house, except for what went on inside. McCarter couldn't hear the children, and suspected they couldn't hear him: each room was soundproofed individually, with the convenience of the customer in mind. McCarter reckoned he could fire off ten or fifteen magazines downstairs and never wake the prisoners who slept upstairs.

There was a panic button, though, installed to give the customers and staff alike some kind of edge if they were raided. One of his intended targets had a fat thumb on the button, poised to mash it, when McCarter stepped in front of him, the AK-47 pointed at his chest.

"Please do," McCarter said.

The Russian looked at him uncertainly, the pistol in his hand still pointed at the floor between his shoes. He didn't press the button, but his hand remained in place. At last McCarter nodded to him, cocked his head in the direction of the button, using pantomime as if he were attempting to communicate with a baboon. Except, he thought, that would have been a grievous insult to baboons.

The gunman blinked once more and pressed the button. No alarm was audible downstairs, but they would hear it in the rooms above, and that was all that mattered. Two rounds from McCarter's AK-47 punched his target over backward, dead before he hit the floor, the pistol still unfired as lifeless fingers lost their grip and let it fall.

McCarter waited by the stairs, where he could also keep watch on the hallway to his left. A sound of automatic-weapons fire from that direction told him Manning had flushed out more enemies. It was another

AK firing, but they were too common in Russia for the sound to mean anything by itself. He would still have to keep his eyes open, watch his back.

Meanwhile the parade had started, three men rushing down the stairs in various states of undress, clutching shirts, slacks, jackets, shoes, all stopping short as they beheld death waiting for them, standing with an automatic rifle in his hands.

McCarter couldn't think of anything to say, nor would the slimy bastards understand him if he spoke. Instead of trying to communicate, he simply shot them where they stood, not caring whether they were businessmen or clergy, young or old, intimidated or defiant. When they tumbled down to join him, they left crimson blotches on the wall. Their blood all looked the same, and he wouldn't have touched it with a ten-foot pole.

A sound behind him made McCarter turn, relaxing at the sight of Gary Manning. "What about the kids?" his fellow warrior asked.

"Upstairs," McCarter said.

He took a piece of paper from his pocket and unfolded it as he was walking to the telephone. There was a number written down, with several sentences in English characters, the Russian words and phrases sounded out phonetically. McCarter dialed the number, waited for an officer to answer and began to read. He took his time, ignoring interruptions, then hung up and left the note beside the telephone.

"We're finished here," McCarter said, and almost felt that he were talking to himself.

GROMYLKO RESERVED one of the fattest targets for himself. Not literally, of course—the man was tall and lean, far from obese, but his authority within the Chechen *mafiya* was second only to the power held by Gregori Vasiliev himself. He was Gennadiy Zanilov, a longtime pimp, narcotics dealer and "suspected" murderer who doubtless had mixed feelings when it came to the events in Moscow. He wouldn't be pleased about the carnage suffered by the family, but at the same time part of him was bound to look ahead, imagining his own promotion to the role of godfather if something fatal happened to Vasiliev. He was the next in line to rule the roost...assuming he was still alive.

The Sokol'niki district, in northeastern Moscow, was another privileged enclave, once a neighborhood of ranking Communist Party members, now the home of up-and-coming businessmen, since communism's unexpected fall. Bank balances were more important than credentials, though the neighborhood was not entirely blind to class. Gennadiy Zanilov was known as an investment banker to his neighbors, always smiling when they chanced to meet in public, never taking time to mingle with them socially. He was a busy man, they understood, and dedicated to the hot pursuit of material wealth.

But at the moment Zanilov was more concerned with living through the night than rolling up a fortune. Dead men had no use for money, after all.

A phone call flushed the target out from under cover. Leonid Gromylko didn't give his name, but simply told the man who answered that his boss was marked to die. Gunmen were on the way, and if the Chechen doubted him, he read off the address to prove his point. The target had no way of knowing that the call came from a mobile telephone, or that Gromylko and his two companions were already waiting on the street outside his home.

Zanilov sent two men out in front of him, one to start the car while the other stood guard in the shadows, posing with a Skorpion machine pistol behind his back. Gromylko watched and waited, peering through the sights of his Kalashnikov, wedged in the stout fork of a tree across the street. It was uncomfortable, but he didn't care, as long as he could make the shot. His two companions had the flanks, one stationed half a block in each direction, to prevent the mark from slipping past in case Gromylko missed.

In case he died.

The car was running now. Its driver stayed behind the wheel and sent the gunner back to fetch their boss, along with any other soldiers who were waiting in the house. A moment later the lieutenant saw his man emerging, two men leading him, while two more followed on his heels, one pausing long enough to lock the door behind them. That made six guns altogether, but Gromylko concentrated on the one man he had come to kill, whatever else might happen there tonight.

He framed Zanilov directly in his sights and followed the tall man along the concrete walk that led his party to the waiting car. When they had covered half the distance from the front door to the vehicle, Gromylko fired a long burst from his rifle, saw the gangster lurch and stagger as a stream of bullets ripped into his shoulder, neck and face. One of the soldiers close behind him soaked up three rounds for himself, and then the rest of them were firing, sighting on the muzzle-flashes from Gromylko's AK-47.

Bullets struck the tree trunk, inches from his face, and ripped the leaves apart on either side of him. He felt his balance going, toppled over backward from his perch and saw the ground rush up to meet him as he fell. Gromylko clutched his weapon, twisting in midair to land feetfirst, and still the shock of impact drove him to all fours. The stout tree stood between him and his enemies, but they were rushing toward him now. Gromylko knew he didn't have a prayer of dropping them all before they got at least one lucky shot and brought him down.

He struggled to his feet regardless, grimacing as pain lanced through one ankle. He was turning toward the enemy when his American partners opened fire from either side, their bullets slicing through the Chechen gunmen, breaking up their charge and leaving bodies scattered in the street like so much overripe fruit.

Moving in to check on him, the black man told Gromylko, "Hey, I didn't know you were an acrobat."

"Neither did I," Gromylko said.

"You're limping. Can you make it?"

"*Da.* I won't be stopped that easily."

"Okay, your call. Right now I think we'd better split."

"By all means," Gromylko agreed. "We have work to do."

BOLAN CONSIDERED that it would seem a waste of time to trash the downtown office where Vasiliev did business with the world at large. The place was obviously shut down and deserted in the predawn hours, and whatever paperwork a fire might manage to destroy, the chances were that Gregori Vasiliev would have it all backed up on a computer somewhere else.

But he was going in, regardless. It was something Bolan felt he had to do, a gesture to the Chechen godfather, to tell Vasiliev in no uncertain terms that nothing he possessed, no private sanctum, was secure against the grim, implacable opponents who were stalking him.

Two uniforms were posted in the lobby, the equivalent of rent-a-cops in the United States, with pistols on their hips but no great urge to use them in their hearts. They gave up quickly when the Executioner and Hawkins showed their weapons, and another moment saw them handcuffed, lying on the floor, their radio disabled and the telephone unplugged. Hawk watched the lobby, just in case, while Bolan rode the elevator up to nine and made his way to Vasiliev's public office.

The door was glass, and there was no alarm tape showing, since they posted guards downstairs at closing time. Two rounds from Bolan's AK-47 blew the lock apart, and he was well inside the office in a heartbeat, checking out the place. The OD canvas satchel slung across his shoulder held four Semtex charges, two pounds each, with detonators you could set so that a silent signal flashed from one would blow the others all at once.

The marvels of technology.

He placed one charge atop the spacious desk where a receptionist would normally be seated, greeting any visitors. The door was locked, and Bolan used another round from the Kalashnikov to open it, intruding on the space where Gregori Vasiliev spent six or seven hours on an average business day. One charge could easily have done the job, but Bolan used all three— one underneath the desk, one in the private bathroom, one wedged in between two heavy filing cabinets. There would be no repairing this place once the smoke cleared, and he didn't care much what the impact on adjoining offices might be, since Vasiliev owned the whole building.

On his way out through the outer office, Bolan paused to set the detonator that would spark the others, giving himself enough time to get back downstairs before it blew. His plans did not include a long night stranded in an elevator if he could avoid it. Hawk was waiting for him in the lobby, talking to the rent-a-cops as if they had a clue what he was saying, telling them a joke about a horse who tries to order whiskey in a bar.

"And the bartender says, 'Why the long face?'"

"You finished?" Bolan asked him.

"Just about. These guys have trouble with the punch lines."

"Maybe it's a problem with delivery," Bolan said.

Hawk looked stricken, tugging an imaginary necktie into place as he fell into step with Bolan. "See," the young man complained, "I don't get no respect."

CHAPTER TWENTY

The dacha forty miles northwest of Moscow was designed for pleasure, but it served as well in war. The house was isolated from its neighbors—no one else within two miles—and since the spacious grounds were wooded, it could not be seen by passersby. There was a metal gate across the entrance to the driveway, guarded at all times, so that attackers would be forced to either crash the barricade or reach the house on foot by crossing several hundred yards of rugged ground.

And still Vasiliev felt unsafe. He *did* feel better than he had in Moscow, more secure, but all security was relative. If there were men out there who hated him enough to throw their lives away, just for the sake of killing him, then he would not be safe on board a submarine beneath the polar ice cap. There is always some way to reach out and kill another human being.

Always.

Vasiliev was glad that Yuri Renko had retired immediately after supper, leaving him alone. Their drive from Moscow, in the predawn hours, had been tiring in itself; then came the daylight hours while they sat around and waited for the other shoe to drop. Reports from Moscow told him that Gennadiy Zanilov was dead, and also that the violence had ceased, from all appearances. Police were still investigating, but there had been no more raids since dawn.

What did it mean? The press reported nothing on the capture of the terrorists, and when Vasiliev reached out for his lieutenants who were still alive in Moscow, none of them had any word of casualties on the other side. Of course, there was an outside possibility his enemies had suffered losses that prevented them from pressing the attack, somehow contrived to take their dead and wounded with them when they fled, but he wasn't inclined to think so.

They were on the move, but what did *that* mean? Were they tracking him or pulling back? The tension brought his throbbing headache back to life with a vengeance, making his skull feel as if it would burst. He would allow the pills a few more minutes to kick in before he went to have a soak in the Jacuzzi, but he wasn't sure that anything would help—except perhaps the personal extermination of his enemies.

Assuming they had given up and he was in the clear, Vasiliev knew it was still too early to assess his damages, in terms of his standing with his fellow bosses in the Thieves' Society. If it was over, even though he lived, Vasiliev would doubtless be perceived as someone who had failed to solve a major problem, losing men and merchandise on every side, while total strangers taunted him at will. The damage to his reputation might well be irreparable, but he would have to wait and see.

One thing was certain: he would need more soldiers in the days and weeks ahead. If any of his *mafiya* associates should feel like muscling in on him while he was still recovering from the attacks in Moscow and abroad, Vasiliev would need to be prepared. Half-hearted measures would not do. If challenged, he would have to go all out, respond with savage force and thereby demonstrate that he was still in firm control.

But not tonight.

He would consider all those problems in the morning, when he had survived another night. Right now his mind was still on those who might be hunting him across the darkened countryside.

How could they know where he had gone? The dacha was no secret, in the sense that many of his soldiers knew about it, as did other members of the Thieves' Society and almost certainly some officers of the *militsiya*. He hadn't used a front to make the purchase, but he kept the house swept clean of bugs and wiretaps, with technicians checking twice a week when he wasn't in residence and three times a day when he was on the property. It may have been excessive, but he took no chances. Paranoia served him well as a security device.

Vasiliev topped off his glass of vodka, thinking of the forty soldiers he had stationed in the house and on the grounds, all armed and linked by two-way radios. He wouldn't say it was impossible for an outsider to surprise him there, but it would be damn difficult.

He willed himself to finally relax. From all appearances the storm had passed him by. Survival did not equal winning, but it was the most important thing, and he couldn't be rightly labeled as a loser if his enemies gave up and ran away.

A few more peaceful hours, Gregori Vasiliev decided, and he would declare a victory, perhaps make up some tale of wiping out his adversaries in a secret ambush, cleaning up the evidence to hide it from police. Who could dispute him if the raids didn't resume?

Besides, he told himself, the Russians had a long tradition of rewriting history.

THE DAYLIGHT HOURS seemed to last forever. Bolan and his friends deliberately abstained from a new round of attacks, but finally the sun went down, and they were on their way. Gromylko marked their maps ahead of time and navigated from the lead car, Hawkins driving, Bolan seated in the back with Calvin James. McCarter, Manning and Encizo had the second car, their military hardware evenly split up between the two. Three-quarters of an hour after leaving Moscow, they were on the site and cruising with their lights off, looking for a place to hide the cars.

A narrow access road that wandered through the forest offered adequate concealment from the highway, and they found a turn-out where the cars would not obstruct whatever traffic came along. Gromylko put *Militsiya* stickers on the dashboard of each vehicle and hoped that any farmers passing by would show respect instead of venting peasant anger and defiance in a fit of vandalism. Either way it was the best that he could do.

They suited up in camouflage fatigues, strapped on their gear and primed their weapons, hiking eastward, using Bolan's compass as a guide. Another twenty minutes, and there could be little doubt that they were trespassing on Gregori Vasiliev's retreat. A final quarter of an hour, and they saw the house, ablaze with lights, cars in the driveway, gunmen on patrol around the grounds.

Each man was detailed to command an arc of the perimeter, like wedges on a pie chart, so that they would have the house surrounded. They agreed that fifteen minutes should be adequate for all of them to take up their positions and be ready when the signal came for their attack. The three men packing RPGs— James, Hawkins and McCarter—would initiate the strike at 2230 hours.

It all came down to this, thought Bolan as he crouched in shadows, waiting for the first wave of triangulated rocket fire. It was a long way from New York to Turkey, farther yet to Moscow and beyond. How many men had died since he stood waiting in another darkened forest, waiting for the proper time to strike? How much blood had been spilled in the pursuit of justice?

Not enough.

The dragon was alive, inside his lair, but Bolan still had one more chance to bring him down. The odds were with his enemy, but that wasn't unusual; in fact, it was routine. The Executioner did not fear the numbers, though he would respect them, take nothing for granted as he moved into the killing ground.

Bolan checked his watch again, glanced back in the direction of the house and braced himself. There had been no gunfire so far to indicate that any members of his team had been discovered by the enemy. If they were in their places, the attack should be beginning...*now!*

Three rockets blazed through the darkness, sizzling toward the house and leaving trails of fire. He saw them detonate and waited for the shock waves of their thunderclaps to reach him, watching as the Russian sentries started to react downrange. They had no targets yet, only a vague idea of where the missiles came from, but a few of them were firing anyway, off toward the tree line.

Bolan waited for the next barrage to make his move. Before the RPG rounds reached their target, he was on his feet and breaking toward the house. A hundred yards or so to Bolan's right, another running figure left the shadows, Gary Manning holding up his end.

The sentries hadn't seen them yet, no doubt preoccupied with two more rockets as they slammed into the house, a third round taking one of the cars parked in the driveway. It wouldn't be long, though, until someone saw the infantry advancing and responded with defensive fire.

As if in answer to Bolan's thoughts, one of the Chechen gunners pointed toward Manning, shouted something to his fellows and began unloading with a submachine gun, firing from the hip. The range was long for pistol ammunition, and a trick of lighting had betrayed the shooter, showing him a distant target in the flare of an explosion, while the Executioner moved closer, unobserved.

Before the nearest gunmen could find their mark, Bolan unleashed a burst from his Kalashnikov. His bullets dropped the shooter with the SMG and startled two of his companions into losing track of Gary Manning as they turned back to face the nearer threat. They both had automatic weapons, and while Bolan was within their range, they were too shaken at the moment to respond effectively. He cut them down while they stood gawking at him, and swept past their huddled corpses toward the house.

THE DACHA WAS BURNING. When he stuck his head outside the bedroom where he had been quartered, Yuri Renko smelled the smoke and heard men shouting as they tried to stop the fire from spreading.

Clearly it was time for him to cut and run.

He had been dozing, groggy from fatigue and too much vodka, when the first set of explosions rocked the house, but he was wide-awake and stone-cold sober now. In all of his experience, there was nothing like the close proximity of violent death to cut through mental haze and bring the faculties to full alert.

The colonel fumbled with his trousers, finally got them on and stuffed bare feet into his boots. The leather would leave blisters on his heels, but he didn't have time to hunt around the unfamiliar room and find where he had tossed his socks when he stripped for bed. The Makarov was more important at the moment, and he found it instantly, still waiting for him on the nightstand, with the safety off.

Where could he go? It hardly seemed to matter now. Step one would be for him to find a way out of the house and off the property, out of harm's way. Beyond that he would trust himself to find the nearest town, obtain some form of transportation, even if he had to steal a car at gunpoint to escape. The niceties of law and order were the last thing on his mind right now.

The colonel shrugged his jacket on—no point in freezing when he got outside—and checked the corridor outside his room again. One of Vasiliev's hired guns ran past, some fifty feet away, without a glance at Renko. He was carrying a fire extinguisher in one hand and an AK-47 in the other, cursing as he passed.

And there would never be a better time to slip away.

Renko closed the door behind him, softly, as if frightened that he might awaken some imaginary roommate. Renko guessed that no one would come looking for him, but he didn't wish to telegraph the fact that he was gone. It would be difficult, perhaps, to dodge the gunmen who were stationed all over the grounds, but they were smart enough to know that he wasn't the enemy.

He hoped so, anyway.

The hall ran north and south, with most of the commotion emanating from the southern end, toward the front of the house. Renko turned north, to his left, and moved along the corridor with hurried strides. No time to waste. He felt it running out.

Ideally he would try to find a car outside with keys in the ignition. Failing that, he was prepared to walk all night, if necessary, until he could find the highway, pick a safe direction and proceed to the next house or town. His overcoat would hide the Makarov if he had to knock on any doors. And once he was inside, the colonel could decide if pulling rank or pulling guns seemed like the way to go.

One of Vasiliev's people came around the corner up ahead, and slowed down to a rapid walk as he approached the colonel. He stared hard at Renko for a moment, but the man had other problems on his mind, and kept going, passing by with a silent nod of acknowledgment.

Renko was just about to congratulate himself on clearing one small hurdle when another explosion rocked the house. Grenades? It felt more powerful than that, but Renko drew a momentary blank on weapons nomenclature.

The key right now was to avoid involvement with the enemy, no matter what hardware the bastards might be carrying. Renko was not a front-line soldier anymore. Rank had its privileges, and one of those was to avoid the trenches, where a man could get his ass shot off for almost anything at all. Renko told himself that he hadn't entirely lost the killer instinct of his youth, so finely honed when he was in the military, but he had his doubts. It had been years—hell, decades—since he fired a shot in anger. The mechanics were familiar to him, as was the feeling in his gut, but any skill needs practice to ensure proficiency.

But he would do his best. There was no other choice, no one he could rely on to assist him in this hour of need. He couldn't trust Vasiliev to help him, knowing that the mobster only cared about himself, his interests. That was understandable, of course, since Renko felt the same. And at the moment Yuri Renko's interest was in living through the night.

He reached an exit without meeting any more of Vasiliev's soldiers and hesitated for a moment with one hand on the knob, the other clutching his weapon. Finally the smell of smoke made up his mind, and Renko stepped outside. There was nowhere to go but forward, in the darkness, whether it should lead to life or death.

MCCARTER'S FINAL ROCKET stood a limousine on end and dropped it back into a roiling lake of fire. He saw a sentry running, trailing flames and flapping arms that suddenly resembled bright orange wings. The runner's comrades ducked and sidestepped, dodging, leaving him to burn.

McCarter dropped his empty RPG and picked up the Kalashnikov. A couple of Vasiliev's defenders had him spotted, tracking the muzzle-flashes, and he watched them moving closer, squeezing off short bursts at random as they came. They didn't have a perfect fix, but knew where he had crouched a moment earlier, when he unleashed his last round from the rocket launcher, and they hosed the tree line down for ten or fifteen feet on either side.

Unfortunately for the shooters, their intended prey

had faded ten yards or so to the left, and he already had them covered as they closed the gap. McCarter's first rounds took the nearer gunman, ripped the AK-47 from his hands and swept him off his feet before the pull of gravity took over and he went down in a boneless sprawl.

The other watchdog saw his comrade die and tried to rethink his attack, but there was no time left. McCarter's weapon rattled off another burst and dropped the shooter where he stood, his last rounds churning sod around his feet as he collapsed.

McCarter left the trees and started moving toward the burning line of cars where he had spent his last two rockets, touching off a veritable bonfire of the vanities. He knew about conspicuous consumption—rich folks showing off their wealth with cars that cost the same as houses, watches worth enough to feed a peasant family for life—and he would never tire of putting such men in their place by blowing up their toys.

McCarter wasn't opposed to wealth per se, but rather to the means some persons used to fatten up their bank accounts. No moralist as such, he still knew where to draw the line between aggressive businessmen and predators in human form.

Another of Vasiliev's defenders was advancing from McCarter's left, the firelight casting a gigantic shadow out in front of him. He was a small man, but size in this case would be measured by the semiauto shotgun that he carried, squeezing off his first shot in a rush, before he came within effective range.

One of the pellets stung McCarter, drew blood where it had creased his thigh through the fatigues. If his assailant had been any closer, he would probably have scored a torso hit or two, with potentially fatal results. It was time to shut the gunner down, before his aim or luck improved.

McCarter framed the runner in his rifle sights and stroked the AK-47's trigger, rattling off a 6-round burst that caught his target lining up another shot. The Russian looked surprised as bullets tore into his rib cage, punched him backward several paces, dumping him like so much dirty laundry on the grass.

Several of Vasiliev's hired goons were trying hard to save the cars. Of six vehicles lined up nose to tail, two were not burning yet, and drivers were attempting to extract them from the spreading lake of fire. Three other men were running up and down the line of cars with fire extinguishers, as if they had a prayer of salvaging the twisted wreckage left by rocket blasts.

McCarter veered in that direction, bent on finishing what he had started with his RPG. One of the more or less undamaged cars was almost out of line now, scraping past the bumper of the smoking hulk in front of it, the driver craning forward for a better view. McCarter shot him through the tinted windshield, saw his head snap back and heard the engine as his lifeless foot jammed down on the accelerator. With a grating sound the car leaped free and started off across the lawn, tires scoring turf, until it met a tree and jolted to a halt, the engine stalling out.

The second driver, still focused on the task of salvaging his vehicle, was oblivious to his companion's plight. McCarter had already closed the gap to forty feet, and knew the foot soldiers had spotted him, but still he concentrated on the wheelman, lining up his shot. Another burst from the Kalashnikov smashed windshield glass, the dead man slumped across his steering wheel and the machine lurched backward, nudging one behind it that was already in flames.

That left the motley firefighters. McCarter turned on them with a vengeance, raking them with automatic fire. They tried to stand and fight to save themselves, but nothing in a life of bullying the helpless had prepared them for such wrath. Two were cut down before they had a chance to use their weapons, while the third broke ranks and ran.

McCarter tracked him with the AK-47, put a 3-round burst between his shoulder blades, turned away before his human target hit the ground. He had more-pressing work to do than counting bodies, and the job would not get done unless he put his ass in gear.

So many enemies, so little time.

McCarter fed another magazine into his AK and went off to find the war.

GROMYLKO FELT as if his whole life had been leading to this moment. How often he had wondered what it must have felt like for another generation of his people, in the Great Patriotic War, to risk their lives in desperate battle with a ruthless enemy who plotted the destruction of their homeland.

Now he knew.

He didn't feel heroic—whatever that meant—nor was he terrified of dying at the hands of strangers. He was somewhere in between, a man of flesh and blood who intended to succeed or die in the attempt to honor his duty. He almost felt as if it were *expected* of him, something that humanity required—a way of paying dues, as the Americans would say.

A burst from his Kalashnikov surprised two of Vasiliev's hired guns, as they were facing in the opposite direction. The lieutenant felt no qualms about shooting them in the back. This wasn't a Western movie, after all, where good guys always let their enemies shoot first, to prove that they were fighting on the side of truth and justice. In real-life combat situations, hesitation was a killer, and the man who let his enemy shoot first couldn't expect to live and fight another day.

He stepped around the bodies, drawing closer to the house. A pall of smoke obscured the dacha, but it wasn't thick enough to hide the leaping flames that had begun to spread from rocket impact sites, endangering the house at large. Another twenty minutes, give or take, and the lieutenant guessed that there would be no saving anyone inside the house.

That wasn't good enough, of course. He wasn't ready to *presume* his adversaries dead; Gromylko had to *see* them dead. Only then would his need be satisfied, the debt he owed Alexei Churbanov repaid. He felt as if this moment had been sneaking up on him for years, and now that it had finally arrived, Gromylko would not flinch from whatever he was required to do.

A bullet warmed the air beside his face. Gromylko turned toward its source, the echo of a gunshot ringing in his ears. The shooter held his pistol in a stiff two-handed grip, like something he had seen on television, but his hands were shaking, and the perspiration on his face might be produced by heat from the expanding fire or by a killer case of nerves.

Gromylko ducked beneath the second shot and rattled off a hasty burst from his Kalashnikov. He almost missed the target, but a round or two struck home below the Chechen's belt, a hip shot, dropping him to one knee with a cry of pain. The man was wounded but still dangerous, as he immediately proved by squeezing off another round.

Gromylko forced himself to take his time, line up the shot and do it right. His next burst found the gunman's chest and slammed him over backward, to the ground. Gromylko started forward, through the smoke, intent on getting to the house while there was still a chance for him to have a look inside.

He almost made it.

There was someone coming at him through the smoke. Gromylko hesitated, wanting to be sure it was an enemy before he opened fire. He had six comrades on the field, somewhere, if all of them were still alive, and he didn't intend to let his zeal cost any one of them a life. He could afford to wait and glimpse the face, before—

"Lieutenant."

Yuri Renko didn't sound surprised to see him. He was out of uniform, but still well dressed, considering the circumstances of their meeting. One cheek smudged with soot didn't detract from his normal imperious bearing. Fear had done no damage to his ramrod spine. The pistol he held pressed against his right leg didn't rise as he approached Gromylko, moving cautiously.

"That's far enough," Gromylko said.

"I don't suppose we can discuss this," Renko said. A small, sardonic smile twisted one corner of his mouth.

"There's nothing to discuss."

"I thought perhaps—"

"You murdered Vanya."

"Technically you're wrong," Renko said. "He was sent to mark you for the others. I had no idea Vasiliev was planning to kill both of you."

"Would it have mattered, *Colonel?*"

Renko thought about it for perhaps two seconds. "No."

"I didn't think so. What about Alexei?"

"That's on your head," Renko told him. "How would your Americans describe it? I believe the saying is, 'You bit off more than you could chew.'"

"You did not warn Vasiliev?"

"There wasn't time. Your damn impromptu raid prevented it. I might have saved your partner for you, if you'd only gone through channels. Now you simply have to live with it. In time the nightmares will begin to fade."

"I will sleep well tonight," Gromylko promised him.

"Sleep well, and long."

The colonel brought his pistol up and fired in one quick motion, pumping off three rounds in rapid fire. Gromylko felt a bullet strike his ribs, the impact making him stagger, but there was no real pain to speak of as he held the AK-47's trigger down. The jagged bolts of lightning from its muzzle seemed to make his target dance, Renko disintegrating, bits and pieces of him flying off in all directions. Even so, he managed one more shot, a wasted round, before he fell.

Gromylko's legs refused to hold him up, and he wound up on his knees, one hand clasped to his wounded side, the other bracing his Kalashnikov as if it were a stubby walking stick. The pain was coming now, exacerbated by the hot blood spilling through his fingers.

The lieutenant wondered whether he was dying, thought he wouldn't care and suddenly discovered his mistake. It mattered very much, though why he couldn't say.

Gromylko simply knew that he was desperate to survive.

HAWKINS WENT IN LOW, beneath the hanging pall of smoke. They taught you that in basic: hot air rises, and the smoke goes with it, filling up the ceiling space before it works its way down to the floor. In burning houses hug the deck and keep your ass in motion. If you stay in one place too long, it's a safe bet that you'll fry.

The place was coming down around his ears, and while it would have been a safer bet to stand outside and watch it burn, Hawk had surrendered to an urge that drove him past the edge of common sense. He had to have a look inside, find out if Gregori Vasiliev was in there—or at least be able to report that he had made the try.

At first he took the sound of shots for ammunition detonating in the fire, like lethal popcorn, but the bullets came his way with a consistency that ruled out chance. Not close enough to graze him yet, but they were getting there. He peered ahead and saw a crouching shadow in the doorway leading to a corridor, some twenty feet in front of him. One of Vasiliev's defenders, unwilling to desert his post no matter what.

Hawkins returned fire from the prone position, missed his shifting target, but the AK rounds came close enough to make the gunner duckwalk backward, looking for a place to hide. The young American edged forward, pushing it, convinced that in the present situation, backing off would only have a tendency to get him killed.

He fired another short burst into smoky darkness, knowing it was wasted, hoping that he might provoke his adversary into some mistake and thus tip the balance in Hawkins's favor. You could never tell.

The screaming, when it came, was not produced by one of his AK rounds striking home. The Russian gunman burst from cover, charging forward, wreathed in flames from head to toe, a living human torch. A heartbeat from collision and the burning man's embrace of death, Hawk shot him in the chest and dropped him in midstride, the screams cut off as if someone had slammed a soundproof door.

And it was hopeless to advance, Hawkins realized. The dacha was becoming an inferno, portions of the roof already crumbling inward, while the walls began to sag. There might be other angles of attack, but they would all stop short of penetrating far enough for him to really check the house. If Gregori Vasiliev was still inside the dacha, he would have to find an exit now.

Hawkins retreated, crawling backward on his stomach till he reached the foyer, rising to a crouch from there and homing on the door. Three of Vasiliev's house troops were standing back to watch the house burn from several yards away as he emerged. The smoke obscured his face and clothing, giving Hawk time to level his Kalashnikov as one of them called out to him, taking him for yet another member of the home team.

Hawkins killed them where they stood, emptied his magazine as they went down, reloading as he put the burning house behind him. It was hot enough to bake right through his clothes, and he already felt as if his face were sunburned. He was grateful when the night breeze shifted, blowing toward the fire and sparing him a measure of the heat. He thought about Vasiliev and wondered how it felt to have your dreams go up in smoke.

Life's hard, he told himself, and then you fry.

"NO WAY I'm going in there," Calvin James declared. "No way."

Encizo frowned agreement. "No one could survive that."

"Maybe in a fire suit," James said, "but I forgot to pack mine when I left the house."

"Let's check the other buildings," Encizo suggested.

"I heard that."

Besides the dacha, there was still a rustic-style detached garage, together with a larger building, not unlike a barn, although the property was clearly not a farm. James and Encizo moved toward the garage, which had been spared by rocket hits as all three soldiers armed with RPGs had concentrated on the house and cars outside.

"I should have nuked this place while I was at it," James muttered to himself. But it was too late now. If there was anyone in the garage, they would be forced to root the bastards out by force and take them one-on-one.

Or maybe not.

As if in answer to his thoughts, the wide door opened on its own. A black sedan burst through the opening, impatient with the door's slow progress, smashing wood to splinters with its grille. Behind it, coming loud and fast, two motorcycles cleared the open maw of the garage and raced off parallel to the sedan, their drivers hunched low over stubby handlebars.

"I've got the bikes!" Encizo shouted, breaking off

to intercept them, firing with his AK-47 as he ran and leaving James to face the car.

"Well, shit!"

He stitched a rising burst across the grille, then unleashed another on the windshield. Cracks like spiderwebs were visible before the glass blew inward, and the car began to swerve, its rear tires spewing gravel from the driveway, then digging into grass and sod for better traction, taking off across the lawn.

Wondering if Vasiliev was in the car, James followed in a headlong sprint, still firing at the car, rewarded with another crash of glass from the rear window. Shiny patches marked the body where his bullets struck, but he couldn't keep up the pace. His lungs were bursting, and his heart was thumping solidly against his ribs, as if it wanted to escape.

James veered off track to give himself a clear shot from the right side of the car. He halted, aimed and fired off half a magazine before he got results. The starboard tires exploded, rubber flapping on the rims as they were torn apart. The vehicle began to swerve again, and then it flipped into a roll, kept rolling— two, three, four, five times.

It came to rest upside down, its two good tires still spinning. James reloaded as he closed in on the wreck, and he was ready when a body started worming out through the back window, crawling hand over hand, wriggling clear of the auto and trying to stand. His next burst, from a range of forty feet, undid the lean survivor's progress, left him stretched out on the turf.

James crouched to check the car and counted two

more dead inside. They both had faces—one of them just barely—and he saw that neither was Vasiliev. Ditto the gunner who had almost managed to escape.

"*Damn* it!"

Angry, James turned back toward the sound of automatic-rifle fire in time to see Encizo finish off the second biker. It would have amazed him to find out that one of them was Gregori Vasiliev.

And he was not amazed.

"Let's finish it," James said, unclipping a grenade from his combat harness as he advanced on the garage. He yanked the pin and made his pitch from thirty feet, stood back and waited for the blast that tore a new door in the wall.

He went in through the smoke, Encizo close behind him, to discover that the place was empty. Five men had escaped the house, to seek refuge in the garage, and now all five of them were dead.

Vasiliev was either toasting in the dacha, even now, or he was still at large.

"We're not done yet," Encizo said.

The barn. James nodded, wondering if there was such a thing as any kind of limit on bad luck. They were alive, of course, and that was excellent, but he wouldn't be satisfied until he knew the purpose of their strike had been achieved.

The barn.

"Let's go," he said, and moved back toward the killing ground.

IT WAS A FLUKE that Bolan ever saw Vasiliev at all. Another moment either way, and he would certainly have missed the three men charging through a side door of the house, stampeding toward the barnlike structure thirty yards away. He had been pinned down by a pair of gunners on the east side of the dacha, touch and go until he faked them out by playing dead and then surprised them with the fact that he was still alive.

Back on his feet and closing on the house that had become a burning ruin, Bolan was surprised to see three figures exit in a puff of smoke that trailed them through the open doorway. None of them was injured, from the way they ran, and it was all that he could do to keep pace with them as they sprinted toward the barn.

The middle of the three was Gregori Vasiliev.

He chased them with a burst from his Kalashnikov and missed all three, but still got their attention. Two of them kept running, but the third man stopped and turned to face him, firing from the hip with a compact SMG. Bolan returned the fire and saw his target stagger, reeling, going down on one knee, crimson blotches spreading on his shirt. Still, he kept firing, forcing Bolan to expend a few more rounds to finish it and stretch him on the grass.

By then, his two companions had already disappeared inside the barn.

It was a dangerous approach, but Bolan had no choice. He didn't have the luxury of hanging back and waiting for old age to claim his enemies. Both men were armed, and they might have more weapons stockpiled in the barn. More to the point, they might have vehicles in there, a chance to leave him in the dust and flee to God knew where.

Even with that in mind, it came as a surprise to Bolan when the barn's roof suddenly began to open like the jaws of a titanic clam. His ears picked up an old, familiar sound, and Bolan cursed, began to sprint the last few yards, afraid that he was already too late.

The helicopter rose up into view, a giant prehistoric insect shape against the velvet Russian sky. It should have kept on rising, but the pilot hesitated, hovering, and Bolan saw his last, best chance.

He started firing, held the AK-47's trigger down and gave it everything he had. When two more rifles joined the fusillade, he didn't turn to see which members of his team were firing, simply knew that if the bullets were not striking him, it must be friendly fire. Converging streams of armor-piercing rounds tattooed the underbelly of the helicopter, ripping through the floor and fuselage, exploding through the windscreen, striking bright sparks from the engine cowling and the rotor blades. Another moment, and the chopper farted thick black smoke, then plummeted straight down and disappeared once more inside the barn.

The crash was loud enough, but even that was lost in the explosion that immediately followed, flattening the four walls of the barn and spewing fire in all directions. Bolan, James and Rafael Encizo hastily retreated, putting space between themselves and the rapacious funeral pyre.

"Vasiliev?" James asked when he could make himself be heard.

"He's done," Bolan said, reaching for the little two-way on his belt. He raised it to his lips and thumbed the button down. "Break off," he said. "Repeat, break off. Confirm!"

"Confirmed," McCarter told him seconds later.

"Done," Gary Manning added, sounding small and faraway.

"I hear you," Hawkins said.

They stood waiting for another moment, Bolan frowning at the silence, feeling sweet relief uncoil inside him at the sound of one more voice.

"Confirming that," said Leonid Gromylko. "But I'm not sure I can join you at the moment."

"Are you hit?" Bolan asked.

"So it would appear."

"Where are you?"

"On the south side of the house," Gromylko answered. "I'm keeping Comrade Renko company."

"I'm there," said Hawkins, picking up on the exchange.

"Two minutes," Gary Manning promised.

Between the two of them, Gromylko would be in good hands. There was no point in everybody rushing over to inspect his wounds, especially while there were Chechen gunners still alive and prowling in the neighborhood.

"We'll meet you back on the perimeter," Bolan said, and returned the little two-way to his belt. He found the others watching him, and finally allowed himself a smile.

"Okay," he said, "who's ready to go home?"

EPILOGUE

"The word is, you'll be out of here by Thursday, maybe Friday at the latest."

Bolan stood beside Gromylko's hospital bed, half turned so he could keep a sharp eye on the door. The guard outside had let him in, but despite the years of change it was still an eerie feeling, counting on a ally in a Russian uniform.

Old habits die hard. Old enemies, too.

"I should not have to stay at all," Gromylko said. "The bullet barely grazed me."

"Tell that to your lung," said Bolan. "You could use a rest."

"Perhaps." Gromylko didn't sound convinced, and there was clearly something on his mind. "They're making me a captain."

"So I understand."

"They think I should return to duty."

"Was there ever any doubt?" asked Bolan.

"*I* have doubts," Gromylko said. "I've seen and done too much. It's like I'm on the other side now, with the bastards I've been fighting half my life."

"Not even close," the Executioner replied. "I know the sickness when I see it. You're no carrier."

Gromylko scowled and shook his head. "My work will never be the same."

"Is that so bad?"

"You still don't understand," the Russian said. "I *liked* what we were doing. Can you grasp that? Every time I pulled the trigger, saw one of them fall, I *loved* it."

"Maybe, maybe not," said Bolan. "You could use some distance, take some time to think it through. I have a hunch it won't look quite the same this time next week."

"And if you're wrong?"

"Whatever happens," Bolan said, "you've got a job to do. You've done it by the book for years. There's no law saying that you can't keep right on doing it that way. The past week was a detour into hell, but you survived it. Give yourself some credit."

"Credit? I'm a killer," said Gromylko.

"You're a soldier, doing what you have to do. You'd do the same again."

"And that's what worries me," Gromylko said.

"The difference being, that you may not *have* to," Bolan explained. "You've made a difference, Leonid. Believe it. Maybe it's enough to get things back on track."

"Americans. I'll miss our little chats." Gromylko chuckled to himself.

"You'll have your hands full," Bolan said. "Besides, the general still knows how to get in touch if necessary.''

''Maybe for a talk sometime,'' Gromylko said. ''As for the rest...''

''I'll keep my fingers crossed.''

''But not your trigger fingers, eh?''

''That wouldn't do.'' Bolan glanced at his watch. ''I hate to run, but—''

''You have business,'' Leonid Gromylko said. ''Of course. We all have work to do.''

''Good luck.''

''I make my own,'' the Russian said. ''Is that not right?''

''That's right,'' the Executioner replied.

And thought, *Damn right.*